PRAI

MW01137711

Heartbreak Hill

"In *Heartbreak Hill*, McLaughlin weaves a poignant tale of love, loss, and second chances. Grab your tissues . . . you're going to need them!"
—Taylor Delong, author of *Waiting on Forever*

"*Heartbreak Hill* is a heartbreakingly beautiful novel. Greyson and Reid's journey to love is emotional until the very last page. You don't want to miss this read."
—A. M. Guilliams, author of *Bring Me Back Here*

"*Heartbreak Hill* is a beautiful, heart-stirring, stick-with-you-for-days story of several lives that are intertwined through loss and an extraordinary act of giving."
—M. E. Montgomery, author of *Call It Fate*

"*Heartbreak Hill* took me on a roller coaster of emotions. Heidi has a remarkable talent for creating characters that leave a mark on you."
—J. C. Hannigan, author of *Riverside Reverie*

Before I'm Gone

"*Before I'm Gone* is a heartbreakingly beautiful love story about finding your soulmate against all odds."
—*USA Today* bestselling author Ashley Cade

"A heartbreakingly beautiful story about love, friendship, perseverance, and learning to live life to the fullest."
—Samantha Baca, author of *Just One Time*

"This book is absolutely gut wrenching and broke my heart into a million pieces, but the story hit me in such a beautiful way."
—Vanessa Valencia, Goodreads

"Beautiful and emotional—I cried buckets."
—*AC Book Blog*

"I am not okay. And that's okay. Damn, this book wrecked me with all the feels. Such a cathartic cry I hadn't realized I needed."
—Courtney, Goodreads

Cape Harbor

"I love a good second-chance romance, and Heidi McLaughlin did NOT disappoint."
—*New York Times* bestselling author L. P. Dover

"This is a story that will stay with me for a long, long time."
—Sara, Goodreads

"A beautifully written story that will pull you in and tug at your heartstrings."
—Nikki, *Crazy Cajun Book Addicts*

"The reader will instantly fall in love with Cape Harbor."
—Nicki, *The Overflowing Bookcase*

"McLaughlin knows how to put a person in touch with their emotions."
—Isha Coleman, hopeless romantic

The Beaumont Series

"If you want to read a book that is all heart—full of characters you will instantly connect with and love from the first page to the last—then *Forever My Girl* is the book for you."

—Jenny, *Totally Booked Blog*

"*Forever My Girl* is a sweet, loving, all-around adorable read. If you, like me, have a thing for musicians and reconnections, then this read is for you."

—*Jacqueline's Reads*

"This is an utterly moving story of second chances in life, of redemption, remorse, forgiveness, of loves lost and found again, of trust regained. Through alternating points of view, we feel both Liam's and Josie's emotions, fears, and sorrow. These are well-developed characters whose love for each other survives time and distance."

—*Natasha Is a Book Junkie*, on *Forever My Girl*

"*My Unexpected Forever* completely outdid my expectations and blew *Forever My Girl* out of the water. *My Unexpected Forever* is without a doubt a book that I would recommend, and Harrison is officially my new book boyfriend!"

—Holly's Hot Reads

The Beaumont Series: Next Generation

"Heidi McLaughlin delivers a breathtaking addition to the Beaumont series. *Holding Onto Forever* is everything you want it to be and so much more. I fell in love all over again."

—*USA Today* bestselling author K. L. Grayson

"A roller coaster of emotions. McLaughlin takes you on a journey of two hearts that are destined to be together."

—*New York Times* bestselling author Kaylee Ryan

"Heidi McLaughlin delivers yet another heartfelt, emotional, engaging read! I loved every second of *Fighting for Our Forever*! You will too!"

—*USA Today* bestselling author M. Never

The Archer Brothers

"I *loved* everything about this book. It is an emotional story that will have you begging for more. Even after I finished reading, I can't stop thinking about it. A *must* read!"

—Jamie Rae, author of *Call Sign Karma*

"McLaughlin will have you frantically turning pages and make your heart beat faster because each page has something more surprising than the one before it. You'll be dying to see what happens next!"

—*New York Times* bestselling author Jay Crownover

"I needed this book. I didn't even realize how much until I read it!"

—*USA Today* bestselling author Adriana Locke

The Boys of Summer

"Heidi McLaughlin has done it again! Sexy, sweet, and full of heart, *Third Base* is a winner!"

—Melissa Brown, author of *Wife Number Seven*

"*Third Base* hits the reading sweet spot. A must read for any baseball and romance fans."

—Carey Heywood, author of *Him*

"*Third Base* is sexy and witty and pulls you in from the first page. You'll get lost in Ethan and Daisy and never want their story to end."

—S. Moose, author of *Offbeat*

"McLaughlin knocks it out of the park with her second sports contemporary . . . This novel goes above and beyond the typical sports romance with a hot, complex hero and a gutsy, multidimensional heroine. McLaughlin keeps the pace lively throughout, and just when readers think they have the finale figured out, she throws them a few curveballs. This novel will appeal to McLaughlin's fans and will win her many more."

—*Publishers Weekly* (starred review), on *Home Run*

"Heidi McLaughlin never fails to pull me in with her storytelling, and I assure you she'll do the same to you! *Home Run* is a home run, in my book."

—*New York Times* bestselling author Jen McLaughlin

"Top Pick! Four and a half stars! McLaughlin has hit the mark with her third Boys of Summer novel. There's more than one great storyline to capture the imagination."

—RT Book Reviews

The Art of Starting Over

Other Titles by Heidi McLaughlin

THE BEAUMONT SERIES

Forever My Girl

My Everything

My Unexpected Forever

Finding My Forever

Finding My Way

12 Days of Forever

My Kind of Forever

Forever Our Boys

Forever Mason

THE BEAUMONT SERIES: NEXT GENERATION

Holding Onto Forever

My Unexpected Love

Chasing My Forever

Peyton & Noah

Fighting for Our Forever

NASHVILLE NIGHTS

Sangria

THE REALITY DUET

Blind Reality

Twisted Reality

STAND-ALONE NOVELS

Before I'm Gone

Heartbreak Hill

HOLIDAY NOVELS

Santa's Secret

It's a Wonderful Holiday

Stranded with the One

Love in Print

The Art of Starting Over

HEIDI McLAUGHLIN

 Montlake

Text copyright © 2025 by Heidi McLaughlin
All rights reserved.

Published by Montlake, Seattle

www.apub.com

Amazon, the Amazon logo, and Montlake are trademarks of Amazon.com, Inc., or its affiliates.

ISBN-13: 9781662521461 (paperback)
ISBN-13: 9781662521454 (digital)

Cover design by Ploy Siripant
Cover images: © Shobeir Ansari, © Walter Bibikow / Getty; © FTiare / Shutterstock

Printed in the United States of America

The Art of Starting Over

ONE

DEVORAH

There's a moment in everyone's life when their world crumbles around them. For Devorah Campbell, her moment came while she sat in a nail salon, getting a pedicure and scrolling through her phone on one of those popular vlogging apps.

She thought of her nine-year-old daughter, Maren, who was addicted to the videos, always laughing, dancing, and begging her parents to let her have an account. Devorah and her husband of fifteen years, Chad, had banned social media from their home. They felt that, while social media had some advantages, they didn't outweigh the negatives for an impressionable young woman like Maren. To appease her daughter, Devy had signed up with one of those user1227985812426 numbers, left the profile and bio blank, and allowed Maren to watch on her phone. Together, they followed their favorite actors, actresses, musicians, and vloggers. A few fun accounts were mixed in from some of Maren's classmates and Dev's best friend, Ester.

While her favorite nail tech, Kristin, painted her toes hot pink, Devy moved her thumb up the screen to switch the video. She smiled when Ester's newest video came on the screen, and she popped her earbud in so she could listen to what she had to say. She was always talking about their homeowners' association drama, which they had quite a bit of—the "Don't let your springtime lawn get over an inch and a half, or Nicole, the overzealous HOA president, will come knocking on your door" sort of thing.

"Am I the asshole? Ugh, I am. I truly am. I did the unthinkable, and I don't know what I should do." Ester sighed and shook her head. "I've been having an affair with my best friend's husband, and I'm in love with him, and he loves me. I don't know what I'm going to do when my best friend comes to me after her husband leaves her. What am I going to say?"

Devy's heart hit her stomach and didn't bounce back into place. Tears filled her eyes. *She* was Ester's best friend. They had been since college and now lived one block away from each other, living the suburban mom life with PTA meetings, school plays, and whatever sport their kids were involved with. She'd held her hand when Ester's husband filed for divorce. Ester's daughter, Rita, was Maren's best friend. They often spent the night at each other's houses, sat next to each other on the bus and in class, and were generally inseparable.

Was Devorah the best friend?

Was Chad the other man?

She didn't know what to do or what to think. The video started again, and Devy found herself listening to the words on repeat. Each time stung more than the next. There was no way Chad would ever cheat on her. They were happy and in love, high school sweethearts who went away to college together and never looked back on their small ocean-side hometown. Most of their classmates stayed, working in various family businesses or joining fishing or boating charters. Jobs neither she nor Chad wanted. Nor did they want the small-town life for Maren. They wanted her to experience life and go to school with more than ten kids. They wanted her to have more than they'd had.

After they graduated from Northwestern, Chad took a job in finance, while Devy went to work as an estate curator. She loved going into homes, especially older ones, and helping families liquidate their possessions. Her job was fun and never stressful, even when she had to work on weekends. The job, and her career, brought her a lot of satisfaction, and it allowed her time to always be present for Maren and whatever activity she had going on.

Ester's voice brought Devy back from her reverie. She shook her head and looked at her friend's face, frozen on her screen. She didn't look sad, upset, or distraught. Shouldn't she be, if she was having an affair with her best friend's husband?

Chad would never do this to her. Nor could she fathom Ester being so classless as to make a video about their affair and put it online. Were people inherently evil? Devy had seen some truly nasty things on the internet, but this one took the cake, and she couldn't stomach thinking this was about her.

"Devorah, please don't move," her nail tech said.

"Kristin, I need to go."

"You're almost done," she said. "Five more minutes."

Five minutes seemed like a lifetime. She sat there, with her phone clutched in her hand, while Kristin put the last coat of polish on her toes. One more drying cycle and she'd be free to go.

To where, Devy had no idea. She couldn't do anything irrational, like burst into her husband's office and ask if he was having an affair, or do the same at Ester's office, demanding to know why she would post such a horrible video for someone to find. And if it wasn't Chad, then why would Ester say "best friend" in her video?

Devy paid and left without scheduling her next appointment. Her mind was elsewhere, with no direction. She got behind the wheel of her car and chided herself for thinking the video was about her husband. Chad wouldn't cheat. He wouldn't ruin the life they had built together. Yet something deep down inside told her he had. For the life of her, she couldn't understand why. She'd never had a reason not to trust him. At least none she could recall.

Never in her life had she thought about spying on Chad until now. She drove to his office and around the parking lot, looking for his car. It wasn't there, despite it being lunchtime. He'd told her he never left for lunch; why would he need to leave when they had a fully functioning cafeteria on-site? Those had been his words to her ever since he'd started his job there. And she'd believed him. She had no reason not to.

Devy drove around again, this time much more slowly, looking at the bumper of each gray car to find the PROUD PARENT sticker Maren had put on her father's car.

But she couldn't find it. Chad wasn't at work.

Devorah pulled over and called his office. His phone rang through to voicemail. She hung up and pressed his name on her contacts. Voicemail. She closed her eyes and rested her head against the steering wheel as tears of frustration welled in her eyes, tipping over the rims and falling down her face. That was when she saw the shiny pink of her toes and noticed she hadn't bothered to put her shoes on, and she didn't know where they were.

As if on autopilot, she drove to Ester's house. They had plans later, and it was very unlike Devy to show up early, yet she was going to do just that. The entire drive, she told herself the video her best friend had posted wasn't about her. Ester had other friends, people Devy didn't hang out with, especially the ladies from Ester's fiction book club. Their form of reading consisted of drinking bottles of wine and spreading town gossip. Devy liked to stay away from the rumor mill. The less she knew, the better. She never wanted to be caught in the middle of something.

Devy turned onto Ester's street. Maren and Rita often cut through the neighbors' yards to get to each other's homes. Thankfully, the neighbors never seemed to care that the girls had worn a path in their yards. Their safety was far more important than some missing grass.

Ester's car was in the driveway, but not in her usual spot. It was off to the side, as if she'd needed to get in and out of her garage. Devy parked and chided herself for looking at anything and everything possible to make it seem plausible her husband was there.

He wasn't.

Chad wouldn't do this to Devy. To Maren. To their family.

Devorah parked and got out of her car, barefoot. She walked across the grass until she reached the walkway, then went up the two concrete steps to the front door. Her hand was poised to knock. She hadn't knocked on Ester's door in years. Devy set her hand on the handle, pressed the lever, and pushed the door open.

Inside, the house was quiet and empty. She turned toward the hall and paused. The moans were undeniable. Ester was with someone.

Someone who hadn't parked out front or in her driveway.

Against her better judgment, Devy crept down the hall. The moans grew louder, the squeaking of the bed the telltale sign of people having sex. She knew better than to turn the doorknob but couldn't stop herself. Not now.

From what she could remember, Ester had an ebony four-poster bed. She'd spent lavishly on curtains, duvets, and sheets. The finest thread counts. According to her, this was her sanctuary and where she wanted to feel the sexiest at all times. Devy had tried the same at home, finding the rich colors and fabrics to bring her bedroom to life. The problem was, she bored easily with colors and wanted to change them often. Bright colors in the spring and summer and soft dark colors in the winter. Chad never cared. "Whatever makes you happy" was all he'd ever said.

Devy stepped into the room. Ester and whoever she was with kept going. At first, she told herself it wasn't her husband. The bare back, strong arms, and toned legs visible to her prying eyes weren't those of the man she'd vowed to love until death did they part.

She watched as her husband, the man she'd loved since high school—he the star quarterback of their small high school and she the head cheerleader—turned and looked over his shoulder at her while he was balls deep in her best friend.

Her stomach rolled, and she fought back the urge to lose its contents on the white Persian rug Ester loved so much. Yet she couldn't look away, even though every voice in her head told her to run, to run and never look back.

Devy stood there, eyeing her husband, as her knees weakened and threatened to give out from under her.

Still, as they stared at each other, neither said anything.

"Why'd you stop, Chad? I'm close." Ester spoke in a breathy voice, clearly in the process of reaching her peak.

"Devorah." He said her name quietly and then scrambled off Ester, taking the sheet with him and leaving her naked as the day she was born.

Words failed her. The anger Devy thought she'd feel when she found her husband cheating on her didn't come forward. Gut-wrenching pain and anguish did, along with tears. She covered her mouth in a failed attempt to stifle a sob and ran from the room.

Chad didn't follow.

When Devy got outside, she bent at the waist and vomited all over Ester's spring perennials, heaved in gulps of air, and choked. She felt a hand on her back and flinched. "Don't touch me," she screamed. "Don't you dare touch me."

"Devorah, lower your voice," Chad said through gritted teeth. He looked around as if he was embarrassed by his wife losing the contents of her stomach in his mistress's front yard. The irony of the situation was, if someone came outside and saw his rumpled shirt and messed-up hair, they'd know what he was doing there. It didn't take a rocket scientist to see what was going on.

"Don't you dare tell me to lower my voice." Devy stood, wiped her mouth with the back of her hand, and looked into her husband's brown eyes. He was full of shit; that's what everyone always said about him. *Chad Campbell is full of shit. You can see it in his eyes.* She never could. She was blinded by love. Devy had fallen for him at the beginning of their junior year of high school and never looked back. Smitten by his charm and good looks. He'd always kept his brown hair short and gelled off to the side. The wild mane before her was a result of fingers brushing through it. She'd done it more times than she could count and loved how he looked after they'd made love. And now he'd allowed someone else to do it. That someone being her best friend.

"We'll talk about this at home."

"Why wait?" She raised her voice and threw her hands up in the air.

The front door opened. Ester, with her long blond hair and lean legs, stood against the door casing, wearing a short pink silk bathrobe. Devy knew in her heart there wasn't anything she could say or do to save her marriage. Chad had already made his choice.

Devy looked at the ground. Her freshly painted toenails matched the color of Ester's robe. It was a color Chad had mentioned he liked on her.

My bad for assuming he meant me.

"Where are your shoes?" he asked her.

She let out a strangled cry. "You know, I'm not really sure. I think they're somewhere between here and the video I saw of my best friend admitting to sleeping with my husband. It's pretty high quality," she told him. "Do you want to see it?"

Chad said nothing. His expression didn't even change.

Devy looked at her best—now former—friend. She wasn't sure why. Maybe an explanation for the utter humiliation, betrayal, and hurt she and Chad had caused her.

Instead, Ester spoke. "He loves me, Dev."

Devorah's eyes met Chad's. He didn't break eye contact. "It's true. I've fallen in love with her."

"How long has this been going on?"

Chad looked around. Devy didn't care if any of Ester's neighbors came outside.

"How long, Chad?" she screamed.

"A year," he told her under his breath. "Look, I'm sorry, Dev. I love her, and I'm moving in with her."

"Wonderful, thanks for letting me know you planned to destroy our family with my best friend," she muttered as she stepped around her mess in the yard and headed toward her car. It was a good thing her heart was already broken because watching her husband reach for Ester was enough to break Devy in half. He hadn't even waited for her to pull away from the curb before he'd gone back to his mistress.

TWO

HAYDEN

Hayden McKenna dropped the speed of his dually truck to a crawl at twenty miles an hour when he pulled within the city limits of Oyster Bay, his hometown and a place he never thought he'd move back to. The once-a-year visits had been plenty to appease his parents, especially since they preferred to travel now that they were both retired and had nothing holding them down.

He drove across the bridge slowly, angling his head in every direction to make sure the camper he towed behind his truck had clearance. Normally, once he was across, he'd turn right and head through the heart of town, but with the size of his truck and the extra cargo behind him, he was liable to get stuck. With no choice but to take the long way around, Hayden readjusted in his seat once he'd cleared the bridge and mentally calculated another fifteen minutes to the piece of land he'd bought a few months back. There he'd unhitch and then head to his parents' place, even though it was getting late.

Conor, Hayden's nine-year-old son, stirred in the passenger seat. Hayden watched his son out of the corner of his eye, waiting to see if he'd wake. Conor yawned, then rubbed his eyes, and then ran his hand through his short dishwater-blond hair. Hayden had taken him to get it cut before they made the cross-country trip, in time to start at his new school. It had been the first time he'd done so since Conor was a baby, when his wife, Sofia, had made his first haircut a huge celebration.

"Where are we?" he asked groggily.

"Almost there," Hayden said in the darkened cab of the truck.

"To Grandma's?"

"Shortly. We have to drop the camper off first."

Conor looked behind them. Hayden did the same through the rear-view. Everything they owned was in the back of the truck. The important things were in the extended cab. The camper held their clothes and whatever household supplies Hayden had kept or could fit in there. He'd live in the camper on the piece of land and break ground on their new home, while Conor would live with his grandparents. As much as Hayden hated to admit it, he needed help with his son. The single-parent life was hard, and the past year had proved he couldn't do it alone.

Conor sighed and straightened. "I miss Mom."

"Me too," Hayden said automatically. It'd been his response every time Conor said it. The truth was, as much as he missed his wife, he was angry with her. Her death could've been prevented if she had called him for a ride home.

Hayden turned slowly and drove a half mile until the empty lot came into view. He turned and pressed the gas until his front tires slowly climbed the curb and repeated the action until the camper was on the land. In the dusk of twilight, Hayden unhitched and secured his temporary home and then drove over to his parents' house.

As soon as he pulled up, Conor was out of the truck and running toward his grandmother, who stood at the top of her porch with out-stretched arms. Hayden parked and took his sweet time getting out of the truck, pausing to gather their overnight bags.

"Hayden," his mother said as he approached the porch.

"Hey, Mom." Darcy McKenna hugged her son and let him go only when Hayden's father, Lee, interrupted. "Hey, Dad."

Lee and Darcy McKenna were well-known and well-liked pillars of the community; not a soul in town didn't know and love the McKenna family. Lee had been the town doctor and Darcy his nurse. Both were born and raised in Oyster Bay. Darcy was petite, with blond hair and bright-blue eyes, while Lee was a bit taller than the average person, with light-brown hair and hazel eyes. Since retirement, he liked his beer, but his beer didn't like him much and went right to his waistline.

His parents hadn't been able to make Sofia's funeral. They were on a cruise in Europe, and by the time they received Hayden's message, they hadn't had enough time to get to Wyoming for the service.

"Need me to get anything from the truck?" Lee asked.

"Nah, we're good. Hungry, though. Right, sport?"

"Sure," Conor said as he headed inside.

Darcy sneaked under her son's arm, placed one arm along his back, and patted his stomach with her free hand. "Food, we have."

"That's about all he wants these days," Hayden said as they made their way inside.

The house Hayden grew up in had drastically changed over the years. Long gone were the wood-paneled walls, mustard-colored carpet, and aged linoleum. Five years ago, the McKennas had gutted their house from top to bottom and created an open-concept living space in grays, whites, and shades of blue. They'd remodeled the bathrooms with walk-in showers and a soaking tub in the primary. When all was said and done, the property value skyrocketed, which made Lee happy. This home was the one thing he owned, and no one could take it away from him.

Conor sat at the island bar, munching on chips and drinking a soda, knowing full well that doing so was against the rules. Hayden eyed him and said nothing. There was no point in arguing with his son right then. He'd give Conor one night, and then he'd enforce the rules.

"Grandma, where am I sleeping?"

"In Aunt Allie's room," Darcy told Conor.

Hayden's sister lived in Los Angeles, enjoying the single life and vowing never to get married or have kids. Allie's room was a room in name, a place to direct visitors to instead of saying "Upstairs, third door on your right."

"When you finish, you need to brush your teeth," Hayden told Conor. "It's going to take some time for me to find you a dentist. I don't need your teeth rotting out of your head."

Conor rolled his eyes but agreed. Eye-rolling was such a nine-year-old thing to do. Hayden cared only when Conor sassed back, which thankfully wasn't often. His son was sad, and there wasn't much Hayden could do except be there for him.

When Conor finished his snack, he grabbed his bag and headed upstairs. Once Hayden heard the bathroom door shut, he let out a long sigh.

"That bad?" Darcy asked. Hayden nodded.

"Sometimes I wonder if things would be easier if Sofia had died from cancer or something."

"Probably," Lee said. "Then at least you can say goodbye."

"And not be so pissed off all the time." Hayden tugged on his hair and groaned.

"Things will get better," Darcy said. "You both need to heal and find some semblance of normal. You can do that here and start anew."

While Hayden knew his mother was right, words were easier said than adhered to. "I'm worried how he's going to fit in."

"He'll be fine," Lee said. "There are plenty of kids his age, and baseball season is right around the corner. He hasn't missed tryouts."

"Yeah." Hayden went to the refrigerator, opened the door and looked around, and then closed it. "Any beer?" he asked as he looked at his dad.

"I'm supposed to tell you no, but you know better than that." Lee rubbed his hand over his midsection. "If you promise to go running with me tomorrow, I'll show you where the beer is."

Hayden laughed. "Sure, Dad."

"Come to my office," Lee said as he walked to the back door.

"Tell Conor I'll be up in a minute to say good night," Hayden said to his mom as he followed his dad to the garage.

Out the back door, he stepped onto a wide, wooden deck with five white rockers. From here, they had a view of the bay. During the summer and into the early-fall months, cruise ships passed by as they headed into port. Hayden took the stairs to the paved walkway and went into the side door of the garage.

"We're thinking of building an apartment up there," Lee said as he pointed upward. He popped the top on a bottle of beer and handed it to his son. For being a two-car garage, it was spotless. Even with his parents' cars parked in there, they had enough space to move around without bumping into something or having to move the vehicles out. The size was a rarity for Oyster Bay, but when Lee had purchased the lot next to the house, he'd increased the lot size and had a nice garage constructed.

"Are you hurting for money or something?"

Lee shook his head and took a drink of his own bottle. "Nah, just trying to help the community out. The housing shortage is hitting hard. I'm thinking of going into land development. We need affordable housing."

"It's the cost of building materials," Hayden said. "When I saw the construction bill for my house, I about lost it."

"This damn economy." Lee shook his head again. "You going to drink that?"

Hayden studied the label. The beer was from a local brewery. "Wait, is this Colt's?" Colt Crowley had been Hayden's best friend in high school. They were still friends, but they saw each other only when Hayden came to visit.

Lee chuckled. "Yep. He opened about five months ago and took over the Lazy Lamb."

"No shit. Huh, how come no one said anything?" As soon as he asked, he knew why. Because for the past six months, he'd been mourning his wife, and everyone had treated him with kid gloves. No one felt they could tell him about their lives because his had changed drastically in the blink of an eye. "Right." Hayden took a sip and nodded. "Not bad."

"You'll have to go to see him tomorrow for lunch."

"Definitely will, but right now, I need to go inside and tuck my son in."

The men went back into the house. Hayden set his beer down while avoiding eye contact with his mom, and he took the stairs two at a time and headed into his sister's old room. Conor lay on the bed, staring at the ceiling. Hayden tapped his son's leg, a request for him to move over so he could lie next to him.

For a long moment, they sat in silence, staring at the nothingness.

"Do I have to start school tomorrow?"

The responsible thing would be for Hayden to say yes. "No," he told Conor. "But we'll go in, get you registered, and hopefully meet your teacher. Then on Monday, fresh start."

"What does that even mean?"

"I have no idea, bud. It's just a saying."

"It's stupid."

"Yep." There wasn't anything fresh about having to start over. But here they were, living back in Hayden's hometown because he wanted his parents around to help raise Conor. In hindsight, if it hadn't been for Sofia, Hayden never would've left Oyster Bay.

"Can we get a dog?"

Hayden liked the idea. "After the house is finished?"

"Why do we have to wait?"

"Well, because you're living here and I'm going to live in the camper."

Conor turned onto his side and draped his arm over Hayden's mid-section. "Why can't you stay here?"

Hayden rested his hand on top of Conor's. The only reason he planned to stay in the camper was for space. He hated the idea of living at home, especially at almost forty. He felt like a failure, even though he couldn't do anything to change what had happened.

"Grandpa said baseball tryouts are coming up. We can drive to the city to get some new cleats. I think last year's are too small. Your glove is with mine, in the back of the truck. Wanna toss the ball around tomorrow?"

Hayden felt Conor shrug. "What if I don't want to play?"

"Well," Hayden said with a sigh. "I'd be sad because I really like watching you play. I think you're really good. But, ultimately, it's up to you."

"You played for the team here?"

Hayden nodded. "Yep, from the time I was five until I graduated high school."

"Then you met Mom?"

"Yeah, I did. But she's not why I stopped playing," he told his son. Hayden had gone to college to play, but his heart wasn't in it.

"Was it because of me?"

"Of course not," he said. "When I got to college, things changed. I met your mom and realized I wanted a different life."

"Do you think she can see us?"

Hayden's throat tightened. "Sure do. She's watching us. Definitely you, Conor. Your mom loved you more than anything."

"I love her too."

"Yeah, bud. Me too. Close your eyes," he told Conor. "We have a big day tomorrow."

Instead of leaving, Hayden stayed next to his son and closed his own eyes. When he opened them again, rays of sunshine came through the window, and he was alone.

Three

Devorah

From inside the home she had loved for as long as she could remember, Devy watched her daughter load the last of their bags into the SUV parked in the driveway and wondered how in the hell they were going to survive.

It was one thing to find out your husband was having an affair, but to find out the other woman was someone you considered your best friend since college added salt to the gaping wound. Ester knew everything about Devy and Chad's marriage, from how he made Devorah feel in the bedroom, as a wife, and how she'd struggled to find her footing in their marriage. Ester knew Dev strove to be as perfect as possible for Chad, to give him everything he wanted and more, and how she never felt it was enough. Years of Ester telling Dev to dump Chad, to find a better man, now all seemed like a ploy from Ester to get Chad for herself.

Despite knowing better, Devy opened the video and went right to the comments section. This was a place where Dev's feelings were validated. Numerous women had lambasted Ester for what she'd done, calling her a "home-wrecker" while also blaming Chad. But the comments that stood out the most were the ones asking Ester why she would post on social media, in a place where Devy and her daughter could find the video. It was simple, at least in Devorah's mind—Ester didn't know Dev followed her. It was the app-generated username that Ester likely didn't pay attention to. They hadn't posted any videos. To anyone looking, the account probably looked like spam.

Would Ester have posted the video if she'd known Devy followed her?

Yes, Devy thought. Ester wanted the attention, and she wanted Chad.

Now Ester had him, while Devy and Maren had a carful of their belongings and broken hearts.

To make things even worse, Devorah had tried to hide the truth from Maren. No child should have to deal with adult situations. Nor should any child have to see how imperfect their parents are. Dev thought she could keep everything under wraps by saying Maren's father needed some space and that he was moving out for a bit. They certainly wouldn't be the first couple to separate. But then Maren saw the video, thanks to a classmate whose mother had seen it. When the school called and said Maren needed to come home, Devorah knew her daughter had found out.

As soon as Dev saw Maren in the nurse's office, they both broke. They held each other and cried in the hallway. On the way home, Maren said she didn't want to go back to school. Devy agreed and suggested they go away for a bit. They needed to get out of Chicago and away from the stares.

That night, after they'd eaten a quiet dinner, Maren walked out the front door, with Devorah hot on her heels and pleading for her daughter to come back to the house. Maren walked to Ester's place and pounded on the door until Chad answered. Dev stood there in the yard, waiting for her daughter to come back to her, while Chad fed their daughter the same bullshit he'd given Devy—he was in love, everyone else be damned. Chad didn't seem to care that his daughter was losing her best friend in the mix. As long as he was happy, that was all that mattered.

"Rita was my best friend," Maren had screamed, her fists clenched at her sides.

"And I'm going to be her dad now," Chad had said as he tried to put a comforting hand on Maren's shoulder. "Everyone wins."

She'd jerked away. "You're supposed to be my dad! Mine. Not hers."

Chad could've handled the situation differently, but he thought only of himself in that moment with Maren. He ruined not only his marriage but also the friendship between Ester and Devorah, as well as between Maren and Rita. Although the girls were completely innocent, they were forever changed by his and Ester's actions.

Devorah would survive. She'd pick up the pieces of her shattered heart and move on.

Maren would forever remember the time when she found out her father was having an affair with her best friend's mother and had chosen the best friend over her.

"Selfish prick," Devy muttered as she wiped angrily at her cheek. She tore her gaze away and looked around the house.

Devy surveyed the damage she had done to Chad's clothes—she'd shredded them and left nothing more than rags as a result. Their dinnerware set, the one they'd chosen before they got married, sat in heaps of shards on the counter and floor. She didn't bother to clean up. Chad had made a mess of their lives. Dev had done the same. In fact, aside from what she'd packed and planned to take with her, Chad didn't have much of anything left.

The front door opened, and Maren called out for her mom.

"In the kitchen."

"I guess I'm ready when you are." Maren was dressed casually, in a pair of sweatpants and matching sweatshirt, for the long ride back to Oyster Bay. She had long, thick brown hair with natural blond highlights and expressive green eyes. Maren had sprouted early, growing taller than most of her classmates.

They were going home. Well, back to the only place they could go. Staying in Chicago was out of the question, at least until the video was yesterday's news, and for people to forget the utter humiliation she had experienced. As it was, she couldn't even face her neighbors and didn't even want to look at the other parents on the PTA. At the end of summer, they'd return to Chicago with their heads held high, and Devy would be ready to tackle next year's PTA schedule.

Only, they wouldn't return to the house Devorah loved so much. It held far too many memories, all muddied by Chad admitting he and Ester had been together in the home, the foundation he'd built with Devorah.

So she was going back to the father she barely spoke to and to a brother who already hated Chad. As soon as they found out, every conversation would have a long line of "I told you so's."

"Are you sure you have everything you want to take?"

Maren nodded.

"Your father can mail you whatever."

"I don't plan to talk to him," Maren said as they headed toward the front door. Devorah wanted to cheer, fist pump, and give her daughter a high five, but she wouldn't. Chad needed to work out his relationship with his daughter, without any interference from Devy or anyone else. Fat chance it would happen anytime soon. When she told Maren they were leaving, all Maren could say was that her dad had chosen someone else to be his daughter. That knife to the heart twisted more than the cheating. Devorah never wanted to see her daughter in pain. Especially not at the hands of her dad.

Devy fought back tears as she drove out of the neighborhood she loved. Past the homes she'd visited for various parties, past people she'd called friends. She hadn't told anyone they were leaving, other than Maren's school, but Devy suspected people knew. Hell, everyone in the surrounding area knew. Within hours of the video posting, she'd had to shut her phone off. The calls and texts were too much, and she had nothing to say. She didn't need to hear people tell her how sorry they were or ask if she was the one Ester had talked about in the video. Everyone knew. Ester had done a stand-up job not hiding anything and putting their entire messy situation on full blast for everyone to witness. Ester and Chad easily could've saved Devorah from embarrassment and told her outright. Life could've been a lot easier for everyone involved. But no, Ester wanted the drama.

Ester wanted the views.

"I will find a place here later," she said to her daughter. "We'll come back in the fall, in time for school to start."

"Do you think people will have forgotten?"

No.

Devorah hated that she wasn't able to protect her daughter from any of this. No child should have to bear witness to something of this magnitude. Maren should grow up thinking her father was perfect. But instead, at nine, Maren worried about people never forgetting what her father had done.

"We can only hope. If not, we can try for a different school." They definitely needed a fresh start.

"Maybe." Maren stared out the window. Devy reached for her daughter's hand and held it tightly. She would do whatever it would take to make things right for her little girl again. Her brother, Colt, would step up. He'd be a father figure, and her dad . . . well, he'd remind Devy how he'd told her not to follow some wannabe to college. Which was exactly what she had done. While she loved her job as an estate curator, she wasn't rolling in the dough, according to Chad. And her income definitely wasn't enough to continue the lifestyle she'd grown accustomed to in Chicago.

As soon as she pulled onto Interstate 80, Devy turned on the playlist she'd put together for their fifteen-hour drive, turned the volume up, and started singing. When her favorite song came on, she danced in her seat and did everything she could to get her daughter to smile.

At the end of all this, Maren wouldn't see what the affair had done to her mother. Devorah would mask everything until her child was tucked away at night. Then and only then would she allow her emotions to come through, allow herself to feel. She'd be brave for her daughter and for anyone else she ran into once she was back home. All she could hope for was that no one in Oyster Bay had seen the video—or, if they had, that they hadn't realized it was about her. She didn't need any more embarrassment in her life. Enough of that would be coming from those who had never left Oyster Bay, people who would be happy to see the "Pearl of the Ocean" four years running fall flat on her face.

They were only an hour into the drive when Maren started singing and dancing. Her smile was enough to keep Devy's foot on the gas and moving forward.

It was after dinner the next day when they pulled into town. Antique streetlights and lamps kept the street lit, and the sound of the foghorn reminded Devorah how close they were to the water. Devorah pushed a button, sending her window down. She leaned her head out of the window and inhaled, almost gagging on the smell of brine. No one enjoyed the odor, but it meant home to her. They had Lake Michigan in Chicago, and while it was massive, she missed the ocean. She missed the constant ocean mist the air held from being this close to the water and the sound of fishing boats returning to harbor, along with the constant ting of the buoy bell wind chimes.

"How far does Grandpa live from the water?"

"Not far," Devy said as she turned onto Main Street. "You can walk there in two minutes if you don't get stopped by someone who knows you."

"No one knows me here."

Devy let out a small laugh. "Oh, sweetie, everyone knows who you are here. And by tomorrow morning, they'll all know Tremaine Crowley's only granddaughter is in town. Especially since the last time you were here, you were three."

"Really?" Maren looked like she didn't really believe her mom.

"Yep. Small-town living definitely has its drawbacks." She pulled into the driveway and put the SUV into park. She stared at the yellow house and wide porch. The railings looked freshly painted to match the picket fence in the front. The house and subsequently the fence sat too close to the main road but had been built long before Oyster Bay ever became a town. Blue-and-white hydrangeas took up most of what little front yard they had, and she was surprised they looked well kept and weren't growing over the fence.

To the left of her was a small road, leading not only to their back-yard but to a few cottages out back. At one time, thanks to a social studies assignment, she'd learned that her house had been owned by Joe Updike, the founder of Oyster Bay. He'd built the cottages behind what was now her childhood home for his employees.

Devy sighed and shut her car off. She was ready to get out, stretch, and head to the beach.

"What's the perk?" Maren asked when they met at the back of the car.

"This." Devy pointed across the street, where if you looked through the somewhat empty parking lot, you could see the water and the masts of sailboats tied to the docks. Dev, her brother Colt, and all their friends had spent plenty of time on those docks back in the day. Doing things she'd rather not tell her impressionable nine-year-old daughter about.

"We can go there?"

"Yep. There's a paved walking path over there." She pointed in the general direction of where the pathway started, between two old buildings that had been there since the early 1700s. The one on the right of the path had always been a law office, passed down from one generation to the next. The building on the left used to be a bait-and-tackle shop, but from the looks of it now, it seemed to be some sort of gallery. "With a lot of spots where you can walk down to the water. We'll go tomorrow."

"What about school?"

Devorah opened the back and reached for her suitcase. "School can wait until Monday."

"Awesome."

It was the least Dev could do. She wanted to give Maren time to adjust and get to know Oyster Bay before she threw her to the wolves. She wasn't wrong when she said there were drawbacks to living in a place like Oyster Bay. Sure, it was beautiful and had a lot to offer people, if a town this small was what people looked for. It was great for visiting, but you either fit in or you didn't. There really wasn't a middle ground. Maren had a lot going for her, though. She was outgoing, charismatic, smart, and athletic. Devy hoped that would be enough.

With what they could carry, they headed toward the concrete pathway, where the fence opened near the house, which would lead to the wide-planked steps and then to the front door, where, if memory served correctly, the screen door would be old yet sturdy and still squeak when opened and closed.

With her arms full, Devorah looked toward the house and saw her father standing on the porch. Tremaine Crowley, Crow for short, was the town sheriff, or, as he liked to tell everyone, he was the law around town. He was the epitome of what most people would think a small-town sheriff would look like. Big and burly, he kept his dark hair high and tight. Every kid in town was afraid of him, including his own.

"I heard you were coming," he said gruffly as he descended the stairs. Crow wasn't one for pleasantries or change. He liked his life to stay the same, day in and day out. Which was why Oyster Bay was the only town with a sheriff and deputies, while every other place had a chief and a police force.

"Hi, Daddy," Devorah said. "I can't imagine who you heard it from."

"That man you . . ." Crow stopped when his eyes met his granddaughter's. Maren was one of the reasons Devy had stayed away from Oyster Bay for so long—her daughter looked identical to her mother, who had passed away when Devy was ten and Colt was twelve. Crow never got over the death of his wife.

"Hi, Grandpa," Maren said as she stepped around her mom. Maren wrapped her arms around Crow. The gesture seemed to take him by surprise. Devy cocked her eyebrow at him, in challenge, wanting to know how he was going to react. He slowly placed his hands on Maren's back and patted her. Dev said nothing. She couldn't remember the last time her father had hugged her.

The wooden screen door popped open, and a light-brown puppy trotted out.

"Grandpa, you have a puppy?" Maren went immediately to the fluff ball standing on the porch, with its tail wagging back and forth.

"She was the runt of the litter, and no one wanted her," he said as he reached for the suitcases. "Your uncle brought her home."

"What's her name?" Maren dropped to her knees and cuddled the dog.

"Cordelia," Crow said. "Your uncle says her name means 'goddess of the sea' or something like that. Hell, I mean heck. I don't know."

"I can help take care of her," Maren said without taking her eyes off the puppy. "We're going to be best friends."

Devorah watched this unfold and found herself smiling. This puppy could turn out to be a good thing for Maren.

"Colt lives here?" Devorah asked as she followed her father up the stairs.

"He does. Don't worry, we have room. Come on, Cordelia," he barked out as he entered the house. Much to Devy's surprise, the puppy followed on command.

Nothing had changed. Not the house nor the man who ran it. The door slammed behind Devy. She jumped, lost in thought as she looked around the entryway of the home she'd grown up in and couldn't wait to leave as soon as she graduated from high school.

While the bones of the house were old, dating back to prerevolutionary days, the interior had been redone sometime in the seventies or eighties and was in desperate need of another remodel. To the left was the large dining room, with built-in cabinets and buffet. The last Devy knew, those cabinets and drawers were filled with dishes and linens her mother, Marguerite, had acquired. Either passed down to her or something she'd bought. Devorah couldn't imagine her father throwing anything out. The dining room table still looked the same, from what Devy could see. The tablecloth was lace, yellowed from age and lack of washing, with a vinyl protector underneath. There wasn't a doubt in her mind the wooden tabletop was in pristine condition.

Separating the dining room from the eat-in kitchen was a robin's-egg-blue swinging door. It was something you'd find in an old diner. Devy and her friends often used it for their grand entrances during their days of dress-up.

To the right, the outdated living room, with its floral wallpaper, brown wood trim, and well-used fireplace. The room was in desperate need of a paint job and probably a hammer. In front of the large picture window sat her father's recliner. Crow sat there and watched over the town he'd sworn to protect thirty-plus years ago.

Straight ahead, a glass door, and behind it the hallway, her parents' bedroom, one of the two bathrooms, one of the two entrances to the kitchen, and a door that led to the upstairs bedrooms and attic.

"Jesus, it's like a time capsule in here. Don't you get tired of looking at the same stuff, day after day?"

"No," he said pointedly as he opened the door to the hallway. "Upstairs you go," he said to Maren and Devy. They climbed the stairs after him and Cordelia. Maren followed her grandfather to the right, but Devy paused at another large picture window. That was one thing she loved about this home—the windows. Each room had massive windows, letting in as much natural light as possible.

She moved the sheer curtains to the side, coughing at the amount of dust that had accumulated. If she had to bet, she'd wager her father hadn't washed the curtains since Dev had done it last time. The house would be cleaned, top to bottom, before she went back to Chicago, whether Crow liked it or not. It was the least she could do. She rested her head on the pane of glass and sighed, remembering that if she opened the window and leaned out, she could see the water from here. Otherwise, there was nothing but the rooftops of the other homes on Main Street and the old bank building at the end of the road.

Behind her was her old room. Devy walked toward the threshold and sighed. It was exactly as she'd left it. She expected to find a thick layer of dust, but the room was clean. Had her father cleaned it after Chad called him? Had Colt? Did her father have a girlfriend? The latter idea made her heart swirl in ways she didn't expect. She wanted her dad to be happy, but imagining him with someone other than her mom was hard.

Devy walked through the Jack and Jill bathroom and found Maren chatting animatedly with her grandfather and Cordelia snuggled next to her. He seemed to be listening, which Dev appreciated.

At a break in the conversation, Devy asked, "Where does Colt sleep?"

"Converted the garage into an apartment."

"Really? Isn't it kind of small?"

Crow pointed to the window. Devy walked over and looked into the backyard. The wooden fence had been replaced with white vinyl, and the garage Dev remembered as falling down looked brand new. Her father could build a new garage but not update the interior of their house.

Because my mother never went into the garage.

"Looks nice. Where's your car?" she asked without turning around.

The last Devy knew, her father still had his '72 Chevelle, black with black leather bucket seats. She used to love riding around in it when she was little.

"Still there. Colt built his apartment above the garage."

Devy turned around in time to watch her father leave the room without another word. She glanced at Maren, who stared at her. Dev shrugged.

"Grandpa's complicated."

"He'd probably say the same about you."

Maren's words gave her pause. History was about to repeat itself if Devy wasn't careful. The last thing she wanted was for Maren to have a strained relationship with Chad, even though he didn't deserve any kindness from her. Either of them, for that matter.

Four

Hayden

Hayden's mood matched the dreary weather. It had rained for over twenty-four hours, ruining any weekend plans he'd had with Conor. He'd wanted to show his son Oyster Bay, take him down to all the best fishing holes by the water, and give Conor a chance to acclimate himself to the area before he started school. Conor would be walking to school most days, and he needed to learn the way. Not that he could really get lost. Oyster Bay was the definition of small-town living. By the end of the week, if not already, the people in town would know who Conor was and where he was supposed to be.

Instead, Hayden drove Conor to school, along Main Street, with cars parked along the side of the road, in his oversize truck. He cursed as he turned the corner and barely escaped taking off the side mirrors of a couple of parked cars.

"Maybe you need a smaller truck," Conor said as Hayden drove at a snail's pace along the road, slowing even more to allow others to pass by.

A new vehicle wasn't in the budget, nor was it something he planned on doing, but his son had a point. Hayden would have to see if his father was up for a trip to the "city" for a possible trade-in. A truck was still a necessity, especially with the camper and the need for supplies to build a house.

Hayden pulled into the school's parking lot, shut the truck off, and stared at Oyster Bay School, or OB, as the locals called it, where he'd spent his entire youth. The K–12 building had grown over the years as the population increased but was still small.

"Maybe you want to try homeschooling me?" Conor asked.

"You'll like it here," Hayden said as he looked at his son. "People will like you, and you'll make some great friends. Don't forget, baseball sign-ups are coming up."

"Yeah."

"When I played, we were good."

"Back in the olden days?"

Hayden smiled and chuckled. "Come on, sport."

Conor walked two steps ahead of his dad and kept his eyes trained on the ground. Hayden felt for his son. He'd been through so much in the past six months; adding a new school to the mix was yet another stressor for the boy. Still, Hayden stood by his decision to move back to Rhode Island. He needed his mother's help—not only with Conor but with himself. Being among family was what they needed.

"Hayden McKenna, is that you?"

The stout woman in front of him caught him off guard. It took him a moment to recall her name. "Mrs. Pierson?"

"Of course. Who else would I be?" she said with a laugh.

Hayden couldn't believe the school receptionist he had back in the "olden days," according to Conor, was still the receptionist now. He figured she would've retired ages ago.

"Now this must be Conor. I'm Mrs. Pierson. I've known your dad since he was in diapers." That was a slight exaggeration, or at least Hayden thought it was.

Conor looked at his dad and grinned brightly. A lot of times over the next few weeks, someone in town would say something like this to Conor about Hayden. But this one would stick with Conor for a long time, and he'd never let his father live it down.

"Hi, Mrs. Pierson," Conor said after Hayden gave him the eye.

"Follow me into the office."

Hayden held the door open. She passed through, followed by Conor. As soon as the door slammed shut, Hayden's heart lurched at the sound, reminding him of the one too many times he'd spent in there, sitting on the hard wooden chairs, waiting for the principal to call him back to the office for something he likely did but would deny until the cows came home.

Mrs. Pierson walked around the tall counter, which she was barely tall enough to rest her elbows on. "Let's see, I have your schedule right here," she said as she handed it to Conor. "You'll spend most of your day with Mr. Raze, but sometimes you'll go to other classrooms. That'll all depend on your testing."

Conor groaned. "Testing?"

"You'll be fine, bud. The school needs to see where you are intellectually with your peers," Hayden said, and then he looked at the receptionist. "Testing won't be all day, right? I really want Conor to have a chance to get to know his teachers and his classmates."

"Nope, one hour a day for the week. We have another new student, so he won't be alone."

"Perfect." Hayden set his hand on Conor's shoulder. "Want me to walk you to Mr. Raze's class?"

"Do you know him?"

Hayden hesitated and then shook his head. "No, but I believe I had his dad as my math teacher."

Conor rolled his eyes. "I really hope you were a good student."

Hayden laughed, as did Mrs. Pierson. All his antics would need to remain under wraps. He didn't need his son learning about the things he did in elementary school. Or junior high. Or high school, for that matter.

Mrs. Pierson handed Conor a map of the school, then gave a stack to Hayden. "You have homework, Hayden," she said with a hint of laughter. "And you: Mr. Raze is waiting." She gave him directions and then shooed them out of the office.

"You sure you don't want me to walk you to class?"

"I'm not a baby."

"Making sure you find your way doesn't make you a baby."

Conor stared down the hall and sighed. "I'll be fine. See you after school?"

"Yep. If the rain stops, we'll walk so you'll know how to get back to Grandma and Grandpa's." Hayden waited for Conor to acknowledge him. When he didn't, he sighed. "I love you, sport. This will be good for us. I promise."

"Yeah, bye, Dad."

Hayden watched as Conor walked down the hall, looked at the map, and turned around. He was tempted to sneak down the hall but didn't want Conor to spot him. He had to let Conor grow up.

With his head down, Hayden pushed the metal door open and stepped out. He barely had time to stop himself from bumping into the woman hiding under the awning from the current downpour.

"Shit, sorr—" He paused and took her in. Hayden wasn't great at recognizing people from the past, but this face he knew, without a doubt.

Devorah Crowley, the one he'd crushed on, loved even, through his formative years and the one he'd lost the day Chad Campbell weaseled his way into her life. She was still as beautiful as the day he last saw her. He'd come home from college to see her, only to find her smiling and happy with someone else. He'd missed his opportunity, again.

But it was the first time he ever kissed her that flashed in his mind on this dreary morning.

"What are you doing here?" Colt groaned when his sister walked into the basement of Sheldon Gene's house. Hayden smiled, though, because Devorah Crowley was one smoking chick, and he had the hots for her. He didn't even care that she was two years younger than him. Although, if he ever told any of his friends, especially Colt, they'd tease him. She didn't act like the other

girls in her grade and was way more mature than her brother. Sleepovers with her brother were some of Hayden's favorite things to do on the weekends. Being one room away from her was a definite bonus. Plus, she liked to watch movies with them and always sat next to Hayden. The best part was when she'd get a blanket, and it would somehow end up covering him too. Then his hand could touch her leg, and no one but them would know.

"It's not your party, Colt. Laila and I can come if we want."

"Crow is going to bust your butt if he catches you."

"Well then, it's a good thing you're not telling because he'll bust yours too!"

She stuck her tongue out at her brother, and Hayden coughed to hide his laughter.

"It's time to play 'seven minutes in heaven,'" Sheldon yelled. There was a collective groan among the partygoers, who were mostly classmates at Oyster Bay but also included a handful of those who were excited. Seven minutes to make out with your boyfriend or girlfriend, without getting caught by your parents or teachers, was a nice reprieve. Or at least Hayden thought it would be if he'd had a girlfriend.

Everyone sat in a circle, boy / girl / boy / girl. Each drew a piece of paper from Sheldon's hat, which was sort of gross because Sheldon wasn't the type who washed his hair very often.

"Who has number one?"

Some girl Hayden didn't know raised her hand and spun the bottle. It rotated a couple of times before stopping in front of a guy a few over from him. Hayden glanced at Devorah. She stared back, and Hayden really hoped the bottle would land on her when he spun or vice versa. He had wanted to kiss her for a while now, but there was no way he'd ever make a move. Not with Colt being his best friend.

With each new spin of the bottle, Hayden held his breath. He felt like he had a hundred needles jabbing into his skin, mocking him that he could end up with someone he didn't like or didn't even know. Which was the point of the game. But he only wanted to go into the closet with one person.

When Devy raised her hand indicating that she was next, Hayden couldn't take his eyes off her as she leaned forward to spin, and then his eyes watched every revolution the bottle took. He'd never prayed so hard to be chosen.

His lungs seized as the opening of the bottle pointed toward him. If he had any words, they failed instantly. So had any rational thoughts, until he heard Colt.

"Dude, this is sick," Colt hollered over the music and the snickers of the others in the circle. "She's my sister."

Hayden looked at the bottle, and sure enough, the seven minutes in heaven gods were watching out for him.

He smirked. He couldn't help it but added the classic eye roll to let Colt know it bothered him to have to go in the closet with his sister. "Don't worry. We'll just talk."

"You better, or I'll kick your ass."

Devorah stood and came toward Hayden, grinning from ear to ear. He followed her to the closet, where Sheldon stood with his stopwatch poised and ready to track those precious seven minutes. He opened the door, told them to keep their clothes on, and then closed it.

The space was dark, but nothing was hanging from the bar, from what Hayden could feel.

"So, we just stand here until Sheldon opens the door?"

"No." Hayden kept his voice low and tried to add a hint of seductiveness, although he wasn't sure he'd done it right. "I want to kiss you."

"What about Colt?"

"He's not in here."

Hayden's heart picked up the pace as he thought about kissing Devorah. He'd seen enough TV to know where his hand should go and what his mouth should do, but knowing and doing were vastly different things in the minds of teenagers.

He cupped her face and leaned in. At first, he kissed the side of her lips and got more of her cheek than anything.

Awkward!

He tried again, and this time their lips pressed together. Another try, and he held his lips to hers for longer.

"Can I try with tongue?" he asked.

"I've never done that," she said.

"Me neither."

"You won't tell Colt?" she asked.

"Never."

"Okay."

Hayden kissed her again, but this time he had more confidence and slipped his tongue into her mouth. When his touched hers, an explosion of terror, anxiety, thrills, and happiness rushed through his body. Devorah tilted her head up slightly and pushed her tongue a bit deeper into Hayden's mouth. He moved his head to the other side, just like he'd seen numerous times while watching soap operas with his mother, and then back.

"We should stop," she said, pulling away and resting her forehead against his.

"I know, but I don't want to. That was, wow!"

"Maybe we can do it again."

"When?" He knew he sounded eager. He was, and he had no idea how to control what he felt. His heart raced, and his skin felt as if it were on fire.

"Are you spending the night?"

From that night until he left for college, they made out every chance they could, but he never had the courage to tell Colt he wanted to date his sister. He regretted never saying something.

Now, Hayden stared at Devorah as his mind fumbled for something to say. The first thing that came to his mind was to ask how she was doing, but he could see that, just by looking at her, she was not well. He took her in. The long dark hair he remembered from years ago was still as beautiful as ever. Her striking brown eyes, the ones that had kept him mesmerized for years, were bloodshot and sitting on top of bags that looked bruised.

"What's wrong?" he asked before he could stop the words from coming out. He should've started with "hi" or a compliment. "What can I do to help?"

She blanched and looked away. He fought the urge to turn her chin toward him so he could wipe away the tears rolling over her cheeks. Someone had hurt her.

Who?

Her husband?

Rage boiled in his belly. The last he knew, she'd married Chad Campbell, the biggest piece of shit Oyster Bay had ever encountered. He was an outsider looking in. Not someone from OB, Rhode Island, or even New England. He thought he could come to town and rule the roost. Most of the guys in high school hated the kid, but the girls seemed to fawn over him. Probably because he was a shiny new toy.

Hayden reached for her hand and felt his own hand warm. "Devorah," he said softly. Her name had always been one of his favorites. It was unique and often mispronounced. Anyone who didn't know her and saw her name would say "De-*vor*-ah," when it was pronounced "*Dev*-ra." Her name matched her.

Devorah smiled sadly and took her hand from his. He refused to let the rejection sting. "Hi, Hayden. Fancy meeting you here." She looked back at the school and sighed.

"Yeah, I could say the same. What are you doing here?"

She shrugged. "Oh, you know."

He didn't. He wanted to, though.

"Do you need a ride?" He motioned toward the parking lot.

"I think I'm okay," she said as she leaned forward and looked toward the sky.

"It's not supposed to stop for a couple of hours." He could wait, and then it would be time to pick Conor up, which would probably ease the anxiety Hayden felt about his son starting at a new school today. "I'm going to run over to my truck. I'll drive up. If you want a ride, you'll get in. If not . . ." Hayden shrugged and took off sprinting toward his truck.

He dodged puddles and kept his head down to avoid getting pelted in the face with rain. Inside his cab, he turned on the truck, blasted the heat, and turned the wipers on.

He did as he'd said and pulled up to where Devorah stood. Hayden leaned over the seat, opened the door, and waited. Between the sound of the truck and the rain, he didn't even try to yell because she wouldn't have been able to hear him.

It took her a handful of seconds before she darted for the truck, hopped in, and pulled the door shut. "Thank you."

"It's the least I could do," he said as he put the truck into drive. "I wouldn't want you to melt." When he was one of those annoying prepubescent boys, he did what any normal tween did—cracked jokes about her to get her attention. When she finally gave him the attention he wanted, he was afraid her brother would never approve, which meant Hayden was never truly himself with Devy. By the time he graduated from high school, he was in love with her, and he was certain she loved him right back. When Hayden finally found the courage to come clean about his feelings, he was a bit too late. A trip home from college changed everything. In a way, Devorah had broken his heart, and he'd never truly gotten over it.

"Funny."

"Yeah, that's me, the funny guy."

"Who are you staring at?" Colt elbowed Hayden in the bicep. He was thankful his friend didn't see him flinch or Colt would've razzed him relentlessly for being soft. Hayden was far from weak, but an elbow to the tender part of his arm was never fun.

Hayden cleared his throat and shook his head for good measure. "Uh, no one."

Except she was someone. She was his best friend's sister, and completely off limits.

Hayden couldn't pinpoint what had changed in him, but for the past two or three weeks, Devorah Crowley had been living rent-free in his mind. His infatuation had started when Hayden spent the night at her house . . . well, stayed with her brother, and they'd run into each other in the bathroom.

She'd smiled at Hayden. It wasn't one of those "Hey, how's it going?" types of smiles. It was flirtatious, with fluttering eyelashes and a soft, sexy voice as she said "Excuse me" and tilted her head. But it was when she bit her lower lip and pulled her long braid over her shoulder that Hayden felt a stirring. He wanted to follow her into her room but froze.

What would he even do in there?

Hayden cleared his thoughts and brought himself back to the here and now.

The cafeteria was busy and noisy, with students and teachers moving in all directions. Devorah sat next to Laila Dixon. They were best friends, and Laila was often at the Crowleys' when Hayden was there. Sometimes the four of them hung out, but Colt hated spending time with his sister and her annoying friend.

Hayden definitely didn't mind.

After a few minutes, Devorah grabbed her things, waved, and left the cafeteria. Hayden did the same, telling Colt he needed to go to the nurse. The boys were always going to the nurse with some stomach bug because she was young and very pretty.

He made his way over to Laila, hoping Colt wasn't watching.

"Hey, Laila."

Her eyes sparkled when he said her name. "Hi, Hayden."

He sat next to her, and she tried to flutter her eyelashes, but she didn't do it as sexily as Devorah had. But maybe he was biased. Laila was pretty, but she wasn't Dev.

"Can I ask you something?"

"Yes," she said excitedly.

"Does Devorah like me?"

Laila's face fell, and Hayden regretted the way he'd approached her with his question. But he had to know, and there was only one person who could tell him.

"I'll ask," she said pointedly and went back to chatting with the others at the table, making Hayden feel like an intruder.

Hayden had no choice but to get up and leave. He headed to his locker. From there, he could see Devorah's. He'd lost count over the past couple of weeks of how many times he'd stood there, watching her throw her head back in laughter, wishing he'd been the one to elicit that response from her. He hoped she was there because then maybe he could smile at her, and she'd want to talk.

Before the bell rang to send everyone back to class, Laila came toward Hayden. She sauntered over and had a look on her face like she had juicy gossip to share. His heart rate spiked. The anticipation of finding out was enough to actually send him to see the nurse.

"Hey," he said as casually as possible.

"She thinks you're a funny guy."

"Funny?"

Laila shrugged. "Yep." She walked away, leaving Hayden speechless. He waited for her to turn around and come back with more information, but she continued down the hall without another word or a glance over her shoulder.

"I'm funny?"

A hand slapped down on his shoulder, jolting him. "A laugh a minute," Colt said as he grabbed his book from their shared locker.

"Funny?" he mumbled to himself in disbelief. He closed the metal door and followed Colt down the hall, shaking his head. What had he done to make her laugh?

Hayden smiled at the memory of when he thought he'd test the waters and ask Laila if Devorah liked him.

Hayden drove. He headed out of town, passed her father's house, and continued past the boutiques, banks, and other businesses. She said nothing. He pulled into the parking lot of the pier and parked at the water's edge. The only people who would be able to see them would be anyone who parked next to him. Leaning over, he opened the glove box, pulled out a box of tissues, and handed it to her.

Devorah coughed out a sob and took the box from Hayden. He tried not to watch her, to keep his eyes forward. If it hadn't been raining, fishing boats would've been coming and going. They would at least give him something to watch.

Except, he wanted to keep his eyes on her. It was clear that Chad or whoever it was had hurt her. Hayden didn't know how or why, or even who. But someone had.

"How long are you in town for?" he asked.

"I don't know. If Crow has anything to say about it, not long."

Hayden chuckled. Every kid in town was afraid of Colt and Devorah's father. With a nickname like "Crow," it was hard for them not to be. He saw and heard everything and held a grudge like there was no tomorrow. Once you were on his bad side, you'd never make it to the good one.

"Where do you live these days?"

"Chicago," she said quietly.

Hayden nodded. "Never thought about visiting there."

Devorah fiddled with the tissue in her hands. "Do you not know why I'm here?"

"Nope," he said. "I arrived in town a few days ago. I haven't even seen your brother yet."

"He cheated."

He knew it. She didn't have to specify who she was talking about. "Chad?"

She nodded. "With my best friend."

Stupid fucker.

"I found out because she posted a video about it on one of those popular vlogging apps." Devorah looked out the window. "I was getting a pedicure and thought I'd pass the time by watching some funny videos, and there she was, confessing it all."

"Wait, what?"

"I'm thinking, 'There's no way my best friend is having an affair with my husband.' I mean, Chad and I don't fight, and I think we have a really great marriage. Besides, she's my best friend, and her daughter and my daughter are best friends. We're close. We vacation together. There's no way. Except when I drive over to Chad's work, he's not there and he's not answering his work or cell phone. The only logical thing is to drive over to her house and . . ." She inhaled deeply. "I guess I don't know what I thought I would find."

Hayden didn't ask for details. The fact she was telling him and reliving all this was enough. Devorah could've left it at "He cheated," and that would've been enough for him.

"I'm sorry."

"Me too."

"How old is your daughter?"

"She's nine."

"Does she go to OB?"

"First day," she said.

Hayden smiled. "My son, Conor, started today. He's nine as well."

For the first time since she climbed into his truck, Devorah turned and looked at him. She didn't smile. There wasn't any light in her eyes. Hayden fought the urge to rub his thumb under her eyes.

"Your wife is probably wondering where you are."

Hayden shook his head slightly. "She passed away six months ago."

FIVE

DEVORAH

The rain continued as Hayden's statement lingered in the space of the cab. Would death be easier? Would it be better to live with knowing your spouse had died instead of knowing he'd consciously crawled into bed with your best friend?

Devorah wasn't sure.

The feelings she had—the broken heart, the longing, and the anger—would likely be the same, no matter what.

She stared out the window at the gray. The rain, the cloud cover, and the fog matched her mood. In the distance, the foghorn sounded, warning any boat or ship trying to navigate through the mess. It was unsafe, yet people would try. Even on the water, people had places to go and things to do. Fish, lobster, crabs, and oysters needed to be caught and brought in. Days off were rare.

Devorah turned and looked at Hayden, sitting there with his seat belt still on despite them being parked. He'd changed since she last saw him, thickened out and become more manly. She remembered him as tall and scrawny, and someone who had flirted with her and at times made her feel special. There was a time in her life when she thought they would become official, but Hayden never asked her to be his girlfriend.

He led people to think otherwise, though, and he never dated anyone else until he left for college.

Then Chad took an interest in her, and everything changed.

Was Hayden one year or two years older than her?

She couldn't remember, other than Hayden being best friends with Colt.

Somewhere in her room, she still had her old yearbooks. Later, she'd look through them and see what year Hayden had graduated.

He ran his hand through his sandy-blond hair. While short on the sides, the top had a bit of a curl to it, and Devorah wondered if the curls appeared only when wet or if his hair had always been wavy. For as long as she'd known him, he'd kept his hair short and sometimes even shaved.

"I'm really sorry about your wife."

Hayden sighed and rocked back and forth. "Thanks." He glanced at Devorah. She studied him. His face was tan, with the fine lines you'd expect to see at his age, but when she looked into his ocean-blue eyes, she saw sadness and hope, a life well lived, and worry. How could someone have so many questions and unknowns in his eyes? Devy turned away, unwilling for him to analyze her the way she had him.

"I hear Colt is running the Lazy Lamb," Hayden said, breaking the silence.

"Have you been?"

"No, not yet. I meant to over the weekend but decided to lay low. I guess I'm not ready for the questions to start."

Devy knew all too well what he meant. "Crow's phone rang off the hook once people saw my car in the driveway. A few people came over, brought casseroles. Like they did after my mom died. He's pissed."

"At you?"

Devorah shrugged. "Maybe he's gloating. I don't know."

"There's a lot of pride in a man like him."

"And his daughter is the laughingstock of the social media world." Devy wiped at her cheek. "He doesn't understand the whole vlogging thing, and I don't have the patience to explain how people post stupid shit for likes and views."

"Something tells me she didn't post a video like that for likes, but to come clean."

Devorah scoffed. "How about telling me in private, so I'm not embarrassed and leaving town with my tail tucked between my legs?"

"What does Chad say?"

She looked at Hayden. He seemed genuinely concerned for her feelings. "You know how when you're watching a movie, and the person gets caught with the wrong person and they say, 'It's not what it looks like'?"

Hayden nodded.

"Yeah, that didn't happen. My husband covered himself up and left his mistress lying there, naked as the day she was born. Those words never came out of his mouth. He didn't apologize or beg me to listen to him. He got angry with me because I threw up on her front lawn and didn't have any shoes on."

"Because you'd just had a pedicure."

Devy nodded. "Yep. Then he told me he loved her."

Hayden leaned toward her and gently rubbed his thumb along her cheekbone, wiping away her tears. "I don't mean to make you cry."

"You're not," she told him. "My thoughts make me cry."

"Still, we don't have to talk about it."

"Yeah, you asked about Colt. I haven't been to the Lazy Lamb either. I'm sure I'll go this week sometime and pretend everything's great and smile my way through town while I wait for the other shoe to drop."

"Being?"

"That someone here has seen the video. It's humiliating enough to know my entire community in Chicago saw it, but if it reaches here . . ." Devy groaned. "Maren's been through enough."

"Maybe Chad should ask his friend to take it down."

"We'd have to be on speaking terms."

"Silent treatment, huh?"

Devorah shrugged and readjusted in the seat. "I don't have anything to say. Besides, deep down, I don't want to hear how this is my fault or how happy he is now that I'm not there."

Hayden reached over and touched her hand lightly. "We'll go to the Lazy Lamb together. This way, the town gossips won't know which way to go with the tales."

"Thanks, but I don't need your pity."

"It's not pity," he told her, but that was how she saw it. She didn't need to be seen with him so people wouldn't judge her. Eventually she'd have to face the music, and it would be best to do it with her head held high. Ignorance was bliss, and Devy banked on no one in Oyster Bay having seen the video.

Devorah wrapped her fingers around the door handle and paused. She glanced at Hayden, who stared back at her. "Thanks for the talk." She opened the door and slid out, not giving him a chance to talk her out of walking in the rain. The rain hid her tears, which she needed right now in case she ran into someone on the street. Not that many people would be out, but people were always willing to brave the wind and downpours to do their daily business.

On her walk toward her father's home, she passed by the Lazy Lamb. She glanced at her watch, wiped water from the top, and saw she'd sat in Hayden's truck for almost two hours. It was almost lunchtime, and her stomach was growling. Instantly, her hand covered her midsection to stifle the noise, although it was unlikely anyone else could have heard it anyway. The action was habit, and if Chad had been with her, he'd admonish her for not eating, and then, once she had, he'd mention how snug her pants were or ask how the gym was, knowing full well she hadn't gone.

As hard as she tried not to think about Chad, he flooded her memories. She missed him and didn't know how to turn off those feelings, even though the thought of him repulsed her. After spending the last two decades of her life with the man, the only image she could recall was the one embedded in her mind—her husband thrusting into another woman. It was seared there, playing on constant repeat, to remind Devy of her failure as a wife.

The door to the Lazy Lamb opened, and two men walked out. They didn't see her standing there and speed walked toward a parked car along the curb. The door shut slowly, giving Devorah enough time to tell herself she didn't want to go in and see her brother, especially looking like a drowned rat. Giving the fine people of Oyster Bay more fodder was not high on her priority list.

By the time she walked up the steps to her childhood home, water was sloshing in her shoes. Once she was under the cover of the porch, she kicked them off, along with her socks and jacket, and made her way inside. The house was warm and smelled of tobacco. Her father must've smoked his pipe before he left for work. She stood in the hallway and inhaled the familiar scent—one she hadn't realized she longed for until she'd returned home.

Her relationship with her father was rocky at best. Simply put, Tremaine had no idea how to raise a daughter. He'd always had high and unreasonable expectations of her and Colt, but he seemed to go easier on her brother. The Crowley kids were expected to stay out of trouble, get good grades, and not do anything to embarrass the sheriff.

When Devy started dating Chad Campbell, Crow didn't approve. It wasn't because no one would ever be good enough for his daughter but because Crow had busted Chad for "parking" at the pier. Then, weeks later, he'd asked Devorah out. "Someone who does that with one girl and then moves on to another is not to be trusted," Crow had said.

Devorah should've listened.

She opened the door to the basement and walked down the stairs, carrying her wet shoes and jacket. Downstairs, she stuffed her shoes with old newspaper, put them in a pillowcase, and knotted the opening. Then she stripped off her clothes and put everything into the dryer. Devy was thankful Crow was at work because the thunking sound her shoes made in the dryer would surely annoy him. She rummaged through a basket on top of the dryer, deduced that the clothes belonged to Colt, and found a T-shirt and a pair of sweatpants to slip into. When she got to the top of the stairs, she screamed and placed her hand over her pounding heart.

"What are you doing here?"

"This is my house," her father said gruffly.

Devy stepped into the hallway and closed the door to the basement. "No, I mean why aren't you at work?"

"I come home for lunch."

"Oh." She followed her father into the kitchen and stood there, wringing her hands. In Chicago, this was her space, the place where she would make her family three meals a day and where Maren would come and sit at the island bar after school and tell Devy about her day.

"Would you like me to make you something?" she asked Crow.

"No," he said pointedly. "I can do it."

Devy felt a mixture of rage and hurt boiling. "I know you can do it, but I'm offering because . . . because . . ." She couldn't finish her statement before she broke down. A sob rolled from her toes until it left her mouth in an ungodly sound. She bent at her waist, wrapping her arms tightly around herself, as if she was trying (and failing) to hold everything in.

"I can't . . ." were the only words she could get out before her father pulled her to his chest.

"Breathe, Devorah," he said as he rubbed his hands up and down her back. "You need to breathe before you pass out."

"It h-hurts," she stammered through a hiccup. "Everything hurts."

"It gets better."

Would it, though? Was he better, or was he still bitter and angry that his wife had passed away? Devorah didn't see how any of this could get better. Her husband had done the unthinkable. If they'd had problems in their marriage, he should've come to her. Instead, he'd given himself to another woman, a woman Devy had trusted implicitly. This betrayal ran deep and was unforgivable.

Her father didn't know this sort of pain. His wife didn't cheat or leave him for another man. She was sick, and the doctors couldn't cure her. Yet Crow still golfed with those doctors on occasion. Or at least he had the last Devy knew.

What Crow *had* done, though, was shut himself off from everyone, except for work and his friends, after her mother died. Crow hadn't comforted his children, except briefly, when he'd told them she had succumbed to cancer. He was a man of few words and even fewer emotions.

She still had to comfort her daughter and explain to Maren why her father had done something like this, and why he had allowed his mistress to be so callous in airing their dirty laundry.

Devorah stepped out of her father's grasp, doing so first before he could let go. If he pushed her away, she'd lose it again. The Crowleys were strong and always put on a brave face despite how they felt on the inside.

She left her dad in the kitchen, to fend for himself like he wanted, and climbed the stairs to the second floor. Without changing out of Colt's clothes, she crawled into bed, set the alarm on her phone, and pulled the covers over her head. Sleep would evade her, but she'd try. It was the least she could do for herself.

Six

Hayden

Hayden pulled in behind the last car in the school pickup line, and within seconds other moms—not parents—were out of their cars and coming toward him. This was his personal brand of hell, and he wished Oyster Bay had a busing service.

"Shit," he muttered as a mom approached the driver's side of his truck. He didn't have enough time to determine if he knew her from way back when or not. Thankfully, the rain had stopped. He pushed the button, and his window went down.

"Hayden McKenna, I heard you were back in town."

Any news traveled fast in Oyster Bay.

He made eye contact with the woman and then briefly looked around. Other moms lingered, some in pairs and others in groups. Were they all waiting to talk to him? Did he need to hold court or something?

"Yep, I'm back." He cringed at his wording and the inflection his voice did at the end. It was as if he thought he was the Terminator, who promised to always return. This wasn't Hayden's first time back to his hometown, but it was his first as a single man. That made a difference.

"You don't remember me, do you?"

He shook his head slowly while he studied her face. She seemed familiar, but he had a hard time placing where he'd know her from, other than school.

"Sapphire Fleming."

As soon as she said her name, he remembered both her and her sisters. They all had gemstone names, which stood out among their classmates. If he recalled correctly, she was one of four sisters, along with Ruby, Opal, and Amethyst. Amethyst was in his class and was memorable because she had worked in his father's office as an aide.

"How's it going?" he asked, even though engaging in a conversation in the school dismissal line didn't seem like the right time. The car in front of him inched forward, which confused him since the bell hadn't rung yet. He didn't know what the etiquette was—did he move up as well, or wait?

"Things are well, just picking up the kiddos. You know," Sapphire said in the same bubbly tone he remembered her having back in school. "You're back for good?"

He nodded.

"That's fantastic." She placed her hand on the door, her fingers grazing his arm. "We'll have to get together for a beer and catch up."

They had nothing to catch up on, but he agreed anyway because he didn't want to be rude. The bell rang, saving the day. He caught a glimpse of the others as they looked at him talking with Sapphire, then slumped their shoulders and turned toward the double doors and their cars. Something told him he'd experience this again tomorrow.

Sapphire made her way back to her car, pausing to turn and give him a wave. Someone honked and she scowled. Hayden watched the double doors he'd gone into and come out of when he was in elementary school. His mom would pick him and Allie up, and then they'd go sit in the back room of their father's practice until their mom had wrapped up work for the day. Darcy McKenna never let her children stay home longer than an hour by themselves. Small town or not, things happened when adults weren't around. By the time Hayden was in high school and playing sports after school, Allie went with him, choosing to sit and watch, then being treated like she wasn't responsible for his well-being.

Kids filed out in small groups. Girls talked animatedly, with their little arms and hands flying in every which direction, and boys laughed at something their friends had said. Hayden wanted this for his son. He wanted him to find a good, solid group of friends he could grow up with. Hayden had, until they all went away to college and lost touch over the years. Most of his friends wanted to get the hell out of Dodge and never return. Move to the city and live. Hayden had done the same thing until he'd met Sofia and followed her back to Wyoming. He'd intended to go to law school, but that never seemed to pan out. He ended up putting his criminal justice degree to work by becoming a deputy in the county sheriff's department. He'd never truly found his way once he left Oyster Bay.

But Sofia had made him happy, and that was enough.

Hayden spotted Conor before his son saw the truck. He studied his son as he stood there under the awning with his backpack slung over his shoulder and his sweatshirt tied around his waist. Conor looked left and then right, spotted the truck, and gave his dad a little wave. The gesture brought a much-needed smile to Hayden's face.

He saw Conor wave to a classmate. A girl, with a long brunette ponytail. She reminded him of someone else he knew, someone who had recently spent time in his truck. Hayden would ask Conor later, if only to appease his own curiosity.

Conor walked toward the truck with his head held high, which brought another smile to Hayden's face—he assumed his son's first day went well. Of course, he could've been happy that his day was over. Hayden often hated school as a kid. One Monday in particular always stood out in his mind—the Monday after some Saturday-night party in the eighth grade, where he and Devorah Crowley had made out in the closet for seven glorious minutes. He thought he'd done a pretty damn good job of expressing himself and confidently walked right up to Miss

Devorah Crowley and tried to ask her out—only for her to turn ten shades of red and run from him.

"Hey, Devorah." Hayden said her name with such confidence—he felt like he was on top of the world. Laila looked at him first. He avoided all eye contact with her because he was pretty certain she had a crush on him. But Hayden was also confident Dev liked him more.

"Oh, hi, Hayden."

The air left his sail. He'd hoped for a little more exuberance from her.

"Can I speak with you in the hall?" As soon as he'd asked, he regretted it. Their classmates lingered, staring, and some looked at them questioningly. He should've waited until they were doing homework later, when they'd be alone in the dining room of her house, and while Colt was on the phone with his current girlfriend.

The other girls around the table giggled. Hayden smiled, even though he wanted to run away. Devorah stood, and he motioned for her to walk ahead of him. Like his father often did with his mom.

When they got to the hall, Hayden pointed to the alcove where a lot of the high schoolers went to make out. Dev's footsteps faltered a bit, but she continued.

Once they were safely behind the wall, Hayden mustered all the courage he could. "Would you like to go out with me?"

Her eyes widened, her cheeks turned a fiery red, and she covered her mouth. Before he could ask her if she was okay, she ran away, leaving him there in utter embarrassment.

Later, Colt said that some older dude had asked his sister out. "If I find out which one of my friends did this, I'm going to pummel him."

Dev apologized weeks later, and while Hayden wasn't afraid of Colt, he was afraid of Crow, and he didn't want to do anything to damage his friendship with Colt. Devorah liked Hayden, though, and she flirted.

He flirted back.

Two months after they'd had seven minutes in heaven, he kissed her again, this time under the old oak tree, where no one could see.

Hayden sighed and cleared his thoughts as Conor approached the truck. Hayden leaned over and pulled the handle to help Conor open the door. His son tossed his backpack onto the floorboard and climbed in.

"Well, how was it?"

"It's school," Conor said pointedly and shrugged. "But Mr. Raze is nice. He's very funny."

"Did you make any new friends?"

Another shrug. "I met some kids. They invited me to play kickball with them."

"That's fun." Hayden inched his way out and drove slowly around the crescent-shaped roadway, watching for any youngsters who might dart out in front of him, but also trying to see where the girl Conor had spoken to had gone. Hayden told himself he wanted to confirm the girl was Devy's, but what he really wanted to do was see Devy again. She'd left him in the parking lot, and at first, he was okay with her leaving, until he remembered what she'd said about her husband and how he hadn't chased after her. By then, it was too late. He'd looked around for her, but it was like she had vanished into thin air.

"Yeah, just the guys, though."

"Girls don't want to play?"

"I don't think they're invited. They sit on the bleachers and cheer. Some even have those hand things they shake."

"Pom-poms?"

"Yeah, those things. One girl did some leg thing and had her arms doing funny things. The guys seemed to like it."

"That's called cheer or cheerleading," Hayden said as he made his way down Main Street. "It's actually a popular sport for kids your age and through high school. Some go on to college and cheer for college teams."

"You mean girls?"

"No," Hayden said as he turned onto his parents' street. "Boys can join if they want. Cheerleading is serious business, especially in high school and college. They're responsible for hyping up the crowd."

"Oh, like the announcer at the basketball games?"

Hayden pulled into his parents' driveway and put his beastly truck into park. "Exactly." He turned the truck off and got out, meeting Conor around the front. He placed his hand on his son's shoulder and guided him to the back door.

"Did you start on the house today?" Conor asked as they climbed the back steps.

"No, it rained most of the day. I might head over now, though, and place the flags down, so the contractor knows where we want the foundation."

"Don't forget the pool," Conor said as he went into the house.

"Yeah, yeah." His other grandparents had an indoor pool at their house in Wyoming, and one of the things Hayden said he would consider when building their new house was a pool. As soon as he had said it, he knew it was the wrong thing to do. He'd used it as a crutch or some sort of enticement to get Conor on the same page when it came to moving.

Staying in Wyoming wasn't an option, even though he'd had a good relationship with his in-laws. As much as Hayden needed Conor to be okay, Hayden needed his parents. There was a certain level of emotional support only a parent could give. Sofia's parents would visit, and once Conor settled in Oyster Bay, he'd go back to Wyoming for breaks. Hayden had no intentions of keeping them away from each other.

Hayden walked in after his son and kicked his shoes off onto the wet mat by the door. As he did, he inhaled deeply, and his stomach growled. He smelled marinara, freshly baked bread, and cake. He wasn't sure what type of cake, but he knew they were having cake for dessert.

Darcy was in the kitchen, standing at the island; Conor was across from her, perched on one of the barstools. Hayden kissed her cheek and dipped his finger into the bowl of frosting on the countertop. Homemade chocolate frosting was his favorite. Everything homemade was his favorite. She slapped his hand.

"Knock it off."

"I can't help it."

"Neither can I," Conor said as he reached across the counter and dipped his finger into the bowl as well.

"That's it, no dessert for either of you."

Hayden placed his hand over his heart and pretended to cry. Conor did the same and started wailing. Darcy wasn't buying their act. She did, however, give them two spoons and told them to have at it because she needed to make a fresh batch.

"Only a couple spoonfuls," Hayden told Conor. "You don't want to spoil your dinner."

"Heed your own advice," Darcy said from the pantry. When she returned, she had a container of powdered sugar, but no chocolate.

"Aren't you making more chocolate?" Hayden asked.

"I am not," she told him as she pushed the other bowl toward him. "You couldn't keep your grubby mitts off my frosting—you're not getting any more."

Hayden stood there, stunned. Conor giggled. He looked at his son and failed to keep a straight face when he saw frosting smeared on Conor's cheeks. Hayden shook his head and pulled a sheet of paper towel off the roll, wetted it, and handed it to his son.

"Conor, how was school?" Darcy asked as she put the other batch of frosting contents into her mixer. "Did you make any new friends?"

"Some," he said. "There's another new kid in my class."

"Maren Campbell?" Darcy asked.

Hayden assumed Maren was Devorah's daughter, but he couldn't be sure, even though Chad's last name was Campbell. He hadn't gotten around to asking about her daughter earlier.

"Yeah, she has a funny name. Some of the kids were making fun of her."

"I saw you wave at her," Hayden said to Conor.

"She's nice," Conor said. "Mr. Raze said we had to be reading partners."

"What were the other kids saying to her?" Darcy asked.

Conor shrugged. "Something about her mom being on a video. I don't know. I wasn't listening because I don't know her, and I don't want anyone to think I'm a mean kid."

Hayden happened to glace at his mom, who eyed him warningly; she then looked to Conor. Hayden understood.

"Hey, bud, why don't you run upstairs and do your homework. Grandma is going to need the counter to make dinner."

"Okay," he said as he climbed down and grabbed his backpack. Hayden waited until he heard stomping overhead before saying anything to his mom.

"You know?"

She nodded. "Everyone knows."

"How?"

"According to the gals at the coffee shop, the video went viral. Whatever that's supposed to mean."

"But she doesn't even live here."

Darcy shrugged. "How do you know about it?"

"I ran into Devorah outside the kids' school this morning. It was raining, so I offered her a ride. We chatted for a bit, and she told me."

"You haven't seen it?"

Hayden shook his head. He wasn't sure he wanted to see it.

"Probably for the best," his mom said. "It's not good, and there's a follow-up. This woman . . ." Darcy paused and turned the mixer off. "I don't know what on earth possesses a woman to be as catty as this one on the video. Her parents should be ashamed. Just horrible what they've done to our Devy."

"Your Devy?"

Darcy held a spatula in her hand, covered with vanilla frosting. "Oyster Bay takes care of their own."

"Right," he said, shaking his head. "Spreading rumors and gossip like wildfire in the 'He said, she said' narrative isn't considered taking care of its own, Mom."

"That woman on the video will get hers. You just wait and see."

Hayden scrubbed his hand over his face and groaned. "Devorah is a grown woman. Let her take care of her home, while you take care of yours. She doesn't need a group of Crafty Cathys coming to her rescue," he said, referring to the town's long-standing social group to which his mother belonged.

"She might."

"Believe me, what Devy needs is support. She's going through a tough time. If you want to help, give her a shoulder to cry on. It's not like Crow is the type of guy to lend an ear."

"You can say that again."

Hayden opened his mouth and then thought better of it. "I'm going to go check on Conor, then I'll be back down, and you'll have a list of things for me to do." He kissed his mom on her cheek and went upstairs.

He paused when he came to Conor's door and smiled as he heard his son reading to himself. This move would be good for them. Hayden would make sure of it.

Seven

Devorah

The next afternoon, Devy rushed down the stairs to answer the landline her father still insisted on using. His reasoning was valid. He was the town sheriff, and because everyone already had his home number, he didn't need to make everyone memorize his cell phone. Crow had one of those as well, but he hardly used it.

"Hello?" she answered, out of breath. Next time, she'd let the answering machine pick up. She didn't need to exert herself when the call wouldn't be for her.

"Hey, it's Colt."

"Hi. What are you doing? Where are you?" She still hadn't seen her brother and didn't have any desire to go into the Lazy Lamb to see him. Mostly because she was embarrassed and afraid people would know why she was back in town. She supposed they'd already figured it out, since her daughter was enrolled in school and her husband was nowhere to be found.

"Yeah, sorry. I keep meaning to come in, but by the time I get home, everyone's asleep, and then I leave first thing."

Devorah hadn't been asleep. She hadn't had a good night's sleep since the night before her life turned upside down.

"Anyway," Colt continued. "What are you doing? Do you want to meet up for dinner?"

Devy turned and looked around the kitchen, which had things for her to make, but she was so wrapped up in her thoughts she hadn't gotten around to it.

"Where?"

"Down here at the Lazy Lamb."

"Maren—"

"Can come too. It's a pub, not a bar. She's allowed."

Being out in public wasn't ideal. She hadn't showered, which meant she hadn't done her hair. Devy had already run into Hayden yesterday and didn't really want to see anyone else.

"I don't know, Colt. I—"

"It's dead down here, Dev. And I really want to see my niece."

She thought for a moment and then finally nodded. "I need to shower."

"Okay, take your time. Do you remember where it's at?"

"Yes." It was hard to forget when the town was so small. Oyster Bay was one of those places where, if you got lost, which was near impossible, you followed the snow evacuation route to the water. Then you'd find your way again.

Devorah hung up, went back upstairs, and found Maren in her room, reading a book.

"Hey," Dev said as she leaned against the doorjamb. "Uncle Colt would like us to come down to his pub for dinner."

"Okay," Maren said as she closed her book. "Are you . . ." She stopped talking and sighed.

"Am I going to get dressed?"

Maren nodded, and her lower lip quivered. Devorah went into the room and sat next to her daughter. "I know I'm a broken mess."

"It's okay, Mom."

Devy gave her a weak smile. "It's not. I want to feel better. I'm trying."

"I'll help."

She kissed her daughter on her forehead. "You help by being here with me. I'm going to shower, and then we'll go."

"Okay."

In the shared bathroom, Devy started the water. She held her hand under the stream until it turned warm, undressed, and then stepped in. The last shower she'd taken, she'd stood in there and cried, the rushing water easily drowning out her sobs. She wasn't lying when she'd told Maren she was broken. Everything hurt, and her heart no longer beat the way she remembered it. Now, it felt dull and lifeless. Foreign. It didn't belong in her anymore.

Maren's shampoo sat on the windowsill. Devy poured some into her hand and inhaled the coconut-and-vanilla scent. Tears of joy came instantly. She would be nothing without Maren, and it wasn't fair to her nine-year-old to have to support her.

Devorah managed to wash and condition her hair, as well as coat her body in Maren's sweet-smelling body soap. She washed, rinsed, and felt slightly better than she had an hour ago. After turning the water off, she got out, dried off, and then went into her room. On her bed were a pair of jeans and a sweater. She couldn't help but smile as she looked toward the wall, where her daughter was on the other side. If she didn't have Maren, she'd be so lost.

"I'll be ready in fifteen," she yelled, knowing Maren could hear her. When Devorah and Colt were younger, they constantly yelled back and forth instead of getting up and going to each other's room to talk. Their parents hated it, but it was an easy form of communication for them.

"May I come in?" Maren asked. Devy slipped the sweater over her head and looked toward the bathroom door, where she suspected her daughter to be. She wasn't. Dev took a few steps toward the shared bathroom and leaned to the side and saw Maren standing in the doorway on her side of the bathroom.

"Of course."

Maren walked in, wearing jeans and a similar sweater. "You look refreshed."

"Thanks. Are you mothering me?"

Maren nodded and inhaled deeply. Dev knew this was her daughter's way of warding off tears. Chad had hated it when Maren would cry over anything he thought was trivial, so Maren had taught herself to "suck it up," according to her father.

Devy held her arms out for her daughter. They hugged tightly, each rubbing a hand down the other's back. "I'm just so sad. I think Daddy is sad too."

She froze at her daughter's words. How would Maren know Chad was sad? He hadn't called, which only exacerbated how Dev felt about him. He should have been calling his daughter every day, checking in, and seeing how she was coping after his epic failure as a man.

"What do you mean?" She leaned back slightly but not enough to let go of her daughter. Maren was her lifeline. Her reason for being any semblance of human these days.

"Daddy called while you were in the shower."

"Wha—" Devorah caught herself. This was a good thing—him calling to talk to Maren—but it stung. Dev was sad. Angry. Confused. Pissed off. And every emotion in between. Days had passed, and Chad hadn't even reached out. At least that was what she'd thought.

Deep down, Devy had expected him to and hoped he would. She wanted to hear his voice, hear him tell her how sorry he was for everything, to listen to him cry on the phone and say how he missed her and Maren and wanted them to come home. Those words needed to come from him to her.

He would never. Groveling and accepting responsibility were beneath him.

As much as it pained her, she had to put her feelings toward Chad aside and do what was best for their daughter. Maren was the only priority.

Devorah inhaled deeply, looked into her daughter's eyes, and cupped her cheek softly. "Did you have a good chat with your dad?"

Maren shrugged. "He asked a lot of questions about Oyster Bay. You and Grandpa."

"Did he ask about school? How you are?"

She shook her head.

Devy's heart sank for her daughter.

"He asked if we were done visiting."

Visiting? Is that what Chad thought they were doing?

Devorah ran her hand down Maren's silky hair. "I'm glad you got to speak to him."

Maren nodded and rested her head on her mother's chest, hugging her tighter.

Once they returned to Chicago, Devorah would do so with more questions than answers. Being in Oyster Bay was nothing more than an escape from the scrutiny and finger-pointing.

The two parted, and Devorah finished dressing before following Maren into the bathroom. Maren plugged the hairdryer in and motioned for her mom to sit on the toilet. Devy closed her eyes and tried to relax while Maren brushed and dried her hair. She thought about Chad, Maren, and herself as a family and tried to recall happy memories.

They'd had some lovely family vacations—vacations where Chad would spend hours supposedly working, and Devorah and Maren would go out on their own to explore wherever they were.

Family vacations that included Ester because she was all alone when Rita went to her father's house during vacations.

Realization hit Devorah square in the chest. When Chad worked, Ester never felt well. It was never Dev, Maren, and Ester.

Ever.

Devorah wanted to throw up. Chad was a liar, and he'd ruined every happy memory she had. The affair was right there in front of her face, but she'd been too blind and trusting to see everything. She forced the nausea down and focused on the fact that she and Maren were together.

The sensation of Maren's fingers running through her hair, mixed with the soft sounds of the hairdryer, almost lulled her to sleep. Her eyes snapped open when everything stopped.

"Can I put a little makeup on?"

"Sure. Do you want me to do it for you?"

Maren nodded. They switched places, and Devorah put some blush on Maren's cheeks, added a light dusting of eye shadow on her lids, and coated her lips in a soft baby-pink gloss. She told her daughter to blot and aimed the tissue at her lips.

"You're really so beautiful, you'll probably never need makeup."

"Like you?"

"Yeah." Devorah smiled softly. "I never really wore much until college."

"Mr. Raze says he knows you."

"I'm not surprised. Oyster Bay is a small place. Everyone knows everyone. You'll figure it out soon enough, especially since you're Crow's granddaughter."

"Do I have to try out for the Pearl of the Bay pageant?"

"Pearl of the Ocean." Devy rested her hip against the sink and shook her head as she appraised her daughter. She looked a lot like Devy had at that age but was much wiser. "You have a lot of years before you have to even think about the pageant. It all starts when you're in the ninth grade. Unless it's changed."

"Will we still be here?"

Devy's shoulders lifted. "I don't know, Maren. Probably not. We're just here . . ." Dev trailed off and then added, "Come on, we should go." She went back to the bedroom, slipped into some shoes, and looked around her room for her purse. When she didn't see it on her dresser or the pile of crap on the chair, she lifted the blankets off her unmade bed.

"Where in the hell is it?"

"What are looking for?"

"My purse. Did you take it?" She dropped to the ground to look under the bed.

"I saw it downstairs," Maren said as she headed toward the door. "I believe on the table."

Devorah couldn't recall leaving it down there, but she also couldn't remember bringing it upstairs or taking it out of her car.

Downstairs, she followed Maren to the dining room, where Devorah found her purse. "Thanks."

"Don't mention it."

She smirked at her daughter. "Come on, let's go see Uncle Colt."

The walk from Crow's house to the Lazy Lamb took a whole five minutes. Devy held the door and motioned for her daughter to go in first. As soon as Maren stepped in, Colt let out a very loud welcome.

"My niece is finally in my bar!"

"Pub," Devy said. "You told me it was a pub."

"Same thing to me." Colt came around the bar and pulled Maren into a bear hug, lifting her off the ground and swinging her around. After he put her down, he went to his sister. Devy braced herself for the same level of attention, but Colt simply brought her into his fold and hugged her tightly. "If you had called, I would've come and got you," he whispered in her ear.

Devorah knew this, which was why she hadn't called her brother. If she had, Colt not only would have come to get her and Maren, but he also would've made sure that Chad knew how badly he'd messed up.

"Uncle Colt, can I go behind the bar?" Maren asked, getting his attention.

Colt turned and shook his head. "No, ma'am. Come on, let's sit down and order food. I'm starving." He draped his arm over Devy's shoulders and guided her to a table. "This one works."

As they sat down, Devorah looked around, remembering the Lazy Lamb from when she was a teen. Not much had changed, except Colt owned the place now. The seating area was still a mix of tables or booths, and thankfully the vinyl on the booth wasn't cracked or peeling. The walls

were still adorned with an array of Oyster Bay memorabilia, from pho-
tographs of all the high school teams to various bowling, dart-throwing,
and fishing competitions. Of course, somewhere on the walls were Devy's
photos from being Pearl of the Ocean four years running. She couldn't
wait for Maren to find those.

People she probably knew sat at the bar, drinking beer, cocktails,
soda, or water. Some munched on appetizers, while others ate full
meals. A few watched the television in the corner, while others chatted to their stool neighbors. The Lazy Lamb was busy, and seeing this
warmed Devy. She wanted her brother to succeed.

They sat down, and a waitress brought them menus.

"Wow, you have staff?" Devy said as she opened the menu.

"I do. It's strange. I never thought I'd be able to have my own place.
My own beer is on tap. People come in all the time. They love the food.
The atmosphere. The live music on Friday nights."

"I'm proud of you." Devy reached across the table and squeezed his
hand. "Does Dad come down?"

Colt nodded. "Yep. He's a regular. Sits at the bar, in the same spot."

"Can I have a spot?" Maren asked.

"You can only sit at the bar if your mom sits there with you."

Maren's eyes widened, and she glanced at her mom. "Can we?"

Colt laughed. "I'll bring you down when we're not open and teach
you how to make your own Shirley Temples."

"Can I put the cherry in?"

"You can have all the cherries you want."

Later, when they were home, Devy would tell her brother that, in
a matter of minutes, he'd managed to make her daughter smile brightly
for the first time since everything with Chad had gone down. Devorah
was grateful for him.

They ordered, and while they waited for their food, Colt took
Maren to play arcade games and select songs from the jukebox. Devy
sat back and sort of zoned out. She could hear people around her,
coming and going, laughing and having a good time, but they were all

a blur. She had tucked herself into the corner, hoping to avoid anyone seeing or recognizing her.

"Fancy meeting you here."

Her eyes cleared and focused on a little boy, and then she saw the man next to him. She sat up and cleared her throat. Hayden stood there with his hand on, presumably, his son's shoulder. Her wish of being left alone had gone out the window, but she had to admit to herself it was nice to see another friendly(ish) face, even if the last time she'd seen him, she was crying her eyes out in his truck. Still, she wasn't sure she was in the mood to socialize.

"Devorah, this is my son, Conor," Hayden said proudly as he glanced at his boy. "Conor, this is Mrs. Campbell." The young man stuck his hand out to shake hers. It caught her off guard, and she slowly extended hers.

"You can call me Devy," she said quietly to Conor.

"Are you Maren's mom?"

Devy nodded. "She's in the back with her uncle." She pointed toward the game area.

"Dad, may I go say hi?"

"Sure, bud. I'll be right here."

As soon as Conor ran off, Hayden sat down. Devy sat up straighter and wished she had said no to dinner. Being out in public wasn't her idea of a good time right now, and having to put on a facade for Hayden didn't register high on her social meter. Curled up in bed, wallowing in self-pity was more her speed at the moment. And Hayden seemed so chipper, which was in contrast to her demeanor. Why would he want to sit and talk with someone as down as her?

"How are you?"

She looked at him for a long moment, wondering how she was supposed to answer. "I don't know," she said, shrugging. Devy clasped her hands in her lap. "I'm here, which is something."

Hayden looked around. "My dad said Colt had bought this place. How does he like it?"

"Loves it. He's very proud of it." Devy looked around and then back at Hayden. As soon as they made eye contact, she looked at the table. "Is your dad still the town doc?"

"Nah, he's retired and living the dream."

"Which is?"

"To annoy my mother." Hayden laughed. "They travel a lot, or they did. I don't know that they will until I get my house built."

"Where are you building?"

"Do you remember the orchard?"

Devy nodded.

"I bought a couple of acres there."

"And you're building your house?"

"Not exactly. I'll be there to hold a nail or two. I hired a contractor. I'm good with a hammer, but even I have to draw the line somewhere."

"Where did you live before coming back here?"

"Wyoming. I was a deputy in a town smaller than Oyster Bay. When I wasn't chasing horse thieves, I worked on a ranch for Sofia's family."

The waitress returned with her dinner, followed by Colt, Maren, and Conor.

"Mom!" Maren's cheeks were flushed and her eyes bright with excitement. "This is my friend Conor. We're in class together, and he just moved here too."

Devorah smiled. "Maren, this is Hayden, Conor's dad and Uncle Colt's best friend."

"So cool. Can they have dinner with us?"

Before Devy could say no, Colt spoke up: "Sure they can!" He moved a table next to their booth and sat down. The waitress came over, took Hayden's and Conor's drink orders, and said she'd be right back. Devorah wanted to go home and crawl into bed.

"Mr. Hayden, do you think Conor could come over this weekend? My grandpa won't mind."

Devorah opened her mouth to tell Maren they had plans. Before she could find the words, though, Conor spoke up. "I would love to."

Despite wanting privacy, Devy wouldn't tell her daughter no. She caught Hayden staring at her and offered him her weakest smile.

"Mom, can Conor and I go back to the arcade?"

Devorah nodded. "Go have fun."

EIGHT

HAYDEN

Colt sat down next to his sister, slung his arm around her shoulder, and sighed happily. Hayden noticed Devorah shrink into herself, almost as if she didn't want the attention from her brother. Her fingers played with the condensation on her glass, and she kept her eyes on the table.

Hayden had never considered himself a violent man, but he wanted to maim Chad Campbell for what he was putting his wife through. No one, not even the vilest people in the world, deserved to be treated the way Chad and his mistress had treated Devy.

Chad's attitude or disposition was par for the course. Back in high school, he was a jerk. A rich prick who thought he owned the school and never got in trouble for any of the shit he pulled. One time, he and most of the football team TP'd the trees in front of the high school. Everyone in town knew it was Chad, but the administration refused to believe he would do anything of the sort. Instead, the entire team received marks on their school discipline records. Hayden had a hard time explaining it on his college applications. Had he come forward, he would've been branded a narc and would've been the pariah of the school. Since he didn't come forward, he was branded a disobedient student. He couldn't win.

The one person who knew Chad was responsible was Sheriff Crowley. He was onto Chad's bullshit.

The waitress stopped by the table and took Hayden's order and then returned a few minutes later with his beer. Hayden took a long sip and then studied the label.

"I can't believe you have your own brew."

Colt smiled brightly and let out a little chuckle. "It's a dream come true." Colt looked at his sister and shook her shoulder. "Right?"

"Yeah," was all Devy said.

"Devy, what do you do for work?"

She shook her head and readjusted in her seat. "I organize estate sales."

"That's a thing?" Her profession shocked Hayden.

"It's a lucrative thing," Colt said. "You wouldn't believe some of these people, just handing their keys over to her."

"It's not like that, Colt." Devy looked up and met Hayden's gaze. "People don't want to deal with their parents' belongings. They go in, take what they want, and the rest is up for sale. That's where I come in. I'll go in, organize the house, and make sure everything is out in the open and marked. I'll advertise the estate sale and run it. Then, whatever's left over gets donated to people in need. I make sure to focus on women's and children's shelters, veterans."

"I've seen signs for estate sales, but I had no idea that's how they worked."

Devy nodded.

"And this pays well?"

She shrugged. "It's enough, or it was. Chad took care of our finances and often made comments—"

"Snide ones?" Colt interrupted.

Devorah nodded. "I know I made good money in Chicago, but it isn't going to be enough to maintain the lifestyle Maren and I had there."

"Don't worry, the old man isn't going to kick you out." Colt bumped his shoulder into hers and then looked toward the bar when his name was called. "Be back."

As soon as Colt left, silence fell upon Devy and Hayden. She barely looked at him, choosing to keep her eyes on the table.

"You know, not all men are like Chad. Most men worship their spouse and treat them like queens. They don't cheat, and they definitely don't do so with the best friend," Hayden said before he could stop the verbal vomit.

She glanced up, and he saw the tears build in the corners of her eyes. Instantly, he hated himself for bringing it up. He had no right. He and Devy were barely friends.

"I'm sorry."

"It's fine," she said. "You're not wrong, but it doesn't take the sting out of things. I just . . ." She took a deep, shuddering inhale and shook her head. "I don't know what I did wrong."

"Probably nothing."

"Clearly something, if he cheated."

Hayden wanted to tell her men like Chad did whatever they wanted without consequences. He bit his tongue instead. Devorah would believe whatever she thought about Chad, regardless of what Hayden or Colt said about him.

Conor and Maren returned, both red faced and out of breath.

"Dad, they have the Whac-A-Mole game. Maren and I tried to get the high score, but we couldn't do it."

"I'll ask my uncle to make it so we can have unlimited play," Maren said proudly.

"Every kid's dream," Hayden said, and then he looked at Devy. "Do you remember the arcade?"

She nodded. "Friday night was unlimited night. We used to spend all night there, just being kids."

"And your dad would circle the parking lot every thirty minutes."

Devy chuckled a bit. "He was spying on me."

"Grandpa spied on you?" Maren asked.

Devorah nodded at her daughter. "Yep, and he's going to spy on you too."

"Ugh, no way. I'm going back to Chicago."

Devorah's reaction was slight, but Hayden saw the grimace.

"I've never been to Chicago. Right, Dad?" Conor asked.

"Nope, sure haven't, bud."

"You can come to my house in Chicago," Maren told him. "My dad will say so."

Hayden watched the back-and-forth between the kids, all the while trying to gauge Devy's reaction to Maren talking about her dad.

"Are you going back to Chicago?" Conor asked. If Hayden wasn't mistaken, he sensed some desperation in his son's voice.

"Yep, my daddy said I can come live with him when I tire of small-town life."

This got Devy's attention. "He said that?" she asked her daughter.

Maren nodded and smiled brightly, as if everything was okay.

Devorah said nothing. She picked up a paper napkin and began shredding it into small pieces. Thankfully, they were saved when Colt and the waitress appeared with their food. For the most part they ate in relative silence, with only the kids talking or Colt occasionally asking Hayden about his return to Oyster Bay.

"Permanent," Hayden told him. "I liked Wyoming, but it was time to come home."

"I'm sorry about your wife," Colt said.

"Thanks. I wasn't sure if people knew around here or not."

Colt nodded. "Your dad comes in a lot. He mentioned it when he said you were moving back," he told Hayden. "You know if it wasn't for your dad, I'm not sure my home brew would be so successful. He's one of my best customers. Always has been."

"Yeah, that's how I found out you bought this place."

"My dad likes beer," Conor blurted out. When everyone looked at him, he shrugged. "Am I wrong?"

"No," Hayden said. "But you also don't need to broadcast it, and it's not like I drink beer all the time." In fact, he hadn't even finished the one the waitress had brought him earlier.

"My mom likes beer too," Conor said, as if everyone at the table needed to know. Hayden grimaced at Conor's use of the present tense. He didn't have the heart to correct his son, but he also needed to change the subject.

"Not now, Conor." Hayden's voice was stern, and it sent a message to his son. There were some things you didn't talk about in front of strangers. Not that Colt and Devorah were strangers, but the others sitting near them were.

Conor opened his mouth to say something but closed it quickly. Hayden was thankful Conor was sitting across from him so he could give him a pointed look. It wasn't that Conor couldn't talk about his mother and her passing. Hayden wanted him to do it in the comfort of their own home, where the walls held secrets and didn't spread rumors.

They finished dinner, and when Hayden tried to pay his bill, Colt waved him off. Hayden still put cash on the table for the waitress. She deserved her tip, regardless of the meal being on the house.

"Thanks for the company. It's really great seeing you both again," Hayden said to Colt and Devy as he motioned for Conor to slide out of the booth.

"See you tomorrow, Maren."

"Bye, Conor."

"Stop by anytime," Colt said, while Devy remained silent. Hayden hadn't expected her to say anything. He suspected Maren's comment about her father was weighing heavily on Devorah.

Outside, Conor and Hayden climbed into the truck. Hayden started it and sat in the parking lot for a minute before backing out of his spot. They didn't have far to go, and in hindsight, they should've walked. He wanted time to think about how to approach the topic of Sofia's death but didn't have time before he'd be at his parents'. This being a school night, Conor needed to take his shower and get to bed.

Hayden turned left when he should've gone straight.

"Don't we live the other way?"

"Yeah, we do. We're going to drive around a bit."

"Am I in trouble?"

"No." Hayden sighed. "It's not that I don't want you to talk about your mom, Conor. You should talk about her. She loved you very much."

"Just not the way she died."

"The thing is, bud, people won't understand, and I don't want them to get the wrong impression of your mom."

They drove by Maren's house. Hayden pointed it out.

"Maybe Maren and I can walk to school together."

"Yeah, maybe. I'll talk to her mom."

"Maren said her mom is sad."

What an understatement. Hayden wished there was something he could do to help. While they were both going through a loss, the situations were entirely different. He'd lost his wife, whereas Devy's husband had violated their vows. Hayden didn't have experience there, and it wasn't like he could tell Devy that everything would be okay. She was going to have to learn how to coparent with someone who'd slept with her best friend. He wasn't sure he could get over something like that.

"Yeah, bud. She is."

"Maren said she's getting a new mommy."

Ouch.

"I'm not sure about that." And it wasn't something he planned to ask Devorah about either. That was the last thing she needed from him. "But let's not bring it up in front of Miss Devy. Okay?"

"I don't want to make her sad."

"No, we don't want to do that."

Hayden turned down another street, and, glancing at his son, he saw a little boy caring about a woman he barely even knew. He was a good boy, dealing with his own loss, and yet he found time to care about others.

"Baseball tryouts are this weekend," Hayden reminded him. "We need to head into the city and get you some cleats."

"Okay. How far?"

"It's like forty-five minutes."

"That seems far."

"It's not bad. Pretty easy drive. We can go to a couple of the stores, grab some lunch. Have a guy day."

Conor shrugged. "Maybe Maren can come."

"Sure, bud. As long as it's okay with her mom."

Hayden turned down their road and into the driveway. He parked, shut off his truck, and stared at his childhood home. He had every intention of splitting his time between his parents' place and his camper because he needed space and time to think without any interruptions. His parents, though, wanted him to stay at the house, as did Conor. So Hayden stayed.

They walked in and found Lee and Darcy sitting at the island, eating pie. Last night it was cake. If his mother kept it up, Hayden was going to start looking like his father.

"Hi, Grandma and Grandpa."

"Hi, honey," Darcy said as she kissed his forehead. "I missed you after school. How was your second day?"

Conor shrugged. "Still boring."

Lee guffawed. "School is never boring. I'm sure you learned something."

Conor smiled and rolled his eyes. "I learned I still have a couple more tests to take to see where I'm at in class. But Maren has to take them, too, being as she's the new kid also."

Lee looked at Hayden with wide eyes.

"Head up and take your shower," Hayden told Conor.

As soon as they heard the water turn on, Lee turned to Hayden. "Crow's granddaughter?"

Hayden nodded.

"Huh, I heard Devorah was back, but I had no idea she brought her daughter. Crow must be beside himself. I'll give him a call later," Lee said.

"That poor woman. The situation was a hot topic at my Crafty Cathys meeting." Darcy shook her head.

"Again?" Hayden asked. "Didn't you talk about the whole thing enough yesterday?"

Darcy waved his comment away and handed him a fork from the drawer. He didn't take it, far too pissed off with what he was hearing. "People talk, Hayden. It's not like I can stop them. I just can't believe Chad would do something like that. He was such a good kid."

Even my mom is blinded by Chad Campbell's charm.

Hayden couldn't believe his mom hadn't let this go from the day prior. "Do me a favor, Mom. When you hear people talking about Devorah, tell them to knock it off. She doesn't need this. Not from the place where she grew up. She needs women to rally around her, not talk about her behind her back."

Hayden didn't give his mom a chance to say anything and walked out. He needed fresh air, and once he got outside, he found himself walking down the road until he came to Main Street. He paused on the corner. He could turn around and go back; he could cross the street, head back to the Lazy Lamb, and get lost in a bottle or two; or he could go right.

He went right and walked the couple of blocks to Sheriff Crowley's house, surprised when he came up to the fence to find Devy sitting on the front steps with a bottle of whiskey next to her.

"Hey."

"Hey," she said.

"I'm sorry Chad did this to you."

"Yeah," she said with a sigh.

Hayden kicked a pebble with his shoe. "If you drink that"—he motioned toward the bottle—"can you promise me you won't drive?"

Devy looked down at the bottle and then at Hayden. "Is that what happened to your wife?"

"Yeah, it is." He nodded.

"I'm sorry."

"Me too."

NINE

DEVORAH

She had no intention of drinking the whole bottle of whiskey, but it was there to numb the thoughts in her mind and the ache she felt all over. Being made to feel worthless had debilitated her. Her body hurt. She had physical pain when she thought too much, likely due to the constant *What could I have done differently?* question playing on repeat. Mostly, Devorah was tired, and no amount of sleep curbed the desire to stay under her covers.

Hayden McKenna stood on the other side of the white picket fence with his hands in his pockets. On occasion, a car would drive by, illuminating him in a soft white glow. He stood there, like he'd done many moons ago.

They had dated, sort of. They had been in a situationship. One that was never public, but it wasn't exactly a secret either. Devorah and Hayden had liked each other, but he was also Colt's best friend, and Hayden respected that relationship. So, like all other teenagers, they sneaked around. Hayden was also afraid of Crow, and her being Crow's daughter, no one dared cross the imaginary line without permission.

Except Chad.

Chad never seemed to care that Devy's father was the sheriff, and a mean one at that. Crow never hesitated to put kids in their place, to give them a citation and make them appear in front of the judge (who happened to be Crow's best friend) or handcuff them and put them in the back of his patrol car. It was his way of keeping the riffraff under control. None of those city shenanigans happened in Oyster Bay, not under Crow's watch.

Devorah scooted over a bit on the step. When her ankle knocked into the bottle, she moved it aside and glanced toward Hayden.

"Wanna come sit?"

He nodded, reached over the gate, and undid the latch, even though he could've walked to the end of the driveway and around the cars. Devy found herself smiling at how formal Hayden was making the invite.

"Where's your dad?"

"Inside, snoring in the recliner." She gestured with her hand over her shoulder, toward the house. "If it's quiet enough, you can hear the freight train rumbling through the house."

"Same one from back in the day?"

Devorah chuckled. "Nah. Colt 'accidently' singed the seat. Crow had no choice but to replace it. Although the new one isn't much better. It has built-in speakers, a place to hold the remote control, and an icebox for his cans."

"He doesn't drink Colt's brew?"

"Ha! Are you kidding? Crow doesn't even drink milk or watch what he eats, and don't even think about asking if he takes vitamins. If it doesn't come out of a silver can, the deep fryer, or the grease trap down the street, it's not for him."

"Hey, I happen to like the grease trap down the street."

Devy did as well. Waiting tables at the Nest was her first job. She worked there from spring until school started again, and then she went back to cheerleading.

"Do you remember when we got caught making out in the bathroom?"

"Hey, are you almost done?" Hayden asked as he sat down at the counter. Devorah rested her elbows on the Formica top, chipped from years of abuse, and batted her long, thickly-coated-with-mascara eyelashes at him. She wanted to be his girlfriend, but he hadn't or wouldn't ask her out—at least not recently—because of her brother. Some stupid bro code. She should've taken Hayden up on the offer back in middle school.

"Yeah. Do you want something?"

Hayden eyed the back, where the grill was. Dev followed his gaze, looked back at him, and mouthed, "Bathroom?"

He smiled brightly, and she rolled her eyes but couldn't hide her grin. They made out. A lot. Like, more than any of her friends did with their boyfriends. It was fun, being secretive and sneaky. The other day, she'd let him touch her boob, over her shirt. She teased him by saying he could touch the real thing if he asked her to be his girlfriend. Dev didn't like giving him an ultimatum, but he was leaving for college soon, and she wanted everyone to know Hayden was finally hers.

Not that her father would ever let her go visit. Hayden was going to Idaho for school.

Wherever that was.

Devorah pushed away from the counter. She went into the back, told the head cook she was now off the clock, and punched out. In the break room, she grabbed her purse, took her apron off, and stuffed it in her bag.

As she came out, she met Hayden in the wood-paneled hall. He rushed them into the bathroom and closed the door behind Devorah.

"Did you lock it?"

"Yeah," he said as he picked her up and set her down on the edge of the sink. He stood between her legs, pushed her work dress up, and pressed his hard-on into her.

"Hayden," she gasped and dug her fingers into the back of his neck as he ground against her.

"Is this okay?"

She thought about saying no but nodded. This was something new for them, and she liked it.

"I can make you feel good, Devorah."

"Not until I'm your girlfriend."

"Okay, baby," he said as his lips pressed into hers. Hayden moved his hips enough to send hot waves of ecstasy through Devorah. She knew exactly how classmates ended up in compromising situations. Their teenage bodies were traitors. They want, want, want, the consequences be damned.

"Oh, God, Hayden. I think . . . I don't know . . ."

Bang! Bang! Bang!

Hayden and Devorah broke apart, both panting heavily.

"Who's in there?"

"Shit," Dev said as she stood and pulled her uniform down.

Hayden waited until Devorah nodded, and then he opened the door quickly, startling the person on the other side. She was one of the new girls, in Oyster Bay for the summer to make money. Her eyes widened and her mouth dropped open at the sight of them. There was no mistaking what Hayden and Dev had been doing in the bathroom with the door locked.

"I'm telling your dad," the newcomer said. It took no one any time to figure out Devorah was the sheriff's daughter. Most of the people thought they could tell her what to do or scare her by tattling. What they didn't know was that Dev didn't care. She welcomed a conversation between her and Crow, one that would never happen—he'd rather go out and look for unruly juveniles than talk to his daughter.

Devorah rolled her eyes and adjusted her dress for good measure. If her coworker—whose name she hadn't bothered to remember—wanted to run to Sheriff Crow, then she was going to give her something good to say.

"Tell him."

"I can't believe you were having sex in here," she seethed as she pointed into the bathroom.

"Don't be jealous." Dev reached for Hayden's arm and followed him out of the diner. He opened his car door for her. She got in, knowing he'd drive them out of town to finish what they'd started.

At least, she hoped so.

Devorah's cheeks flushed red at the memory of her first-ever orgasm. It was unexpected and something she didn't really understand until she talked to Laila about it later. "What was her name? The woman that caught us?"

Hayden shook his head. "I don't remember. She was only here for the summer, but she knew you were Crow's kid and threatened to tell him. Shit, I was so scared."

"Too scared to take me home." She popped her eyebrow up and then rolled her eyes. "He wouldn't have done anything to you. He liked you."

"That's because he doesn't know about the things I used to do to his daughter. Even now, if he knew, he'd probably slap the cuffs on me and toss me into the back of the cruiser."

She looked over her shoulder at the window and saw her dad sleeping. Dev wished he would've done that to Chad, or that she'd been smart enough to see through his bullshit.

She leaned her arms and head on her knees and sighed. "Why do men cheat?"

Hayden sighed heavily. "Not all men cheat, Dev. Hell, women cheat too. It's not something I understand. If you don't want to be with the person you're with, leave. I know leaving isn't always easy, but it's a hell of a lot easier than disrespecting the person you've vowed to love and honor, cherish and forsake all others." He shook his head. "I'm sorry, I'm pissed on your behalf."

"I appreciate it."

A line of cars filled with teens passed by. They were rowdy, yelling out the windows and honking their horns.

"That'll wake Crow for sure," Hayden said.

"Yep, he's always had a knack for disorderly conduct."

As if on cue, the screen door opened. Devy turned and looked at her dad, standing there with his belly hanging over his waistband, his hands on his hips, and the perpetual scowl on his face that never seemed to go away.

"Who was it?"

Devy and Hayden shrugged.

"I don't know anyone around here these days," Devy told her father.

"Same, sir."

"These damn delinquents. I tell ya, they're from the city." The screen door opened and slammed closed behind him. Devy used to jump at the sound when she was little, but it had stopped bothering her by the time she was ten and started annoying her when she was dating Chad. She'd cut her curfew a bit too close one too many times, and because of that door, she could never sneak in.

"Or they just know how to press your buttons," Dev muttered under her breath. Hayden must've heard her because he snickered.

The "city," as everyone in town referred to it, was forty-five minutes away and where you'd find the big-box stores, the megaplex movie theaters, and the mall. When Dev lived in Oyster Bay, what later became the "city" had been nothing but farmland until a car dealership went in, followed by a chain restaurant. Those two establishments set off a boom of development that included homes, schools, hospitals, and any business you could think of. Some people left small towns like Oyster Bay for the bigger-city life, but a lot stayed. Something about the idyllic life along the water kept people there and brought in tourists.

After a moment of quiet, the storm known as Crow got started when an Oyster Bay cruiser pulled into the driveway. The deputy got out and made his way toward the front door.

"Evening, Devorah," Miller Farnsworth said as he tipped his hat toward her. The last time Devy had seen Miller, he was hanging his head in embarrassment after he'd asked her to prom. The rejection was his own doing. She'd been with Chad for almost two years at that point.

"Hayden," Miller said. "Didn't know you were back in town."

Devy chuckled. She highly doubted Miller didn't know. He and Hayden hadn't been friends in high school; surely someone had told Miller his foe had moved back.

"How's it going, Miller?" she asked.

"Oh, you know."

No, Devy didn't know and was curious. What did that statement even mean when people said it?

"I'm looking for Crow, is he—"

Crow burst through the door with Cordelia hot on his heels and his duty belt slung over his shoulder, making Dev wonder if it even fit around his waist.

"Let's go, Miller. Stay, Cordelia. Don't wait up, Devorah."

As if she would. The sentiment was still nice and appreciated.

Cordelia barked but sat on the porch as she was instructed.

Miller gave Dev one last look and then got behind the wheel of the patrol car. She shook her head as it pulled away and headed in the direction the wild kids had gone. Devy sighed and brought her knees to her chest.

"How come you always sit out front?" Hayden asked her as he leaned back against the stair. Cordelia took advantage of there being someone new to lick and showed Hayden some attention.

It was funny to Devy how Hayden remembered the littlest things about her. She was never a fan of the backyard because of the houses facing the yard. Everyone could see her. Never mind ever getting to lie out in the sun. She had no privacy back there. Even less than the front. At least out front she could hide behind the hydrangeas.

"Back then or now?" She glanced at him. He watched her and smiled when their gazes met.

"Either. Both."

Devy shrugged. "This is where the action is, and the deck out back needs replacing. Crow doesn't even let us step on it."

"Why doesn't Colt fix it?"

Dev shrugged. "Don't know." She looked down the street in the direction of her brother's establishment. It was late, and most of the businesses had closed. The Lazy Lamb was still open and would be until last call. Then, she imagined, Colt would come home, crawl into bed, and start all over again in the morning.

Cordelia whined to go back inside. Before Devy could get up to open the door for her, Hayden got up and let the dog in.

When Hayden sat back down, Dev noticed he sat closer to her. Normally, she'd shy away or put distance between herself and another man because she wouldn't want to upset Chad. This time, she didn't move.

"I'm assuming she's Crow's?"

"Colt's, actually, but she's pretty obsessed with Maren. She's been sleeping in her bed since we got here."

"Dogs can help with grief."

"Yeah. I like her. She sits with me during the day, when no one is home and I'm alone with my thoughts. She definitely helps."

"Maybe I should look into getting Conor a dog."

Devy nodded and leaned her head on her hands. "Can I ask about your wife?"

"It's not what you're probably thinking." Hayden sighed. "Sofia was out one night with her cousin and friends for a bachelorette party. We lived about an hour from town, and I told her to call me when she was ready to come home. I didn't want her to worry about getting home, and it's not like we had Uber or anything. I wanted her to go out and have a good time with her friends. To let loose and enjoy the night." Hayden paused.

"It was midnight when I started calling her. I think I must've called every five or ten minutes. Each call went to voicemail. The first couple of calls, I left her messages. Things like, 'Hey, hon, I hope you're having fun. Let me know when I should start heading your way.' And then the frantic ones started. I was worried about her. After an hour, I hopped in my truck. About twenty miles from the ranch, I saw the flares, and then I was at the scene of this one-car accident, and I just knew. Like, deep down, I knew it was her, and my life was going to be changed forever the moment I got out of the truck.

"The car she was in had flipped and landed on the passenger side. She was gone by the time the medics arrived. The kick in the nuts is,

Sofia was sober. Her cousin, the one driving, was well past the legal limit and walked away without a scratch."

"Did she go to jail?"

Hayden shook his head. "I'm not sure there will even be a trial. If there is, I won't be there. It's one of the reasons we moved. Her family, they're distraught and they don't want their niece to go to jail for an accident. Whereas I want her to rot there for stealing away my son's mother. We don't see eye to eye, and that put a strain on our relationship. So, I quit my job, moved out of the house my father-in-law had built for us, and came home."

"I'm sorry, Hayden."

"Yeah, me too," he said again. "It's hardest on Conor. The decision to take him away from his grandparents, the life he had there. I just hope he makes friends here and can thrive."

"Maren lost her best friend in this mess."

Hayden looked at Devy. "Maybe her friend can come visit?"

"No, I don't think that'll be possible. Her mother is the other woman."

"Ooh," Hayden said, drawing out the *ooh*. "Shit."

Devorah nodded. "It seems Maren and I are the only ones losing in this situation. I lost my husband, home, business. My friends. Everything I'd built is gone, and everyone knows my dirty laundry thanks to my so-called friend."

Hayden sighed heavily. "Unfortunately, you're right about 'everyone.'"

Her eyes shot to his. "Everyone? Here too?"

He nodded.

"That's just fucking lovely," she said as she wiped angrily at the instant tears. "I can't even escape to my childhood home without this shit following me."

"I think people here will have your back."

Devorah scoffed. "Yeah, something tells me my former classmates will take every opportunity to rub it in my face. I wasn't exactly nice to most of them."

"We were kids. Kids are assholes," Hayden said with some laughter. "You gotta keep your head up. Don't let anyone bring you down."

"I'm pretty much at the bottom of the barrel, Hayden. I'm not sure how much lower I can go."

"If it's any consolation, I haven't seen the video, and don't plan to watch it."

"Thanks. I do appreciate that. Unlucky for me, though, as she's posted more after the initial one."

"And you've watched them?"

Devy nodded. "It's like a train wreck—I can't look away, even though I know it's about my life. At least she doesn't say my name. Even though all my friends in Chicago know it's me. And I guess here as well."

"Have any of those friends reached out to you?"

"They did, initially, but haven't since." Were they truly her friends? Wondering made her feel ten times worse and even more alone.

They sat there on the steps, listening to the foghorn in the distance and the soft melodic cadence of the water crashing against the docks. Every so often a car would drive by and honk, and they could hear people down the street, talking loudly. Mostly, they sat there, saying nothing to each other, just like they'd done many times before back when they were teens. Only now, Devy couldn't look at Hayden, not with her tearstained face and bloodshot eyes. She wasn't the girl he remembered.

Back then, she had a voice. She was loud, laughed a lot, and smiled endlessly. Dev couldn't recall when she'd changed but suspected it was when she went off to college with Chad. It was at Northwestern when he started to assert himself more.

Or she allowed it to happen.

"On Friday, I'm taking Conor into town to buy some cleats. Baseball tryouts are on Saturday. Would you and Maren like to join us?"

Maren would for sure, but the invite was for them both.

Devy risked looking at Hayden.

She opened the door and found Hayden on their front porch. "Colt's not home," she told him.

"Damn, okay. Where are you off to?"

"The beach. Wanna come?"

"Are you walking?"

She nodded. "Do you see wheels with my name on them?"

Hayden chuckled. She liked the sound of his laughter. She liked him. More than she should. But he confused her, a lot. Occasionally, they'd make out. It was usually when he was at her house, or they'd find themselves alone somewhere. Being alone was hard, though. Dev was either with Laila or Colt was around, being an annoying brother.

"I'll drive."

Hayden opened the car door for her and waited until she was fully in before shutting it. He jogged to the other side, giving Dev a few seconds to stare at him. He was so freaking hot. She couldn't stand it half the time. She definitely couldn't stand it when one of the Fleming sisters flirted with him. He was hers.

Well, she wanted him to be. And Devorah thought he would be if it wasn't for her brother. Colt needed to butt out of her life.

Hayden slipped behind the steering wheel. He smiled at her and then started his car. Instead of turning around and heading to the beach, he drove them out of town.

"What beach are we going to?"

"Jamestown Cove," he told her. It was a place where they were unlikely to run into anyone. A place where they could act like they were the only two people in the world.

As soon as they were out of Oyster Bay, her hand went to the back of his neck, where she played with the ends of his hair. She wished she knew how to make him fall in love with her.

The words "I love you" or "I'm falling in love with you" played on the tip of her tongue. She wanted to tell him, to put her heart out there and tell him he didn't have to worry about Colt or her father. That she could handle them.

A horn honked, grabbing her attention.

Devorah tore her gaze away from Hayden and looked out the front window. Colt hung from the window of his truck, hollering at Hayden. Devorah dropped her hand and faced forward, fighting back a wave of tears that threatened to unleash. Life was unfair.

Even before Hayden said the words, she knew they were turning around and following her brother and their friends. She thought about telling him to drop her off at home, but any time with Hayden was time she craved.

Someday, Hayden McKenna would be hers.

She blinked and pushed the memory of their high school days away from her thoughts. Now, when she looked at Hayden, she saw nothing but friendship in his eyes, or least that was what she told herself it was. It was better thinking he wanted to be her friend than to play along in her self-pity game. He knew she was depressed, and he didn't seem to care.

"That would be lovely," she told him. "I know Maren would like to see more of where we're staying."

"Staying?"

Devorah nodded. "We have a life in Chicago. I have a business and . . ." She trailed off. "Oyster Bay is temporary. It always has been."

Hayden nodded, and his lips pressed into a thin line. "Well, it's a date then," Hayden said and then blanched. "Not like a real date, but one of those 'I'll put it in the calendar' sort of things."

"I know," Devy said as she forced a smile.

"Great. I'll pick you up first, and then we'll get the kids from school. Does that work?"

She nodded. "Are you leaving now?"

"I can stay," he told her. "Even if you don't want to talk."

"That would be nice, Hayden." She wanted him to stay, at least until Colt or her father came home. She didn't like the idea of being alone, even though Maren was upstairs sleeping. There was a certain sense of security that came when a man was in the house, at least for her.

TEN

HAYDEN

On Friday, Hayden parked in front of Sheriff Crow's house, left his truck running, and jogged up the steps. He knocked twice on the wooden screen door and stepped back, giving Devorah space to open the door and step out. He heard her walking toward him. The house creaked from old age or, as people in New England would say, "wicked old age." Hayden pulled the metal handle on the screen door and held it open. He smiled as soon as Devy came into view.

"Are you ready to shop?"

She smiled, but it didn't reach her eyes. He hated that he couldn't fix her problems. Not that he could fix his own, but his were much more straightforward to deal with.

"I'm ready," she said as she pulled the door shut behind her and tested the knob to make sure it was locked. He remembered a time when they didn't lock doors or worry about being robbed. Those days were long gone. Even at the ranch in Wyoming, they locked the doors.

When they reached the truck, Hayden held the passenger-side door open for her, waited for her to get in, and then shut it. He jogged around to the driver's side and hopped in, fastened his seat belt, and headed toward the school.

"How were the past couple of days?" he asked.

"They were okay," she said. "I started looking for a job."

"Oh yeah? Doing what?" Hayden turned at the corner and again a block later, then drove straight on until they arrived at the school. He got behind the last car and waited in the pickup line.

"I'm not sure," she said, answering his question. "When it comes down to it, I don't have a whole lot of experience doing much of anything except organizing. And it's not like there are a ton of estate sales around here or I have the clientele to get a business off the ground. I can't wait for someone to hire me."

"I hear ya."

"What about you?"

"Well, right now I'm living off life insurance and parents. I don't know if I want to go back into law enforcement or go to law school like I'd originally planned. Until then, I have a camper on the land I bought that I'm supposed to be living in while my house is being built. But I have yet to stay in it. My mom likes having me in the house."

"I wish Crow felt the same."

"He does," Hayden said. "He just has a hard time showing his soft side."

Devy choked on a laugh. "There is nothing soft about Crow."

"Has he always been this gruff?"

"No." Devy sighed. "He changed after my mom died. She was the love of his life, and . . . I don't know, I think he figured if he loved Colt and me like he loved her, he'd lose us too."

"He's a good dad, though?"

Devorah shrugged. "In comparison to who? Your dad?"

"Valid point." Lee McKenna was everyone's favorite. Being the longtime doctor in town, he knew everyone, and they knew him. It didn't matter what time it was; Dr. McKenna would make a house call. "I'm not sure it's fair to compare the two, though."

"Maybe not."

Hayden inched forward, even though the line hadn't moved. He looked out the window at the parents who'd parked in the pickup lane and then got out of their cars to chat. He scanned the other cars and groaned when he saw Sapphire Fleming heading his way.

"Shit."

"Is that—"

"Sapphire Fleming? Yep."

Sapphire smiled when she got closer to the truck. She stopped at his window, leaving him no choice but to push the button to put the window down. "Hey, Hayden."

"Sapphire."

She put her hands on the truck and leaned against the door. "I didn't know you were doing the carpool thing. I can put you on the list if you want." Sapphire looked at Devorah and said nothing.

"Nah, I'm good. I think Conor will walk home most days, unless it's raining."

"Oh, I see. What about you, Deborah?" she asked, mispronouncing her name.

"Devorah," Hayden corrected her.

"Oh, right. I must've forgotten."

Devorah barely acknowledged Sapphire. Hayden suspected there was some history there. "No thanks."

"You sure?" Sapphire asked.

"Positive. Thanks for the offer, though."

"So, listen," Sapphire continued, attention solely fixated on Hayden. "I was wondering what you're doing tomorrow night. How about dinner at my place? My ex will have my kids."

"Oh, um." Hayden ran his hand through his hair and tried to come up with a plausible excuse. "I'm not sure if my parents will be home to watch my son."

"Well, I'm sure Devorah could do it. She's not busy. Are you?" Sapphire tilted her head to the side in an attempt to get Devy to look at her.

"Nope, why would I be busy?" Devorah stated. "Conor can come over while you go on a date."

Hayden met Devy's eyes and saw defeat. Watching Conor was the last thing she wanted to do. Going shopping tonight was probably at the bottom of her to-do list as well. He turned back toward Sapphire, who had her phone out.

"I'll let you know. It's really up to Conor right now. He's my priority."

"Of course," Sapphire said sweetly. She put her hand on his arm and gave it a squeeze. "Give me your phone—I'll put my number in."

This was the oldest trick in the book, and he had no choice but to hand over his phone. He waited, tried to force a smile without making it look like a grimace, and cringed when she said, "I texted you back, so now you have my number."

"Great, thanks." He took his phone back and set it in the console next to him.

"The kids are coming," Devy said as she got out of the truck. She walked toward Maren and Conor, and the whole time, Hayden didn't take his eyes off her.

"See you tomorrow, Hayden," Sapphire called as she walked back to her car.

"Wh-what? Oh yeah, okay," he said as he got out to greet Conor on the sidewalk.

"Hey, bud. How was school?" Hayden took Conor's backpack and then reached for Maren's. He opened the back door and waited for the kids to get in before setting their bags on the floorboard and then shutting the door. He wanted to be a gentleman and shut Devy's door as well, but she had beaten him to it.

He stood there for a moment, feeling disappointed. The emotion confused him. Yes, he'd been raised to open doors, but he was also aware that women were independent.

He had a niggling suspicion in the back of his mind that Chad didn't open doors for Devorah, and if he had to guess, the only time he did anything gentlemanly was when people were watching.

Back behind the steering wheel, Hayden adjusted the rearview mirror so he could see Conor. "You good?"

"Yeah."

"Maren?"

"Yeah, it was okay," she said in a sad voice.

"Well, that doesn't sound like a fantastic Friday. I guess we better make it better. Off to shopping we go." Before he left the pickup line, he turned on some music: the Top 40–type tunes Conor liked to listen to. Hayden figured Maren would enjoy the same. By the time they were heading toward the interstate, both of them were singing, which was at least a start. Now all he needed to do was turn Devy's frown upside, and things would be better.

Not perfect.

But better.

◆ ◆ ◆

When Hayden had asked Devorah and Maren to come with Conor and him, it was because Hayden wanted to spend time with Devy. He liked her, and seeing her earlier in the week had only brought back those memories from junior high and high school. He didn't live with many regrets, but Devy was one of them. All he'd had to do back then was be honest with her and himself, but he was afraid of what Colt would think.

And Crow. That man still scared the shit out of him.

Even after he left for college, he still called Devorah when he could and when he knew her father or Colt wouldn't be home. He talked to her only a few times before he realized how homesick he was. Not because he missed his parents or Oyster Bay, but because he missed Devorah. He booked an unscheduled trip home to finally confess his feelings to her.

Hayden waited for Devorah after the homecoming game, only to find out his chance with her had sailed from the harbor.

Hayden knew the risks of going home without telling his parents, but he had one goal in mind—to tell Devorah he was in love with her. She was all he thought about. Day in and day out at school. He'd made a mistake in not telling her how he felt, and it was something he should've done the day she started high school. He was a good kid, raised right by a good man; Crow Crowley would've approved of his relationship with Devy, and Colt would've come around.

Eventually.

He took what he had in savings and paid for a flight back to Rhode Island. He didn't want to wait until Thanksgiving, although that might have been easier. Once he was at the airport, he took the train as far as it would go and then hitchhiked from there. It wasn't the best way, but he didn't want to call his parents or even Colt.

Hayden wanted to surprise Devorah, and he'd do it at the homecoming game. It would be like one of those movies they'd seen, where he'd stand there professing his love and she'd run into his arms.

Hayden made it to the high school with four minutes left on the game clock. He waited patiently, hoping Devorah would spot him standing along the fence.

She never looked his way.

When the final buzzer sounded, Hayden walked toward the entrance to the field, careful to stay in the shadows.

That's when he saw the love of his life kissing another guy.

Not just any guy, but the piece of shit known as Chad Campbell.

Hayden's heart lurched. Devorah . . . his Devy . . . looked happy. She smiled.

She wasn't a secret. Not like she had been with Hayden.

He had failed her, and now he was too late.

Hayden went back to school, flipped the switch on his feelings for Devorah Crowley, and met Sofia.

But things were different now. He wasn't married, and Devy was . . . well, she was going through some major shit. None of which was going to be easy on her or Maren. Hayden felt bad for Dev. Not in the sense that he felt obligated to try and make her feel better about herself or her situation, but in the sense that no one should be treated the way Chad had treated her. What her husband did was the lowest of lows. His behavior was despicable.

Hayden looked over at her as he drove along the interstate. Her lips moved to the song, which made him smile. At least she was putting in an effort.

"Do you like this song?" he asked her.

"It's one of Maren's favorites." She looked over her shoulder at her daughter. Hayden did so quickly. The girl was dancing in her seat. Then he caught a glimpse of Conor. His son was playing the air guitar with so much gusto he actually looked like he knew what he was doing.

"Guess I'm the drummer," Hayden said as he started tapping on the steering wheel. He didn't know the words to the song, but he made his lips move anyway. The four of them continued to put on their own concert until Hayden pulled into the sporting goods store parking lot and shut the truck off.

"Whew, that was fun," Devorah said as she got out of the truck. She opened the back door and helped the kids out. She took Maren's hand while Conor walked next to his father.

"I had no idea we were such a good band," Hayden said, walking close to Devorah. "I think after a few more jam sessions, we'll be able to take our band on the road."

"Definitely."

They entered the large store and were greeted by an employee asking if they needed assistance. After declining, they turned down the first aisle toward the baseball section. As soon as they were close, Conor ran the rest of the way.

"He's excited," Hayden said, almost as if he was making an excuse for his son's enthusiasm.

"Is your dad coaching?" Devy asked.

"Not sure. I have a feeling he'll help out, with Conor being on the team."

"Can I play?" Maren asked.

Devorah looked at her daughter. It took her a couple of seconds, but she finally nodded. "This is baseball," she told Maren. "I can see if there are softball tryouts."

"No, I don't mind playing with Conor."

"Okay, let's get you some shoes and a glove."

"Why don't you go over to the shoes, and I'll look for a glove for her," Hayden told them. "I'll find one that doesn't need a lot of breaking in. Are you right or left handed, Maren?"

"Right," she said, holding up her hand to show him.

"Perfect."

"Thanks, Hayden. This means a lot to me. To us." Dev looked from her daughter to Hayden.

He smiled at them both. "It's my pleasure."

Hayden watched them head toward the shoes, and then he started down the aisle with gloves and balls. He tried on three different mitts before finding one that was already soft and would be easy for Maren to squeeze shut. He figured he would take her to the park early tomorrow and play catch and hit some grounders for her. Not knowing her level of playing ability, he didn't want to assume she hadn't played before.

"Dad!" Conor careened around the corner. "Check out these shoes Miss Devy found for me." Conor opened the box to show off the bright-orange-and-black cleats. "Aren't they the coolest?"

"Very cool. Do they fit?"

"Yep. Miss Devy did the thumb test and everything, just like Mom used to." Conor didn't miss a beat, but Hayden's heart lurched. "Can I get them?"

"Of course. What do you think about going to the park early tomorrow to toss the ball around with Maren?"

"Yeah, okay, that'll be fun. She picked out some black-and-purple cleats. They're nice. They're looking at sweatshirts. Can I get one?"

"Let's go find the ladies," Hayden said. He carried a bucket of balls and the glove he'd chosen for Maren. He wanted her to try it on first to make sure it fit. He and Conor found them in one of the clothing sections, looking at sweatshirts. When Conor approached, Devy took one she had draped over her arm and held it to Conor's chest.

Even if Hayden hadn't wanted to buy it for his son, he would now. The motherly side of Devy shined, and she made his son smile.

"Maren, can you try this on for me?" Hayden asked as he approached the group. Maren came over, took the glove, and slipped her hand inside. Hayden asked her questions about comfort and flexibility and to see if anything pinched.

"Nope, it feels good. Thanks, Mr. Hayden."

"You know, you can call me Hayden. No need for the 'Mr.' in front of it."

Maren smiled, and when she did, she looked exactly like Devorah had at that age, which was right about the time when he'd started hanging around with Colt and teasing the crap out of Colt's little sister.

Nah, he wasn't teasing Devorah. He was flirting with her. He did it then, and he was about to do it now. This time, he'd make sure she knew exactly how he felt.

Eleven

Devorah

There was a time in her life when Devorah had wanted four children. Ideally, two boys and two girls—in that order—and no less. She'd loved having a big brother, someone to stand up for her and be her protector, even though she and Colt fought like cats and dogs at times. It didn't matter if they were mad at each other or if he (in her opinion) had done something incredibly mean; he'd always have her back. He was the only one she allowed to torment her.

Until Chad came along.

During high school, Devy and Chad had had what every high schooler in love called the perfect romance. They never fought, at least nothing to cause a breakup over. They always laughed. They had the best time whenever they went out. He loved her and she him.

Chad would hold Devy's hand everywhere they went, even when he was driving. At times, he acted possessively over Devorah, something Colt and Crow had an issue with and expressed many times. But Chad never said a thing if Devy wanted to hang out with her friends, and no one noticed that by the end of her senior year of high school, she only had Chad. Any girlfriends were long gone because she had constantly chosen him over everyone else.

By the time she realized what had happened, they were off to college. There, they hung out with Chad's friends and their girlfriends. Those women became Devy's friends, at least while they were still a couple.

When Chad and Devorah married, it was at the courthouse. Simple and easy, the way Chad wanted it. When they had Maren, Chad declared their family complete without even consulting Dev. She was heartbroken and yearned for another child. Begged him to reconsider, but he was adamant.

Now, as she helped Conor tie his cleats, made him stand, and did the thumb test to see where his big toe was, it hit her how manipulative Chad had been throughout their relationship. Devy never had a say in anything. Not about where they went out to dinner, where they lived, where they went to college, their marriage—nothing. He controlled every aspect of her life.

You should volunteer. So she did.

You should join the PTA. She did that as well.

You should . . . do this, that. Go here, go there.

"Why don't you walk up and down the aisle. See how they feel," she said to Conor as she fought the urge to cry. She cleared her throat, hoping to ease the ache she had there. Conor did as she suggested and even stutter-stepped, as if he were fielding a ball, or maybe he was trying to run.

"Thank you, Miss Devy," Conor said as he wrapped his arms around her waist and gave her a squeeze.

"You're welcome. Why don't you go show your dad."

Conor nodded and headed toward Hayden. She watched his son and didn't turn away until she heard Hayden greet him. As odd as it was, because she barely knew the boy, she felt comfortable about him. Proof to her that she was meant to be a mom of many, not only Maren. Chad had taken that away from her.

She then turned her attention to Maren, who had her cleats tied and ready for the thumb test.

"Are you sure about this?"

Maren nodded. "It'll be fun, and Conor's my only friend. Maybe Daddy will come to my games."

Devorah ignored the reference to Chad doing anything involving Maren. "You know if you try out for the girls' team, you can make some new friends."

Maren shrugged. "The girls in class aren't very nice."

Devy crouched and pressed her thumb into the front of Maren's shoe. "Okay, you walk now. Do the stuff Conor did, and make sure they feel good."

Maren did and proclaimed they were perfect. She didn't hug her mom or thank her, which bothered Dev. Chad would never thank his wife. Not for keeping the house spotless, not for having dinner on the table each night, not for dropping off and picking up his dry cleaning. Everything she did had been expected of her.

Dev packed up the shoes they weren't going to get and headed toward the clothing section. The morning tryouts would be chilly, and Maren hadn't packed all her clothes, and as far as Devy was concerned, Chad could buy his daughter some new things. The thought of going back to Chicago or asking Chad to send her clothes formed a pit in Dev's stomach. She wasn't ready and needed more time. To her knowledge, Chad had called only once to speak to Maren. He wasn't calling Dev's cell phone. She pulled it out of her pocket and glanced at her missed calls.

None.

They needed to talk, but Devorah didn't have the stomach to initiate anything. Walking away from your life because your husband wanted to live with his mistress was one thing. Taking the necessary step forward to end your marriage was another, and it was a move Devorah wasn't sure how to navigate.

She looked through the racks of sweatshirts and came across one that matched the cleats Conor had chosen. She found his size and draped it over her arm, as if it was second nature to buy him things.

She glanced down at it and smiled. It was odd to think that a sweatshirt for a little boy she barely knew would give her a sense of happiness.

Hayden and Conor came toward them, and she instantly held the sweatshirt against Conor's chest, lining the shoulders up with the seam. "I think you need a large, especially if your uniform shirt is bulky."

Devy didn't ask Hayden if Conor could get it. The thought hadn't even crossed her mind. She was in mother mode, and if Maren was getting a sweatshirt to match her cleats, then Conor needed one as well.

She turned back to the rack to find Conor a different size and to hide her smile as Hayden spoke to Maren about the glove he'd chosen for her. Out of the corner of her eye, she watched him with her daughter. He was gentle, guiding, and determined to make sure Maren's hand was comfortable in the glove.

Another smile crept across her mouth when she heard Hayden tell Maren to just call him Hayden. No need for the "Mr." stuff.

"Can you try this one on for me?" Devy handed Conor the sweatshirt, now in size large. She took his shoes from him and set them with Maren's. Conor did as he was asked, messing up his hair when he pulled it over his head, which Devy promptly fixed.

"How does this feel?" She pulled, tugged, and yanked the shirt in places.

Conor made funny sounds and acted as if he were falling each time Devy moved the sweatshirt.

"You're a funny guy, just like your dad," Dev said. "Is it tight?"

"No, it's perfect."

Devy smiled.

"You should smile more," Conor said. "You're very pretty."

She grinned again. "Thank you, Conor. I appreciate you saying so."

The boy smiled brightly and then ran off toward his dad. Devy watched Hayden as he gave his attention equally to both his son and her daughter. It was weird to her how the four of them flowed. Even though she'd known Hayden most of her life, it was also as if she hadn't.

She had no idea what kind of food he liked or what his favorite color was, and she didn't remember when his birthday was.

I want to know.

The thought gave her pause. She shook her head, clearing the tangled mess of those thoughts away, and headed toward the three of them.

"Look, Mom!" Maren tossed a baseball into the web of the mitt and closed it tightly. "It's ready for tomorrow."

"That's great." A thought occurred to her as she saw the excitement on Maren's face. Had they already missed the sign-ups for the tryouts?

"Hayden." Devy said his name to get his attention. "Did I have to sign Maren up beforehand?"

"No, we sign up at the park. It's an open tryout."

Devorah relaxed. At least she hadn't messed that up.

"Are we all set?" Hayden asked. He looked at each of them. Dev and Maren nodded.

Conor spoke. "What about socks?"

Hayden put his hand on Conor's shoulder. "I think the team will give you a pair. If not, we'll come back once we know your team color."

"Cool," Conor said as he fist pumped the air.

As they made their way to the checkout, anxiety stirred in Devy's stomach. She hadn't used any of her joint credit or debit cards since she arrived back in Oyster Bay, and being as she hadn't spoken to Chad about finances, she had no idea if the cards even worked. Sure, some of the money in their bank account was hers, but Chad never saw it that way. He was the breadwinner. The man who "brought home the bacon," as he often said. Her referred to her earnings as a "pittance," even though at times during the spring and summer, when estate sales were booming, she earned in the very high four digits. He'd always looked down on her job, calling it a "hobby."

Hayden motioned for her to go first in the checkout. She set Maren's stuff on the counter and pulled her wallet out. Her heart raced and her hand shook as she slipped the credit card from the holder. In hindsight, she should've said no to Hayden's invite. She and Maren could've gone by themselves later and avoided any possible embarrassment.

The clerk rang the items in and read off the total. As casually as possible, Dev inserted her credit card, pressed the appropriate buttons when prompted, and waited. She saw the word just as the clerk told her the charge had been declined.

"Is the total right?" Hayden asked the clerk. "Did you get everything?"

"Uh, no?" The clerk added the other items and read off the new total while Devorah stood there, speechless.

Hayden stepped forward and removed Devy's card. He looked at it, furrowed his brow, and shook his head. "This one expired months ago. I'll call the bank and see why they didn't send you a new one." He pocketed the card and then handed Devorah his. "This one should work."

Devorah eyed him as she worked to keep her emotions in check and the pending tears locked behind her eyes. She didn't want to cry in front of him, the kids, or the young man behind the counter.

The transaction went through, and the clerk bagged everything in separate bags after Hayden said the kids wanted to carry their own stuff. With little traffic in the parking lot, the kids ran ahead of their parents to the truck.

"Thank you," Devy said when Conor and Maren were out of earshot. "You didn't have to do that."

"I know I didn't," he said. "But I wasn't going to let your husband embarrass you in front of your daughter."

Devy wiped at an errant tear. "I can't believe he did that."

"Have you spoken to an attorney yet?"

Dev shook her head. "I guess I need to, but I should probably find a job first."

"Same," Hayden said, laughing. "I'm not sure what I want to do. The idea of starting a new job while Conor is acclimating doesn't sit well with me."

"Me too," she said as they reached the truck. Hayden pressed the button on his fob, and the doors unlocked. Devorah smiled when Conor opened the back and waited for Maren to get in. Dev looked at Hayden. "You're teaching him to be a gentleman."

"As if there is any other way to be," he said as he opened the passenger door for her. Once she was in, Hayden leaned to the side and asked, "Pizza?"

The kids cheered, which was good enough for Devy.

Hayden drove a few blocks to the nearest pizza place, which was fully equipped with arcade games that produced tickets. It was the kind of place where you walked in, got a black light stamp on your hand that matched your kids' stamps, and then ordered your pizza before sitting down. But not before you had to buy tokens.

Without any hesitation, Hayden requested the largest token package available and then turned to Dev. "What do we want for pizza?"

"I like mushroom and sausage," she told him.

"Me too."

"Maren likes pineapple on her pizza."

"Conor likes cheese."

"How about we order half and half?"

Hayden shook his head. "Nah, let's get them their own. Leftovers are the best part of getting pizza."

Devorah placed an order for one large and two medium pizzas and unlimited refills at the soda fountain. With two very antsy kids, they found a table, and then Hayden worked to distribute the tokens into four piles. Two for them now and two for later.

With their token cups full, Conor and Maren ran off together, leaving their parents alone.

"When we get back to Crow's, I'll give you money for today."

"You will not," Hayden said. "It's fine."

"I'm appreciative, but I don't want to owe you anything, Hayden. The last thing I need is for people to say I'm taking advantage of you."

"People like Sapphire Fleming?"

Devorah rolled her eyes. "She had a crush on Chad back in high school. I bet she's loving all of this."

"I know this is easy for me to say, but who cares what she or anyone thinks? Shit happens. You can't control what others do, but you sure as hell can control how these people make you feel."

"It's karma."

"Why?"

"Because I wasn't nice to them in high school. I was a stuck-up snob, daughter of the sheriff who never got into trouble for anything. The one who shunned her friends for a guy. No one in town owes me any grace."

Hayden reached across the table and took Devy's hand in his, his thumb brushing across her skin in a light caress. "Don't let the people in Oyster Bay bully you into thinking you're not deserving of compassion, Dev. Everyone is, regardless."

Devorah liked the way Hayden's strong hand engulfed hers, even if it made her feel like they were doing something they shouldn't. When one of the staff came toward their table with their order, Devy pulled her hand away and then excused herself to find the kids.

She walked a bit and then looked over her shoulder. Hayden stared at her with a smile on his face. Devy smiled back. It was genuine, it felt good, and it gave her hope that she and Hayden could be friends.

Later that night, after Maren had gone to bed, Devorah told her father she was going for a walk.

"Take Cordelia with you."

Devorah stared at her father and then looked at the dog, who wagged her tail in anticipation. "Why?"

"Because she needs it, and people are less likely to bother someone with a dog."

"But she's a puppy."

Crow laughed. "Cordelia, show teeth."

The dog obeyed and lifted her lips in a snarl.

"Good girl. Now give her a cookie." Crow motioned to the jar on the sideboard. Dev did as she was told.

"What else can she do?"

"Probably anything you ask. Colt sent her to some fancy-pants training school, which is why I let her stay here and not down at the bar with him."

"A bar is no place for a dog."

"That's what I told him when he brought her home." Crow flipped through the channels until he landed on a baseball game. "Ugh, the Yankees."

"I'll be back. Maren's sleeping," she told her dad as she leashed Cordelia. They set out on their walk. Colt and Dev had wanted a dog growing up, but Crow wouldn't let them have one. They were a busy family, and no one was ever home long enough to take care of an animal.

"You're a good girl. Aren't you?" Dev looked at Cordelia, who stayed right next to her leg. She didn't pull on her leash or try to dart into traffic. "I hope you're good for Maren—she needs someone or something."

Cordelia looked up, as if she knew exactly what Devorah had said to her.

They walked toward downtown and then veered toward the water, headed for a bike path that ran along the beach. During the day, the views were impeccable. At night, she'd be able to see out over the harbor, the lights of the last boats coming in, or the strong orb of the lighthouse not far from them.

She used to run this path back in the day. She and Laila would jog to keep in shape after basketball season was over. There wasn't a sport for them to cheer for during the spring, and Devorah needed to look her best for Pearl of the Ocean. She had never planned to enter the pageant, but it was a rite of passage for all high school girls in OB.

Devorah smiled at the people they passed, but mostly she kept her head down. She didn't want to talk to anyone, even if it was small talk.

When Cordelia stopped to relieve herself, Dev looked up and down the path, mindful of the people coming toward her. If her father had taught her anything, it was to know your surroundings.

They continued to walk, enjoying the cool, spring air. The night was calm, and she could barely hear the water sloshing against the rocks. Footsteps caught her attention before she saw who they belonged to. When she finally noticed, she swallowed hard and stood still.

Hayden ran toward her. His shirt was tucked into the back of his shorts, blowing in the breeze created by his stride.

"Shit," she muttered when reality smacked her in the face—he was shirtless. "Shit, shit, shit." She didn't need this.

Wanted it, maybe.

But definitely didn't need it.

In the few days she'd been back, Hayden had clouded her vision. It wasn't that she didn't like him, because she definitely had at one point in her life; it was that he confused her, and she wasn't sure she could trust him or even herself where he was concerned.

Hayden McKenna had a vibe about him. Sexy and cool. Suave and sweet. He was easy on the eyes and hard on her thoughts. They'd been more than friends but never what she wanted them to be. Right now, friendship was the only thing she could afford with him.

He stopped in front of her, panting, and bent at his waist for a second before righting himself. He put his hands behind his head and attempted to smile at her.

His chest glistened. Sweat trailed down the contours of his muscles, around his nipples, and through the smattering of hair leading into his shorts. Devorah swallowed hard and looked at the ground, back to him, and at the ground again and then swore under her breath.

Cordelia whined.

"Hey, girl." Hayden crouched and patted the dog, who lapped at him.

"Sorry, she can't hold her licker."

"I don't mind. Conor wants a dog, but he has to wait."

Hayden stood, his chest at Dev's eye level. Teenage Devorah wanted to do naughty things to him. She blushed at the thought of touching him, like she had years ago.

"You good?"

She nodded. "Just out walking Cordelia. You?"

"Trying to burn off some pent-up energy."

She could understand.

"How about I walk you back home?"

Was she done with her walk? She could be, but she also felt like she needed to be alone more. "I'm going to walk for a bit more," she told him. "Thanks, though."

"You sure?"

"Yeah, it's a nice night."

Gorgeous, half-naked Hayden stepped forward. He touched her hip with his fingers, sending a spark of desire and longing through her. He leaned down and brushed his lips right below her ear. "See you in the morning, Devorah."

Hayden began jogging again, and Dev turned to watch him. Wishing all the same that she hadn't. Why did he have to come into her life when it was such a mess?

TWELVE

HAYDEN

—

People in New England had an old saying . . . if you don't like the weather, wait five minutes and it'll change. Hayden waited. He stood in the front room window, drinking coffee from a mug declaring him the *World's Best Grandpa*. Cars drove along the road, tires hitting puddles and splashing water and road grime onto yards and parked cars. Hayden glanced at the watch on his wrist and then leaned forward to peer out the window and up at the sky, forgetting that the roof of the porch would hinder his view.

The showers had come out of nowhere and, as of the night before, hadn't been on the radar. The random burst hovered over Oyster Bay, threatening baseball tryouts. Hayden set his coffee down and pulled out his phone. He tapped the screen to bring it alive and then clicked on the weather app, scrolling until he found the video of the rain showers.

"It should be clear in a minute," Darcy said from behind him.

Hayden let out one of those *humph* sounds, neither believing nor disbelieving his mom.

Darcy stood next to him and sighed. "Figures."

"Of course it does."

As a kid, Hayden remembered many times when rain would dampen or ruin an outside activity for him. The worst had been his junior year of high school during football season. The team had lost one game all year and were vying for the state championship in their division. It had rained for three straight days, and no one had had the keen sense of mind to push the game off for a week. They'd been lucky all season with little to no foul weather, but when it mattered the most, Mother Nature unleashed on them. The "mud bowl" ended with a score of two to zero, in favor of the other team. Hayden was the one who'd been sacked in the end zone.

"Tryouts start in an hour," he said to his mom. "And I promised the kids I'd take them to the field beforehand to toss the ball around."

"They're not made of sugar," Darcy said. "They won't melt."

"I'm definitely made of sugar," Hayden said with a smile. "According to the radar, this storm will be over in a minute." Hayden picked his coffee up and took another sip.

"Is there an echo in here?" Darcy looked around the room as if she was looking for the echo to come out of hiding.

"Funny," Hayden said. "I'm stressed. I can't help it."

"It's baseball tryouts. They can happen later in the day."

"Yeah, it's not just the tryouts," he said as he frowned at his phone.

"How was dinner last night?"

"Fine. Took the kids to the Pizza Palace. They had fun."

"And you?"

"What about me?" He eyed his mother cautiously and saw the slight lift of her shoulder as she brought her coffee cup to her lips.

"Just, you know."

"No, I don't know." Hayden knew that his mother and her friends were gossips. If you had or wanted news spread, you asked the Crafty Cathys, or the CC Club. The women of Oyster Bay took their blabbermouthing very seriously. The Crafty Cathys were also the first to come to someone's aid when needed. They were the first to volunteer, be there with food when there was a crisis, and set up watch parties when a fishing boat hadn't returned yet or organize a knitting party for babies in need. The group had a purpose and had been around for eons. It was an honor to be part of the CC Club.

"Tabitha may have mentioned she saw you and another recently single resident chatting it up in the parking lot last week, and then again at dinner."

Hayden rolled his eyes, hard. Tabitha was the worst of the worst when it came to the CC Club. She patrolled the streets in her hot-pink spandex pants and matching jogger jacket, and she often wore a head-band to keep her unruly short, curly blond hair out of her eyes. She was the epitome of what people thought the eighties looked like, with all the neon colors. Hayden was curious, though, if Tabitha still wore the same Reeboks now that they were back in fashion and if she had upgraded her Walkman to an iPhone.

"I'm pretty sure I told you I ran into Devorah outside the school and gave her a ride because it was raining. She's going through a lot of shit right now and doesn't need any of you Crafty Cathys adding your two cents."

Hayden excused himself and went out to stand on the porch. He glanced at the sky. The clouds were moving fast, and the blue sky showed a lot of promise. He sent a text to Devy: Please tell Maren I'm sorry but it doesn't look like the rain is going to let up in time for us to get some practice in. Make sure she doubles up on her socks. The grass is going to be wet. I'll be there shortly to pick you up.

He pocketed his phone and went back into the house, made eye contact with his mom, and shook his head. She meant well, but he truly wanted the locals to forget about what they'd seen and let Devy figure things out on her own. She didn't need a constant reminder that her husband had had an affair with her best friend and had chosen the same best friend who'd humiliated her on the internet.

"Conor, you about ready?" Hayden yelled up the stairs.

"Yes, but it's raining."

"Tryouts are still on. Grab another sweatshirt and extra socks. You'll be fine."

Hayden went into the kitchen and prepared Conor's water bottle. He added ice and then water and then grabbed a couple of bottles from the refrigerator for later. The temperature would rise to a lovely sixty-five, and he didn't want Conor and Maren to be without some form of hydration. He knew they'd need it with all the running around they were about to do.

When he heard Conor thump onto the floor, Hayden yelled, "Stop jumping off the steps."

"You used to do it all the time," Darcy yelled back from the living room.

Hayden gripped the edge of the island and gritted his teeth. His parents babied Conor, which at times he appreciated. He was the parent, however, and there were things he and Sofia had tried to instill in their son. One of them was self-preservation. Jumping off steps was never a good idea.

Conor and his grandma came into the kitchen, both with shit-eating grins on their faces. Hayden shook his head and made a mental note to call the contractor, Link Blackburn, on Monday to see when they could break ground on his new home. Link was a local and had grown up with Hayden. They hadn't been great friends in high school but were always cordial. Hayden was more than ready to have his own place, somewhere he could parent his son without his mom undermining him.

"Ready?" he asked Conor.

"Yep, Grandpa put my stuff in the truck already."

"All right, let's go try out for some baseball."

Conor hugged his grandma goodbye and followed Hayden outside. He climbed into the back, without Hayden suggesting it.

"Are we still picking Maren up?"

"Yeah, we are."

"She really kicked my butt at the games last night."

"You didn't let her win?" Hayden asked as he drove toward the sheriff's house.

"What? No way. She's a beast."

Hayden glanced in the rearview and watched as Conor's head bopped to the song coming from the radio. It pleased him how his son was so compassionate toward Maren, especially considering how Conor had lost his mom. Maybe it was good for the kids to be close.

It was definitely a great excuse for Hayden to spend time with Devy. He liked her. Probably more than he should at the moment.

Hayden pulled up to the front of the house and groaned when Sheriff Crowley came down the steps. Knowing he shouldn't hide from Crow, Hayden put his truck into park and stepped out under the light drizzle to greet the man.

"Sheriff," Hayden said as he came around the front of his truck. "Working on a Saturday?"

"Just gonna monitor the activity at the park," he said as he adjusted his duty belt. "I hear your boy is the reason Maren wants to try out today."

Hayden glanced at his truck and smiled. "Yes, sir. They've become fast friends."

Crow nodded. "She needs all the friends she can get right now."

"She" could've meant Dev or Maren. Hayden took it as both.

The front screen door squeaked as Maren and Devy came out. Maren rushed down the stairs and all but crashed into her grandfather.

"See you at tryouts, Grandpa."

"Knock 'em dead, slugger," he said as he gave Maren a hug. When Devorah reached her father, the reception was stilted. Crow started to put his arm around Dev and then stopped. He sighed heavily and then grunted out something that sounded like "Keep your head up." But Hayden couldn't be sure.

"I will." The response from Devorah was clear as day. As soon as she looked at Hayden, she smiled softly and ducked her head.

Was she flirting with him?

He hoped so.

Hayden stepped to the side and motioned for Devorah to walk in front of him. He followed behind and opened the passenger door for her when they reached his truck. Once Devy was in, he checked on Maren and Conor in the back, both deep in conversation about the Pizza Palace, and then jogged around to the driver's side.

He chanced a look at Crow, who stood there watching everything. Hayden gave him a quick wave and then hopped into the cab. "The rain will stop by the time we get to the field," he said as he put his truck into drive and signaled he was about to reenter the roadway—he didn't want to give the sheriff a reason to pull him over—and headed toward the park.

"I love the rain," Maren said from the back. "It means everything will be all muddy."

Devy shook her head. "It's all she's talked about since it started this morning."

"Do you remember the time it rained for days, right before the football championship?"

"How could I forget? Colt complained nonstop. First about the weather and then about losing. Wasn't the score something like three to five? It was an odd one."

Hayden sighed. "We lost because of me by a score of zero to two."

"Ooh, that's right." Devy's *ooh* seemed to drag out forever. "Now I remember."

"Please don't," Hayden said with a bit of laughter. "No one needs to remember that night, especially me. Actually, I take that back. There are a few things from that night that I want to remember." Hayden winked and Devy blushed. "I've never looked at a swing the same since."

"Hey."

Hayden jumped at the sound of her voice. He hadn't expected that she'd want to see him. He turned in the swing as Devorah came toward him, still in her cheerleading outfit.

"Hey."

She stood in front of him until he had no choice but to look up at her. She sat on his lap, facing him. Being tall gave Hayden a lot of advantages. This was one of them.

"I'm sorry."

"Do they all hate me?" he asked, of the football team. He'd fucked up royally tonight and cost the team a championship.

Devorah shrugged. "Coach says the rain and field conditions hindered everyone's game."

"You can say that again."

"I would, but I don't like repeating myself, and I honestly don't understand any of it."

"You're not mad at me?"

She shook her head. "I'm here, aren't I?"

"Yeah, you are." He pulled her close and helped her put her legs on either side of his hips. Hayden was in love with her but couldn't tell her, afraid of what her brother would say or do. The two-year difference in their age had never bothered him until now. He wanted her to come to college with him, where they could be open and free about how they felt about each other.

Hayden's hand trailed up her back, bringing her forward until their lips met. Gently, he pushed his foot into the rain-soaked ground, swaying them back and forth.

"We all have our moments," she said, smiling at him. "It was high school. Who cares?"

Yes, they'd definitely had their moments, and he was having an easy time remembering them. Most of his memories were good. Great even. The only bad one was when he saw her kissing Chad. If Hayden could go back in time and tell her then how he felt . . .

Nope, he wasn't going there. He and Sofia had had a good life together. They had been happy, in love, and thriving. Hayden couldn't change the past, but he'd be damn sure to show Devorah that she deserved better than the likes of Chad "Full of Shit" Campbell.

Hayden pulled into the parking lot of the park. "Those guys care," he said as he pointed to a group of dads, most of them former classmates.

"This is why small towns suck," Devorah said. "People remember everything."

"Especially when you leave and then come back."

Before Hayden and Devy could move a muscle to get out of the car, Maren and Conor had opened the back doors and bolted for the group.

"They don't have any cares in the world," Devy said. "Maren should, though. I tried to talk her out of this, but she's insistent."

"If it makes you feel any better, Conor is happy she's here."

"A little, but I fear—" Devorah paused and shook her head. "I shouldn't have come back here, but I couldn't stay in Chicago. This place was the lesser of two evils."

Hayden placed his hand on top of hers. "You have friends here who will protect you."

Devy scoffed. "I can't even get my father to sit down and talk to me, let alone anyone else. I'm the town pariah."

"Nah, something will happen next week, and everyone will have moved on. You didn't do anything wrong. Remember that," Hayden said. "Come on, I see my dad sitting at the registration table. The sooner we get this started, the faster it'll be over."

Hayden and Devy made their way to the registration table, where several parents were registering their players. They both went to Lee to make things easier.

"It's good to see you, Devorah," Lee said. "I had coffee with your dad yesterday."

"Well, hopefully Crow did his part to keep up the conversation."

Lee chuckled. "A man of few words our sheriff is, that's for sure. He's happy you and Maren are back in Oyster Bay, though."

"Really? Did he say that?" Dev asked.

"He did. He's very proud of you."

Devy stepped back and met Hayden's gaze. Tears pooled in the corners of her eyes, and Hayden suspected that might have been the first time Crow had ever said anything of the sort. Everyone in town knew Crow had a rocky relationship with his kids, so hearing him say this sort of thing to someone else had probably hit Devy square in the chest.

Devorah and Hayden walked side by side toward a set of bleachers. Devy chose the bottom row. Hayden sat next to her and extended his long legs out in front of him.

"Don't want to sit higher up?"

She shook her head. "I'm less visible here."

Hayden looked around. He smiled when smiled at and waved a couple of times. "No one will bother you. Not here at least."

His words seemed to fall on deaf ears, and he accepted that. If someone even came up to Devorah and said something about what was going on, Hayden would have words with them. There was a time and a place, and it wasn't Oyster Bay.

Thirteen

Devorah

The rain stopped before the kids took the field. Devy groaned when she saw Maren step in a puddle. This girl was going to be the death of her. She loved her daughter fiercely but wanted to wring her neck for getting her shoes and socks wet.

"Put newspaper in her shoes when she gets home."

The voice behind Devy caused her to turn around. Beatrice Sherman sat behind Hayden and her, dressed from head to toe in Oyster Bay baseball gear. She pointed toward the field. "My grandson is out there," she said.

Beatrice was part of the Crafty Cathys and one of the women who helped Crow out after Devy's mother died. Each day, Beatrice would come over with some type of casserole or roast and make sure everything was okay. This lasted a month until Crow told her to never come back.

Beatrice looked at Devy, who hadn't taken her eyes off the woman. "It's good to see you again," Bea said. "You need to stop by the office and visit Theo. He'll help you file your divorce papers."

"I—uh—" She planned to say she hadn't thought about filing any papers, but the fact was, it was all she thought about at night. Devy had visions of a process server showing up at Ester's house, with Chad answering the door buck-ass naked. In her mind, the process server laughed at Chad and slapped the papers against his chest. Also in her mind, Devy got everything—the house, the money, and the satisfaction of knowing she was the one who'd filed first.

"You will divorce that disgusting man, and Theo will take care of it for you. Don't you worry about the money, sweetie. Your mom was one of us. We'll take care of it."

Bea left Devy speechless. She turned back around and caught Hayden looking at her. He winked. "See, not all are bad."

"One good apple doesn't give you a viable orchard," she said.

"We have two apples. My mom and Bea."

"Still not enough to make apple pie."

Hayden scoffed lightly. "Just think, if he ever returns to town, the Crafty Cathys will filet him alive."

"I'd like to see that."

"Me too," Hayden mumbled.

He leaned closer to Devy, their shoulders touching. Instead of moving over a smidge to put space between them, she stayed where she was and watched as the group of kids did as the coaches instructed.

"Who's the coach?"

"Dalton Noble. He's two years older than Colt and me."

"I don't remember him."

"Really? He played baseball with us and definitely hung out at your house."

"Hmm, my mind must've been elsewhere." She looked at Hayden and grinned, even though she felt like a fool. She had no right, at least in her mind, to flirt with Hayden. The last thing she wanted was to lead him on or let him think she was interested.

I was interested back in the day, but then Chad . . .

Devy angled her head to get a better look at Dalton but still couldn't recall him. Some faces and names were lost on her. It was like she had forgotten almost everyone when she moved away, but the truth was, she hadn't taken the time to remember people. She wanted to blame Chad and his narcissistic attitude, where he thought he was better than everyone else. Devy supposed that was how he achieved what he had in business, but now it left a sour taste in her mouth. She should've been a better person in high school and not followed everything he'd said.

She had been in love with him and wondered now how'd she feel if he walked up to her and said he wanted her back. A small part of her wanted that to happen—to give Maren the family she deserved—while the rest of her wanted to kick him in the balls and tell him to rot in hell. Maren didn't need a father who'd openly cheated on her mother. No one needed that type of role model in their lives.

Across the field, she saw her father holding court with a group of men. They were undoubtedly chatting about any petty crime happening in town or whatever game was on television the night before. That was one thing about small-town folks—they loved their sports, local and professional. Everyone in Oyster Bay were die-hard New England sports fans, and those who weren't were the outsiders who had moved there. Like Chad's family.

The Campbells moved to Oyster Bay the summer before Devy entered her freshman year of high school. Chad was a skinny teen and then had come into his own the summer before their junior year. That was when he and Devorah really noticed each other. They were the talk of the town, the young man from the big city dating Oyster Bay's Pearl of the Ocean. Everyone in town gushed, while Crow seethed because he didn't care for Chad. Their classmates were indifferent. Lifelong friends of Devy's were no longer her friends because she had given them up for Chad. Something she regretted now.

Shouting tore Devy's gaze away from her father and to the field, where she saw Conor push another kid. She was up and running toward the group without even thinking, with Hayden hot on her heels.

"Hey, what's going on?" she asked Conor and Maren, ignoring the snickering of the group of boys around them.

"He said some really mean things to Maren."

"Okay, but we don't push, bud," Hayden said.

"He pulled her hair first," Conor said as he pointed toward one of the boys. "Then he kept touching her back. Even when Maren said 'stop.'"

"Okay," Hayden said as he put his hand on Conor's shoulder. He crouched, making himself level with his son. "You did the right thing by protecting Maren. I'm not mad at you. I'm proud of you. With that said, we don't push others. But I get it. You know right from wrong, and you did what you felt was right."

"Maren, did he touch you?" Devy pointed at the boy who seemed to be in charge of the posse around him.

Maren nodded. "I said 'stop,' but he didn't listen."

"You have no right—" Devy stopped when she saw the coach running toward them.

"What's going on?" Dalton Noble ran over, seemingly out of breath, while Crow also came toward the gathering. Devy looked around as a quietness fell over the other parents. She knew, deep down, that Maren would somehow get blamed for everything. She kept Maren glued to her side, trying to keep the mama bear in her tame, when she really wanted to demand why the kid's parents hadn't taught their son better.

Devy looked down at her daughter. "Are you okay?"

Maren nodded. "He's not a nice boy."

"Yeah, I agree. Do you want to stay or go home?"

"I'm staying." Maren pointed at the boy. "He's jealous because I can run faster than him."

"Am not." The boy stuck his tongue out at Maren.

To be nine again.

"What seems to be the trouble?" Crow asked.

Maren went right to her grandfather and buried her head in his torso. Devorah's heart sighed. Crow would protect his own.

"Grandpa, that boy kept pulling my hair and touching me, even though I told him to stop."

"Is that true, Noble?" Crow directed the question at Dalton, who set his hand on the boy in question's shoulder.

"DJ?" Dalton asked. Of course the kid would be the coach's son.

DJ shrugged. "I didn't do anything wrong," he said. "My hand just touched her."

"How many times?" Crow's voice boomed and caused Devy to shrink back. She wasn't needed right now, and she was okay with letting her father handle it all.

"Dunno, but he pushed me." DJ pointed at Conor.

"Only because you wouldn't listen to Maren."

"All right, enough," Crow said as he looked at Dalton. "Keep your son away from my granddaughter, Noble, and Conor McKenna. I expect you and your boy to be in my office within a half hour after these tryouts are over."

"Sheriff, they're kids."

"Lessons are taught every day, Noble. Either you teach them or I do."

Crow leaned down and whispered something in Maren's ear. She nodded and then grabbed Conor by the hand and ran off.

Crow sauntered back to the group of men waiting for him. Dalton shook his head and tsked. "I don't understand why she's trying out anyway," he muttered as he walked away.

Devy opened her mouth to say something, but Hayden took her arm and led her back to the bleachers. After they sat down, she leaned into him. "What in the hell just happened?"

"If I had to guess, Crow has a bone to pick with Noble and just used his son to do it."

"And Maren is in the middle."

"Right along with Conor," Hayden said with a sigh. "I need him to make friends, not enemies."

"I'm sorry. I should've told Maren she couldn't try out."

Hayden looked at Devy so fast she thought his head was going to spin around. "Absolutely not. She shouldn't have to sit home because some boy can't keep his hands to himself. It's common courtesy and good parenting."

"Well, you're back for what, like, five minutes and already causing problems?"

Devorah looked over her shoulder and found Sapphire Fleming standing next to her.

Hayden groaned.

"It's none of your business, Sapphire."

"It is when it involves my son."

"You're married to Dalton?" Hayden asked, turning around to face her.

"We coparent, but that's beside the point," she said. "The point is, you come back to town because Chad came to his senses, and now you're making trouble for everyone else."

"She—"

Devorah held up her hand to cut Hayden off. She took a deep breath and glanced up at Sapphire. "I'm sorry there was an incident with your son, my daughter, and Hayden's son. Crow will sort it out this afternoon, and I'm sure all will be just fine."

"If my son is removed from the baseball team because of your daughter, there will be hell to pay."

Hayden shook his head. "You're unbelievable, Fleming."

Devorah couldn't believe what she was hearing. She stood and didn't fight Hayden when he grabbed her arm. "Your son touched my daughter when she asked him to stop. Maybe he shouldn't be on the team."

"I'm sure that's what happened. Go back to Chicago, Pearl. No one wants you here." Sapphire smirked.

"I do," Hayden said to Dev. "Crow and Colt do. Don't listen to the petty high school jealousy, Dev." Hayden shook his head and muttered under his breath.

The "Pearl" reference was a slap in the face to Dev. It wasn't her fault the people of Oyster Bay crowned her Pearl of the Ocean four years in a row. But others didn't see it like that.

"Oh, wait. Come to think of it, no one wants you in Chicago either."

Sapphire didn't walk away after she made the comment. Instead, she sat down right behind Hayden and leaned toward his ear.

He flinched and gave her a dirty look. "Get the hell away from me." He batted at her like she was a fly.

Devorah wanted nothing more to do with her or the tryouts and walked to the other side of the field, away from everyone.

She took her jacket off, spread it over the freshly laid mulch, and sat down, resting against the trunk of an oak tree. Devy pulled her knees to her chest and let the tears flow. People had rushed to take care of whatever had happened on the field, which she understood and knew her dad would resolve later, but the entire incident made her feel more vulnerable than she already felt. Did DJ pick on Maren because she was the new kid? Conor was new as well. Or had DJ singled her out because she was the only female trying out for a male-dominated sport? Most of the girls Maren's age cheered and attended competitions. Devy had asked her daughter if she wanted to do that instead, but Maren had chosen baseball. It would be nice for kids to be able to live in a world where sports weren't divided up by gender.

Hayden made his way over to where she sat or hid. She had expected him to follow her right away, and when he hadn't, she was relieved. Devorah needed a moment. Or ten. Hayden laid his sweatshirt next to hers and sat down with a sigh. Instead of saying anything, he reached for her hand. She gave it to him freely.

His large hand was warm and tender. His thumb lazily rubbed the spot between her thumb and index finger. The motion soothed her. Hayden didn't ask her what was wrong or bring up the fact that she was crying. He just sat there with her.

They had their own demons they were dealing with. Hers were just out in the open for everyone to see and watch, on repeat, whenever they chose.

When the whistle sounded and tryouts ended, Devy stayed where she was.

"You can't let what Sapphire said get to you."

"Why not? She's telling the truth. No one wants me."

"I do," Hayden said. He reached over and gently pulled her chin toward him. His gaze met hers. "I, for one, am damn happy you're here. I'm not happy with the circumstances, but Chad's mistake is my gain, and I fully intend to make the best of it."

Hayden got up and hustled toward the kids, leaving her there, speechless. She swallowed hard as she watched his swagger in those too-kind-for-the-eyes joggers men wore. Hayden was a whole lot of trouble she didn't need right now, but turning a friend away would be a mistake. He was right, though; she couldn't let what others thought of her bring her down. She hadn't done anything wrong. Chad had. If people couldn't see that cheating was wrong, that publicly humiliating someone you said you cared about was wrong, then they were the ones with the issue. Not her.

"I can do this," she said to the birds. Devy stood, picked up her jacket, and draped the clean side over her arm while she waited for Hayden and the kids. As they walked toward her, Hayden had a hand on each of them. Maren and Conor chatted animatedly, while Hayden stared at Devy with a grin on his face.

One that meant *something* . . . she just had to figure out what.

Fourteen

Hayden

Hayden took everyone out to lunch at the Lazy Lamb, mostly because he didn't want to drop Devorah off yet, and he couldn't think of an excuse to see her later in the evening or tomorrow. The best excuse he'd have to see her would be Monday, when the kids went back to school, and frankly that would be too long for him.

The kids ran into the pub and went to the end of the bar and waited for Colt to follow them to the game room. He was going to lose a fortune on video games where these kids were concerned.

With his hand on the small of Devy's back, Hayden directed them to a booth. They sat across from each other and waited for one of the staff members or Colt to come over to them.

It was Colt who graced them breathlessly as he sat down next to his sister. "How do you keep up with them?" he asked.

"They have a lot of energy, which is shocking, since they just had baseball tryouts," Devorah said.

"I heard some shit went down with Noble's kid?" Colt shook his head. "He's such an ass when he's in here. I've had to call Dad or one of the deputies a time or two. And don't get me started when his ex is here. They're oil and water but volatile. I don't know how they survive each other."

"Sapphire Fleming being the ex?" Hayden asked.

Colt shook his head. "No, believe it or not, she's the sane one. Dalton messed around on his wife with Sapphire, got her pregnant twice. They had an off-and-on thing in high school. I guess they never got over it."

"That's rich," Devorah said. "Now she likes Hayden."

Hayden's eyes went wide. "Believe me, the feelings aren't reciprocated."

"Stay away," Colt said. "You don't want to get involved with her kind of drama."

"I'd like to live a drama-free life," Devy added. "But it doesn't look that way."

Colt put his arm around his sister. "The ship will sail soon. Small-town drama comes and goes like the weather."

"Well, this has been the longest five minutes of my life," she said.

"Anyway, what happened?" Colt asked.

"DJ pulled Maren's hair and touched her when she asked him not to. Crow was there and told Dalton to bring his kid to the station after tryouts," Devy said, summing everything up for Colt.

Her brother shook his head again. "Crow's going to show the boy the jail cell. He may even lock him in it for a minute, since the kid messed with his granddaughter. Dalton should've taught him better."

"Well, Sapphire is more than pissed at me for being back, so I'm sure there's more drama heading our way."

"Not if Crow has anything to say about it," Colt told her. He slapped his hand on the table. "All right, enough of the whatever this is." He waved his hand in front of them. Devy smiled at her brother. "What can I get you to drink? Eat?"

Hayden placed his and Conor's order, and then Devy did the same for her and Maren. Hayden waited for Colt to be out of earshot before he spoke.

"I meant what I said under the tree, Devy."

She smiled softly. "I know you did. I just—"

"I'm not going anywhere." He cut her off, unwilling to hear how she needed time or wasn't looking for anything right now. He wasn't, either, but he also couldn't ignore the strong pull he felt toward her. Seeing her at the school was a sign. He was sure of it.

"I think I need to find a job or a hobby. All this sitting around with my thoughts isn't helping."

"Estate curating, right?"

The small smile turned into a wide grin. "Yes," she said with a shake of her head. "Impractical here, though. I was thinking of asking Colt if he's hiring, or maybe my dad needs someone down at the station."

"I'm sure either are viable. What are you going to do about Bea Sherman's offer?"

"Are the Crafty Cathys really still a thing?"

Hayden nodded vigorously. "My mother is still a proud member. I believe they meet here."

"I think I'm supposed to join or something," she said. "My mom was a member, and so was her mom."

"I bet this is why my sister moved away."

"Where does Allie live?"

"Los Angeles," he told her. "Entertainment law."

"Well, that's about as anti–small town as one can get."

"That's what she wanted. To be far away from here and doing her own thing. She likes it. Conor went to her place last year for a week. She took him to the beach and Disneyland and did the whole Hollywood tour thing. He was only interested in seeing the Angels baseball team and, of course, Disney."

"We were supposed to take Maren to Florida for her birthday this year. I guess it's a good thing we didn't tell her."

"It can still happen. Something tells me the parks are never going away."

"True. I don't know how Chad would feel. I know I shouldn't care, but I'm afraid he'll take things out on Maren because of me."

Colt returned with their drinks and said he'd be back in a few with their food.

Hayden held his soda between his hands, and his temper increased. He would never ever understand parents who used their children to hurt their former spouses or took things out on their kids.

"Do you think Chad would do that?"

Devy shrugged. "Right now, I'm more concerned with him taking her away from me."

"He wouldn't," Hayden guessed.

"I can see him saying I can't support her. Not the way he can. She wouldn't have the same lifestyle here as he can provide her in Chicago."

Hayden bit the inside of his cheek to keep himself from saying something someone might overhear and then tell Chad. He might not live in Oyster Bay, but he knew people. "You should go see Theo Sherman tomorrow." Theo Sherman, Bea's husband, was the town attorney who specialized in everything. There wasn't a case he couldn't or wouldn't take. Hayden remembered one case that made national news when a young girl wanted to sue the convenience store on the corner because the owner refused to stock cherry slushies. She threatened to sue him, he dared her, and Theo Sherman filed the lawsuit. It was frivolous, of course, but Theo meant business. The owner relented and stocked the cherry flavor, which sold out every week, much to his surprise.

"An attorney costs money."

"Theo will let you make payments, Dev. Besides, the sooner you get something in the works, the faster Chad will have to pay support to you and Maren. And I imagine after what he did to you, Theo will make him pay your fees. If anything, go talk to him."

"Talk to who?" Colt asked as he brought their food to the table.

"Theo Sherman. Bea was at the tryouts today and suggested it."

"The Shermans are good people, Dev. You know this. You should go see him. Take Dad with you."

"Why would I take Crow with me?"

"To get the Crow discount," Colt said with a shrug.

Colt had a point, but even Hayden knew Devorah wasn't looking for a handout.

"I'll go get the kids." Devy excused herself from the table. As soon as she was out of the booth, Colt sat down.

"I want to fly to Chicago and hunt the asshole down," Colt said under his breath. "I can't believe he did this to her. He all but alienates her from her family and then pulls this shit. His ass needs to be kicked."

Hayden leaned forward. "Is this how you truly feel? Because my tolerance for Chad Campbell is out the window. He shut off her credit card."

Colt's mouth dropped open. He closed it and shook his head, muttering something under his breath. "I have a colorful list of things to say, but I own this place, and the last thing the patrons need to hear is me going off on my piece-of-crap brother-in-law."

"What does Crow say?" Hayden was curious how their father felt. He was really an enigma unless the situation had something to do with the law.

"He's angry, of course."

"How does he feel about Devorah and Maren being at the house?"

"He loves it. Told me the house hasn't felt like a home since Dev left for college."

"Then ask him to tell her, because he makes her feel unwelcome."

Colt's eyes widened. "Shit, really?"

Hayden nodded. "Do your sister a solid and tell Crow to tell her how he feels. She needs to know she's welcome and that he wants her there. Also, she needs a job. I know I probably shouldn't say anything, but Dev needs one thing to go her way right now."

Colt leaned back and sighed. He started to open his mouth to say something, but Devorah had returned with the kids. He smiled at his sister and then Maren. "Did you clean me out?" he asked the kids.

"I'm a whiz at pinball, Uncle Colt."

"I expect nothing less," he said as he slid out of the booth. He pinched her cheek lightly. Maren scrunched her shoulders, squealed, and then took his seat. "Lunch is on me," he told Dev.

"Why, what do you want?"

Hayden laughed.

Colt ran his hand through his hair. "I sort of need a bartender a few nights a week and someone to make desserts."

Devy leaned to the side. Hayden refused to meet her gaze.

"Okay."

"Okay? That's it? Don't you want to know how much you're going to make?"

Instead of speaking, she wrapped her arms around Colt's waist. If they exchanged words, they did so quietly. To busy himself, Hayden made sure Maren was all set with her burger and fries.

"Can you make me fancy sauce?" Maren asked Hayden.

"What's that?"

"It's ketchup and mayo. My mom mixes it together and calls it 'fancy sauce.'"

"Sure can," he said. He took the little cup of mayo Colt had brought with Maren's food and added ketchup to it. Devorah sat down and offered to finish, but he shook his head, determined to make the perfect sauce for Maren.

"How's this?" He showed her his creation.

Her grin spread from ear to ear. "Thank you." She took the sauce and dipped a fry in, swirled it around, and then stuck it in her mouth.

"Can I try?" Conor asked her.

Maren held the dish out for Conor, who dunked and swirled his fry and then stuck it into his mouth. Hayden waited anxiously for his reaction. After a couple of chews, Conor nodded in approval.

"Colt!" Hayden hollered across the bar. "Another side of mayo, please. We need more fancy sauce."

"You got it."

"We can share until yours comes," Maren said. She set her sauce in the middle of the table for Conor to reach.

Hayden appreciated the comradery between the kids. It was nice to see and be a part of. He still needed to speak to Conor when they got home about what happened. Hayden was proud his son had stood up for Maren. It was the right thing to do. Pushing DJ, however, was not, and Hayden needed to find the right way to explain the difference. He didn't want Conor labeled as a bully or have him be in trouble with Crow. Those days would come. There was no need to rush them.

The four of them made idle chitchat through lunch, and when they were done, they piled into the truck and headed toward Crow's. When Hayden pulled up to the curb, he put the truck in park, and the kids got out.

Devorah reached for the door handle, but Hayden put his hand on hers to keep her there for a moment longer. She looked at him for what he felt like was the first time. Her brown eyes widened as she waited for him to say something.

"Can I take you out tonight? The drive-in is still showing movies. I thought we could throw a couple blankets in the back and share a bucket of popcorn."

"Okay," she said. "But I need to check with Crow and make sure he's going to be around. I can't leave Maren home alone."

"Unless I hear otherwise, I'll be here at seven."

Devy nodded and hesitated before she opened the door of the truck. As soon as her feet hit the pavement, she turned and looked at him. "Thank you, Hayden. For everything."

"It's been all my pleasure, Devorah."

FIFTEEN

DEVORAH

Devorah paced in front of the living room window, stopping occasionally to peer at the cars driving by. Cordelia watched her every move, undoubtedly judging her. She'd thought about sitting in the rocker on the porch or even on the step, but she didn't want to seem too obvious. Crow needed to come home. Not only did she want to talk to him about what had happened at tryouts; she also wanted to ask him if he'd be around later.

Earlier, when Hayden had dropped Maren and her off and subsequently asked her to the movies, she wanted to tell him no. Mostly because she wasn't ready to date or even put herself out there to consider the possibility. It had only been a month since she'd found out about Chad and Ester, and while in high school a month was plenty of time to move on, it wasn't enough time when a marriage ended. Especially when it ended because of adultery.

Still, Devy wanted to go to the movies. She wanted to feel alive, and Hayden sort of made her feel that way. His subtle touches, the smile he always seemed to have for her, and his presence made her feel like she could get through the days ahead.

Crow finally pulled into the driveway. Dev's heart lurched in her chest, and her anxiety spiked. It had been years since she'd waited for her dad to come home. They had long given up on having a father/ daughter relationship by the time she began dating Chad. As long as she obeyed his rules, they would have no issues and no need to talk about things.

Devy met her dad at the door. She opened it before he could and startled him. He placed his hand over his heart and breathed deeply. "Devorah, are you trying to kill me?"

Deep down, she knew he meant it jokingly, but his deep booming voice said otherwise. "Sorry," she muttered and stepped aside.

"Don't," Crow said. "Don't act like that."

"Like what?"

"Sheepishly," he told her. "Be strong, Dev. Stand up for yourself."

She looked at her dad for a long moment and nodded. "I'm trying."

Crow sighed. "You startled me because I'm not used to anyone being here when I come home. Thank you for opening the door."

He then did the unexpected and pulled her into his arms. At first, she was rigid and caught off guard. She inhaled his woodsy scent and finally relaxed, putting her arms around him.

They released each other at the same time. Crow cupped his daughter's face and looked into her eyes. "I mean it when I say you need to stand up for yourself, Devorah. That man and what he's done to you is inexcusable and not your fault. Stop letting him win."

Crow stepped back, crouched, and gave Cordelia some loving pets. Devy nodded because it was easier than trying to find the words to agree. The last thing she wanted was to be seen as weak. Once Crow moved away from the door, she shut it and followed him into the kitchen, testing the questions she had for him in her mind. Crow stood at the counter, facing the now-open cabinet.

"What's on your mind?"

She inhaled deeply. "Did everything go okay at the station after . . ."

Crow turned and met her gaze. Her automatic response was to slink back, but Crow's raised eyebrow made her stop. How had she become this meek person? Despite Devy and her dad not having the best relationship while she was growing up, he'd taught Colt and her to stand up for themselves. To face adversity head on.

Devorah squared her shoulders and faced her father. A small grin started to form on Crow's lips, but it stopped, and he shook his head.

"Sorry, I guess I shouldn't ask. It's private."

"It's not private," he told her. "It's between DJ, Noble, and Maren. He will apologize, and if he doesn't or if he tries to pull anything again, he'll be off the team."

"His dad is the coach."

"Don't matter here," he said. "What the boy did was wrong. His father knows better. Lord knows he's spent enough time in my office over the years. If I don't catch them when they're young, they turn into delinquents. His father should thank me."

"I'm afraid Maren will be teased at school because of today."

Crow sighed. "Then maybe her grandfather needs to drive her to school on Monday."

Devy nodded. Most people respected the sheriff, and if they knew Maren belonged to him, then maybe things would be okay.

"Thank you for stepping in today."

"The other boy, Lee McKenna's grandson? I remember Lee saying something on our last fishing trip about his kid coming back to town. Allie's?"

Devy shook her head. "Hayden moved back. He's Conor's dad."

Crow's face brightened. "Ah, yes. Hayden, I remember. He used to be sweet on you. Still is, from what I can see."

"Dad . . ." Devorah blushed. "That was a long time ago. We're just friends now."

Not if Hayden has anything to say about it.

Crow waved her comment away. "I'd like to talk to young Conor and explain that what he did was honorable, but I don't condone putting hands on someone."

"I'll let Hayden know, which brings me to my next question. Will you be home this evening? Hayden invited me to the movies."

Crow pointed his thick finger at her. Cordelia barked, not liking the gesture. Crow patted her on her head. "I knew it. I like him and approve."

"There's nothing to approve of. He's been a good friend since I got here, and he's going through something similar. His wife died not too long ago."

"Go, have fun. Maren and I will order pizza and watch a movie."

Devorah did a double take. "You watch movies?"

"With her, yes."

But never with his own kids.

"Well, thank you. I'll let her know. Her favorite kind of pizza is Hawaiian."

"Pineapple doesn't belong on pizza," he said as he threw his hands up.

"There's a healthy argument on the internet about this. If you want her to eat, order the pizza with pineapple." She turned and started out of the kitchen.

"Devorah?"

She paused in the doorway and turned toward her father.

"I want you to know, this is always your house. You are always welcome. I know I don't always show it, but I love you and hate that you're going through this. I wish there was something I could do to make things easier for you. Believe me when I tell you this—I want nothing more than to wring Chad's neck for how he's disrespected you. You and Maren deserve better. As your father, seeing you go through this is heartbreaking, and it angers me."

Devy's heart jumped into her throat. She swallowed the lump and searched for the necessary words to say back to him. Her eyes watered as she began to speak. "You're making things easier by letting Maren and I live here. I don't know where I would be right now if I didn't have you and Colt." She looked at the wall, closed her eyes, and willed the tears away. When she opened her eyes, she looked at her dad again. "I love you too, Dad."

Crow took two giant steps and held his arms out for his daughter. This moment trumped the earlier hug and would be something Devorah would never forget. She ran the rest of the way to her father and sobbed when his big strong arms held her to his chest. The hug was what most people called a "bear hug." For Dev, it was much-needed attention from a father she longed to reconnect with.

This was the man she had needed many years ago, when she'd lost her mother. She'd longed to feel him hold her, for him to let her cry on his shoulder, to pound on his broad chest in frustration. Devy was young, and aside from the women in the community, she'd had no one to guide her from being an adolescent into her teens, adulthood, and then motherhood.

Standing there in his arms, she didn't want to let go. She wanted to absorb everything she could from the hug and hold on to it so when the moment passed, she'd still have it pressing against her heart.

More tears came, and his grip tightened around her. Coming back to Oyster Bay, back to her childhood home, had been the right decision.

"Don't cry," he said as he brushed his hand down her hair. "It'll be okay. He can't hurt you anymore. I won't let him."

"Thank you."

When they finally parted, Crow looked away and cleared his throat. Devy told herself it was because her rugged and often stoic father had cried a bit, and he was far too macho to let her see. She didn't need to see his tears to know he cared.

Devorah went through the clothes she had and picked the warmest things she had brought with her from Chicago, which wasn't much. With her dad and Maren out getting pizza, she went into Crow's closet and pulled out one of his flannel jackets. He would wear them in the fall, when out chopping wood. She held it to her nose and inhaled deeply, taking in her father's woodsy cologne.

She added the jacket to the growing pile of blankets and snacks and put an extra pair of socks in her purse just in case her feet got cold. It was still spring, after all. The heap was more than they would need, and this was all assuming Hayden wouldn't bring anything, which was silly. He was the one who'd invited her; of course he would bring the necessities.

The rumble of his truck sent her heart into a tailspin. She ran to the door and then waited until she heard him coming up the stairs. When the first sound of the creak in the screen door started, she swung the front door open and scared him. Much like she had done with her father earlier.

"Hey," he said as coolly as possible. He placed his hand on the doorjamb and leaned.

Devorah swallowed hard. There was no mistake in her mind: Hayden was flirting. Everything in her screamed for her to flirt back, but she was hesitant to give him that side of her again. They'd been down that road before. He could never commit, and she'd ended up with Chad.

Still, the sexy, suave, and oh-so-good-looking Hayden was standing on her front porch again, like all those years before. They were both different, grown up, with other responsibilities. Flirting with Hayden wouldn't hurt her.

"Hey," was all her clouded mind could come up with.

They stood there, like two teens going on a first date. It wasn't until someone drove by and honked that they both moved.

"Come in." She stepped aside and held the door for him. "Crow took Maren to pick up pizza, so if we hurry, we can avoid him."

"Do we need to hurry?"

"No, but it's Crow, and he usually scares the crap out of people."

Hayden chuckled, but it didn't sound like a happy laugh. More like he'd been on the receiving end of Crow scaring the crap out of him.

"Don't sound so scared," she said, teasing him. "Crow likes you."

"Does he now?"

"Yep, told me earlier. I mean, it makes sense. He's close with your dad. Did you know they fish together?"

"I may have heard something about fishing. Although, I'm not sure a lot of fishing gets done with those two."

"Do you think they gab as much as the CC Club?"

Hayden nodded furiously. "I hate to say it, but that's what our future looks like."

Devorah laughed and then caught herself. She had every intention of going back to Chicago, back to the life she had in the city, volunteering for the PTA, and running the little company she'd founded. Since being back in Oyster Bay, she hadn't even opened her email to see if anyone had tried to hire her.

Hayden met her confused gaze and shrugged. "I know you haven't made a decision on whether you're staying or not, but for what it's worth, I'd like you to stay."

Devorah nodded and made her way over to the dining room table, where all the things she'd gathered sat in a pile. Thankfully, Hayden was behind her, so he couldn't see her face. She wasn't sure what he'd see, other than confusion, curiosity, and maybe even the teenage longing that used to be there. She could easily give in to Hayden's charm. Part of her wanted to, but she was proof that high school romances didn't last, and she couldn't put her heart through any more pain. Although Hayden hadn't exactly hurt her. He'd just never fully given himself to her, despite her wanting him.

She cleared her thoughts. They were going to the movies. As friends. Right now, she needed all the friends she could get. Even the unbelievably sexy, caring, and downright untouchable kind.

"I put some things together, but then I realized you'd probably bring stuff, so I sort of just stopped." She pointed at the pile. "Except this stuff. I plan to bring it."

"Do you think it's going to snow?"

She looked at the clothes in her arms and shook her head. "I don't like being cold."

"You lived in Chicago and don't like being cold?"

Devy shrugged. "We had heat."

This time Hayden laughed.

"And it's not like I was out in the cold doing things. When I had to go someplace, I would use the auto-start on my car so it would be warm when I got in. I don't ski or anything, and honestly, I hate the snow. And now that I'm thinking about it, I hated Chicago." Those words took her by surprise.

"You hated Chicago?"

"Yes," she said, nodding. "The more I think about my life here and then there, the more I've concluded that Chad has made all my decisions for me. I didn't want to go to Northwestern, but he did, and he made me think it's where I wanted to go. Does that make sense?"

"It's how manipulation works."

"Huh, well, there ya go."

"Does that mean you're staying in OB?"

"It's not just about me. I have Maren to think about. Divorces are messy, and who knows what kind of visitation Chad will end up with? I definitely can't afford to fly her back and forth . . ." Devorah paused and looked at her pile. "Anyway, I hate being cold."

"Well, good. I'm glad we got that out in the open. I have an electric blanket for the back, and I put the air mattress back there to give us some cushion to sit on."

"Oh, well, that sounds lovely."

Hayden chuckled. "It will be," he said as he took the things from her arms. He held up a sweatshirt and Crow's jacket and told her to pick.

She chose Crow's jacket.

As he'd done in the past, he held the door for her and then jogged around the front. She couldn't take her eyes off his backside, even as her mind reminded her of what he looked like with his shirt off. Time had been good to Hayden.

"You know," he said as he pulled onto the street, "I haven't been to the drive-in since I was seventeen."

"Same," she said. "I guess no one really goes when they're in college because who the hell has a car to take everyone, and Chad hated them, so we never took Maren."

"We'll have to take the kids one weekend. They'd have a blast."

"They would. Speaking of . . ." She looked over at Hayden. "Crow would like to speak with Conor about the incident. He's not in trouble or anything. It's just Crow's way of making sure the kids in town know right from wrong."

"Sure, I can bring him by tomorrow." Hayden pulled up behind the last car in line and waited. "What happened with Noble's kid?"

"Crow talked to him, told him to knock it off or he wouldn't be allowed to play baseball this year."

"I'm sure that went over well with Dalton."

"I'm afraid there will be some type of retaliation. I don't know. Right now, I feel like an outsider, watching as everyone talks about me in front of me and not behind my back. I see the stares and people whispering."

"Ignore them, and if Dalton retaliates, Colt and I will take care of it."

"What are you going to do, beat him up?"

Hayden flexed his arm. The short sleeve of his T-shirt stretched over his bicep. "Do you want to touch it?"

Devy laughed and squeezed. "Okay, muscle man. You're just like all the deputies I know. Always working out."

"Nah, this is from working on the ranch on my days off. All the heavy lifting."

"Do you miss it? Wyoming?"

Hayden pulled forward and rolled his window down in preparation to pay. "Yes and no. I don't miss chasing kids through fields because they went cow tipping, but I miss the work on the ranch, the horses, and Conor's grandparents. I can do without the memories or the tears, and the way they coddled Sofia's cousin. My son lost his mother, and her cousin should be in jail."

"I'm sorry."

"Hayden McKenna, is that you?" Devorah's heart jumped at the sound of her former best friend's voice. Laila Dixon and Dev had been inseparable, until Chad. He'd changed everything. Until now, Devy never realized how Chad had alienated her from her friends. Her hometown. From the people she loved. Even though she had a complicated relationship with Crow, Chad had kept Devy and Maren from visiting OB.

Hayden turned at the mention of his name. "In the flesh."

Devorah leaned forward to glimpse the girl-turned-woman who knew her deepest, darkest secrets. Especially those she'd told Laila about Hayden. Devorah waved at Laila, surprised to see her still working the booth at the drive-in. Maybe coming back or even staying in Oyster Bay wouldn't be so bad. Not with Laila and Hayden around. It could be like old times. Minus the make-out sessions with Hayden, because Devorah wasn't going to let herself go there again.

"Hey, Laila. How are you?"

Laila leaned to the side while Hayden pushed himself into the seat cushion. "Um . . ."

"Devorah Crowley," she said quietly. Did Laila not remember her? That stung, but she deserved it after the way Devy had treated her and dismissed their friendship.

"Oh, Devorah. I didn't know you were visiting."

"Yeah, I'm back for a bit." She guessed the rumors weren't flying as fast as she thought.

Laila tried to smile, but it failed to lift her cheeks. Devy gave up. She didn't need any more embarrassment for the day.

Hayden paid and found them a spot in the back, where they wouldn't block a smaller car from seeing the screen. He got out and started setting up the back. Devy helped as much as she could, but he had everything under control.

"You can't let Laila bother you."

"At this point, I shouldn't let anything that happens bother me."

Hayden helped Devy climb in the back. "Think about it this way: Laila has lived here her entire life. She probably married her high school sweetheart and has two point five children. We grew up and left, and now we're back and the talk of the town."

"Correction, I'm the talk of the town, and she remembered you."

"That's because I'm hot."

Devy rolled her eyes. "Ego much?"

"Only where you're concerned. Come on, let's go get some popcorn and sugary snacks."

Hayden jumped out of the truck and then helped Devy out. She walked as close as she could next to him without holding his hand. She wanted to, but there was no way she'd make a move like that.

She would wait for him and kind of hoped he wouldn't wait too long.

Sixteen

Hayden

Devorah Crowley—because Hayden refused to use her married last name—made him feel like a sixteen-year-old all over again, and even though they were in middle school when they had their first kissing encounter, those feelings never subsided, at least until he'd simply given up.

The jitters were back. Those heart palpitations that made him feel like he was about to shake right out of his skin. He felt anxious and energized, like he'd drunk a four-pack of Red Bulls and was ready to run a marathon.

The worst part—he needed to put his hands somewhere, and his pockets didn't suffice. When they entered the snack shack, it was crowded. Granted, the space was tiny, so more than ten people made it feel like there wasn't any room to move around. Hayden used this as an excuse to reach for Devy's hand.

You know, so she wouldn't get lost.

Her fingers slipped between his effortlessly, and when she gave his hand a light squeeze, he smiled, thankful he was taller than her because he didn't want her to see his cheesy grin. They got in line and stared at the illuminated menu.

"That thing has never been updated," Dev said.

"Probably not. I can't imagine this place brings in a ton of money with the giant megaplex forty minutes down the road."

"I think that's sad. Granted, I live in a megacity, but there's something about the nostalgia a small town has."

"Like fish fries."

Devy's eyes widened as she looked at Hayden. "I haven't had a fish fry in a long time. Is Hank's still open?"

Hayden nodded. "Does Maren like fish?"

"No, but my girl can put away corn dogs like there's no tomorrow."

He laughed as they stepped closer to the counter. "Conor is the same. His favorite are chicken fingers, and now with fancy sauce."

It was Devorah's turn to laugh. "Who knew ketchup and mayonnaise would be so popular together." They took another step toward the front, still holding hands. "Some company bottles it, but I can't remember who. Doesn't matter because it's not the same."

"See, you get it. Ranch dressing from a restaurant isn't the same as the bottle. I say this all the time, and no one believes me."

"Believe me, I do." Dev laughed again.

They approached the counter. The teen behind the cash register mumbled, "Can I help you?"

"We'll take a bucket of popcorn, a box of M&M's, and two large sodas. One Coke, the other Sprite." Hayden looked at Devy for confirmation. She nodded. Hayden paid and then walked to the end of the counter.

While they waited, Hayden played scenarios over in his mind on how he was going to carry their snacks and hold Dev's hand back to the truck. No matter which way he configured things in his mind, hand-holding was out.

After they got their things, Hayden put the candy in his back pocket and carried the sodas while Devy wrapped her arm around the warm bucket of popcorn and started munching on pieces.

"Is there going to be any left for me?"

"I'm not sorry," she said, laughing. "I love the warm buttery pieces. In my mind I know I should try and shake them to the middle of the bucket, but my stomach is like, 'Give me.' I caved."

Hayden chuckled and shook his head.

They reached the truck, and Hayden set their drinks down and then contemplated whether he would be able to pry the bucket from Devorah's arm. He held his hand out. She looked from him to the popcorn, sighed heavily, and gave him her free hand. Hayden laughed hard—until Devy's foot slipped, and she almost fell. Hayden caught her before she hit the ground. Miraculously, none of their popcorn spilled.

"Shit, are you okay?"

"Yes, thanks to you," she said. "I think your truck hates me."

"Well, I can't have that. I guess I need to buy a new one." Hayden scooped Devy into his arms, much to her shock, and set her on the tailgate. He didn't want to risk any more incidents. As soon as she moved out of the way, he hopped into the back and brought their drinks to where they'd sit and watch the movie.

Hayden poured the candy into the bucket of popcorn and gave it a good shake. Thanks to Devorah eating most of the top layer off, there was some room to avoid any spillage. He set it between them, adjusted the volume on the radio so he wouldn't have to do it when the movie started, and then took his spot next to Devy.

"It's a beautiful night," she said as the sun continued to disappear over the horizon.

"You know, for the first few months after Sofia died, I hated nights. Most of them were sleepless. I'd lay in bed and stare at the ceiling, asking myself the same questions over and over. 'Why didn't I insist on driving her? Why didn't I tell her I'd pick her up at a certain time? What the hell am I going to do now? How do I raise Conor?'"

"I think things would be easier if . . ." Devorah trailed off. "I know it's mean to say, but then I wouldn't have minor panic attacks when my phone rings or be afraid to look at a video on the app. I used to enjoy scrolling, watching funny dog videos or learning a new recipe. They took so much away from me because of how selfish they are."

Hayden reached for her hand and gave it a squeeze. "I suspect the video dies down eventually?"

Devorah shrugged. "Once it's on the internet, it's there for life. I tell Maren this all the time. It's such a scary place. Everyone is always going to remember the video of the mistress coming clean, but no one is going to care about the damage it's done to me and my daughter."

"Conor and I will just have to work harder to help you and Maren overcome it all."

Devorah smiled. "Maren really likes Conor. He's a great kid."

"Thanks. I wish I could take all the credit, but I can't. Sofia was a great mom."

"I'm really sorry you lost her."

He was as well.

But then he wouldn't be sitting next to Dev.

His heart was torn.

The movie screen changed from advertisements to previews for upcoming flicks. Hayden moved closer to Devorah and spread the blanket he'd brought across their laps. She also inched closer to where their shoulders touched.

At some point during the movie, she reached for his hand. Hayden tried not to smile, but he couldn't hold back. Halfway through, he put his arm around her shoulder, and she snuggled into his chest.

During the second movie, he found himself watching her more than what was playing on the screen. Each time she laughed, his heart soared. The sound was like music to his ears. He thought back to the day he'd given her a ride in the rain. She was a shell of herself. In the days they'd spent together since, she had blossomed, and the girl he remembered had begun to return. Devorah was beautiful. Now and then.

She looked at him. The wide grin she had stayed. Hayden trailed his finger along her cheek, and then he tilted her chin up, angling her lips to meet his. It may have taken a handful of years, but he was kissing Devorah Crowley again, and this time he wasn't going to let her go.

For the first time since Sofia passed, Hayden felt hope. He hadn't set out to find someone, but fate had a funny way of showing him what had been in front of his face for most of his life.

He deepened the kiss but kept his hands to himself. This was enough . . . for now. They both needed to move slow because it wasn't just them anymore. They had children to think about. To put first. And Devorah needed to heal. Thankfully, Hayden had the cure. He'd show her that she and Maren needed to stay in Oyster Bay, and what he and Dev could've been had he admitted his feelings years ago.

When they broke apart, they both sighed. He wanted to go right back in for more, to pull her down and under the blankets like the horny teen he had once been.

"That wasn't awkward at all," she told him.

"It wasn't our first kiss."

"In public it was."

Ouch, that stung and was well deserved. Hayden ducked his head and sighed. "I've grown up a lot since then. Believe me, I wish I had done things differently."

"Same," she said.

Hayden leaned in and kissed her again. Old habits were hard to break.

When they parted, Devy sighed. "You know, we pretty much perfected the art of making out back then."

"Let me know when you're ready to write the sequel."

Devorah smiled. "When I'm ready to trust again, you'll be the first to know."

He sighed, kissed her forehead, and then put his arm around her. She snuggled into his side and rested her hand on his abdomen.

Returning to Oyster Bay had scared him. He'd worried he wasn't making the right decisions for Conor and himself. Sitting there in the back of his truck, with a woman he used to be in love with, was now proving he had.

On Monday morning, Hayden felt nothing but relief when he saw the bucket loader and a rather large pile of dirt on his property. They'd finally broken ground on his and Conor's new house. He got out of his truck and walked to where Link Blackburn stood with a clipboard. They shook hands and patted each other on their backs.

"It's good to see you, Hayden."

"You too, Link. How's it looking?"

"The plans for the house look great. There shouldn't be much bedrock here. I think our biggest issue will be tree roots, but we'll get those taken care of."

"Thanks. I appreciate it. I'm eager to start building. If all goes well, how long are we looking at?"

"We'll pour the foundation at the end of the week and start framing next week. Do you still plan to help?"

Hayden nodded. "I do. I need something to do."

Link told Hayden to follow him to his truck. There, he handed Hayden a hard hat and some protective eyewear. "Always wear these," Link said. "I don't want you getting hurt."

"Safety first." Hayden put the hat on.

"Once we get the dirt out, we'll start leveling. We can use extra hands for sure."

"I'm your guy." Hayden looked at the bucket loader digging into the ground. Each push was oddly satisfying for him. Hayden figured if he worked on the house every day, it would get done faster. He wanted Conor to have his first Christmas without his mom in their new home. The McKenna men needed a fresh start.

"Link, what do you think about a pool?"

He lifted his shoulder. "If you want one, we can dig the hole while the bucket loader is out here."

Conor definitely wanted a pool.

He wondered if Devorah and Maren would want one.

The thought jolted him and was completely out of the blue. Hayden stared at the ground as he tried to reconcile why he'd thought about Devy in that way. Sure, they'd had a great date and shared a deep and meaningful kiss, but . . .

But what?

Were either of them ready to start something serious?

A smile crept across his lips. He was. He still loved Sofia and always would, but he had fallen in love with Devorah first, and there she was at the forefront of his mind.

"Yeah, let's do it," Hayden said. "A pool would be great. I'll figure out the size and all that." He reached for Link's clipboard, took his pencil, and mapped out where the pool would go. Hayden would have to add more decking, but it would be worth it.

Around lunchtime, a truck pulled into the lot. Everyone stopped what they were doing when two women got out and went to the back. Hayden recognized Devy instantly but couldn't place the driver.

As much as he wanted to walk over to her and see what was up, he stayed with Link and the others. The driver came around the front of the truck, carrying a box. Link's employees started hooting and hollering.

"Who ordered lunch for everyone?" Link asked, but no one answered him.

Hayden watched as Dev approached carrying another box. He went to her and took it. "This is a nice surprise."

"I think I've been set up by my brother."

"What do you mean?" Hayden asked, laughing.

"He said Blackburn Construction needed this delivery, but by how excited the guys seem to be about getting food, I'm questioning Colt's business tactics."

Hayden owed Colt, big time.

"Well, I'm happy you're here. Come on, let me show you the house." Hayden dropped the second box off for the guys to pick through and hoped someone would save him something. He reached for Devy's hand and took her over to where they were digging.

"I know it's going to be hard to picture, but bear with me." He stood behind her.

"A wide farmer's porch, wrapping around to meet a sizable deck, which will be perfect for entertaining."

"Party planning already?"

"I'm sure there's a high school reunion coming up."

Devy groaned.

"You'll walk in, and the kitchen will be to the left, along with the dining room. On the right, the living room, with one of those massive windows, because Oyster Bay has the best sunrises. On the back side, the primary suite will lead to the deck. I'm thinking French doors and maybe a bistro set to enjoy morning coffee. The staircase will be somewhere in the middle, leading to the three bedrooms."

"This is a huge house, Hayden."

He shrugged. "I'm thinking ahead with resale value."

"Makes sense."

"I decided this morning to put in a pool."

"Definitely a party house. Don't tell Crow, or he'll be over here all the time," she said, laughing. "Poor Conor. He won't be able to get away with anything."

A horn honked, and Devy sighed. "That's my cue to go back to work."

Hayden was tempted to kiss her, but he held back.

"Maybe I'll stop in later. I think I need to check out the new bartender at the Lazy Lamb."

Devorah smiled. "I know how to pull the tap for a beer. That's about it. Oh, and order corn dogs." She started walking away and then turned. "Thanks for showing me your house, Hayden. I really like it." Devy walked to the truck and never looked back. If she had, Hayden probably would've run toward her and kissed her in front of everyone.

Seventeen

Devorah

Devy couldn't remember the last time she'd waited on a table. It was almost like a rite of passage for any teenage girl to work at the diner. While working as a waitress there, her biggest challenge had been remembering orders.

Now, as a bartender, her biggest challenge was going to be remembering which beer was which, and how to pour the perfect draft. According to Colt, there was an art to it, and she needed to master it, mostly because she was Colt's little sister, and with him being the brewmaster and owner of the Lazy Lamb, expectations were high.

By a couple of hours into her shift, she had learned the difference between an India pale ale (which patrons would refer to as an IPA) and a DIPA. The DIPA was double the alcohol percentage. Colt had a strict rule—no more than two DIPAs were allowed unless the customer had a designated driver, and the DD got free soda all night. He didn't want anything to happen to any of his patrons or the people of Oyster Bay. This stuck with Devorah. Not only as the sheriff's daughter, but also knowing how Hayden's wife had died. Colt was doing his part to keep people safe, which meant a lot to her, and if Hayden ever found out about Colt's rule, it'd mean everything to him.

It was also on her first day when she found out she would have to go on a food-delivery run. She thought that by telling Colt she hadn't driven to the Lazy Lamb, he'd go in her place, but nope. One of the employees would go with her and drive.

When they returned to the bar, Devorah walked right up to her brother and kicked him in the shin. "That was a setup."

Colt hopped on one foot for a quick second and then put his hands up in the air. "It was a nudge."

"I don't need a nudge."

A nudge wasn't the issue. It was her heart. Hayden had already put himself out there by kissing her at the drive-in. She would never admit this to him, but he'd made her toes curl. Something he'd been doing ever since they'd kissed in the closet, way back when. She wanted to kiss him again, to relive their many shared moments from growing up together. That kiss under the stars, with the movie playing, had woken something in her that had been dormant for a long time.

Passion?

Enthusiasm?

The more she thought about Chad and his affair, the more she realized the passion had long dissipated from their relationship. Sure, they made love, but it was like a calendar: Sundays after Maren had gone to bed, and Wednesdays after her PTA meeting. Long gone was the fervor. They no longer tore at each other's clothes or couldn't wait to feel one another. Sex had become a chore. Or Chad had become an obligation.

But was she ready?

If Hayden had kissed her inside her house or his, and no one was around, there wasn't a doubt in her mind she would've taken him to bed. He'd reignited something in her, something she'd felt for him long ago.

They were both in a place where they could move on together and didn't need any outside interference.

Colt winked and pulled Devy into his arms for a hug. "I'm sorry. I'm trying to help."

Dev stayed there for a long minute, basking in the strength of her brother's hug. When they parted, she looked up at him. "Are you okay with Hayden and me dating?"

Her brother acted insulted by the question. "Why wouldn't I be?"

"Because I used to be in love with Hayden, but he was afraid to lose you as a friend."

Colt sighed and ran his hand through his dark hair. "We were kids back then. I didn't know it was okay for my best friend to like my sister."

They'd more than liked each other.

"But now you do?"

"Hayden's a great guy, Dev. I wish I wasn't so against things back then. Maybe life would be different."

"Yeah, maybe." Dev let out her own sigh. "Doesn't matter because I'm not ready for anything, Colt. The last thing I want to do is lead Hayden on. So no more nudging. I need time."

Colt sighed. "I get it. I do, but I feel like some of this is my fault."

Devorah's eyebrow rose. "You told Chad to cheat on me?"

Colt's eyes widened. "Hell no, but I knew Hayden liked you back in high school. Everyone knew. But being your older brother and his best friend, I think he was afraid to ask you out. I should've been a better brother. Hayden's a good guy, and I'm glad he's back. I'm also glad he's pursuing you, because this smile"—Colt poked at her cheek—"it's worth seeing every day."

She absorbed his words and did smile again. "I appreciate you, but I need time. There's this little thing called 'trust.' I have none to give right now, and I'm not sure that would be fair to Hayden."

"Time. You got it. Now here." He handed her a bottle opener, for those who ordered light beers or something they didn't have on tap, and left her alone at the bar. Thankfully, the lunch rush was over and there were very few people left in the bar.

She started wiping the bar down and thought about what she'd said to her brother, about her not wanting to lead Hayden on. They had kissed at the drive-in. It felt nice. She had wanted to kiss him and didn't push him away. The problem started when she got home and went to bed. Instead of thinking about Hayden and what they had shared, Chad was on her mind. Devy hated how he invaded her thoughts when he didn't deserve them anymore.

And yet, he was there in her mind, mocking her. Pointing out how he controlled every part of her life, from where she lived, who her friends were, and what her job was to how much money he allowed her to spend. He belittled her existence by simply implying she wasn't his equal.

How had she not seen any of this before?

Everything was clear as day—he had brainwashed her into thinking this was how relationships worked.

As she wiped down the counter, she couldn't keep her thoughts straight. Her mind swirled with Chicago—and having to go back there—to Oyster Bay and staying. If the decision was hers and hers alone, she'd stay. Until her return, Devorah hadn't realized how much she had missed her dad and brother. Despite the strain she had with her dad, being with him brought her peace.

Maren's needs had to come first. She'd promised her daughter they would go back to Chicago in the fall, but the more Devorah thought about it, the more she questioned why. Nothing would have changed by then. Ester would still be there. As would the looks, the finger-pointing, and the whispers behind their backs. People would always know about the affair.

Would Maren feel replaced if they moved back, and she saw her father with Rita?

The words Chad had said to Maren echoed in Devorah's mind. *And I'm going to be her dad now.* He was foolish for saying that to Maren. She should've come first in his life, but no, he was a selfish prick who only cared about himself.

Why had it taken her two decades to see this about him? Especially since that was how everyone saw him? Devorah could live without Chad. She could put him out of her mind and never look back.

She also wasn't unaware when it came to Hayden. She knew he liked her. Devorah liked him as well. She had in high school and had waited for him to ask her out. She never minded when they flirted with each other or would sneak off to make out where no one could see. Devy had hoped Hayden would make things official before he left for college, but he hadn't. Chad saw an opportunity and pounced.

Since she'd bumped into Hayden at the school, he'd been the one constant she could count on. They had kissed at the movies, and it had been wonderful. There was nothing awkward about it, and had they not been in public, she might have rekindled one of their old make-out sessions. They had never lacked chemistry back when they were teens, and they definitely had it in spades now that they were adults. The urge to straddle him the other night, like she'd done so many times back in high school, was there, encouraging her to just give in and let herself be free.

Her cheeks flushed hot as she imagined herself crawling onto Hayden's lap and kissing him. She stopped and looked around the bar to see if anyone had noticed her blushing. She couldn't go there.

Not yet, even though her body had no problem remembering how the teenage Hayden used to make her feel.

But at what expense?

Was he still afraid of Colt's reaction? Crow's?

Devorah shook her head. They were adults. What people thought shouldn't matter anymore. And Hayden had said he wished he had done things differently back then, but what did that mean?

She could easily see herself with him, more so if the circumstances were different and she didn't have Maren to worry about.

Devorah might not have been sure of many things, but one thing was for certain: Hayden wasn't going away, and it was up to her to trust him again.

"He wants a part two," she said to herself.

The door opened and voices carried. She thought she heard Hayden's, but when he didn't come through the door, her heart dropped. He'd told her he'd be by later, to check out the Lazy Lamb's new bartender. The thought excited her until her mind took her right back to earlier, when he'd described the house he planned to build.

It was huge. Big enough for a family, and she got the sense that he anticipated her spending some time there. Part of her wanted to, but she told herself she was being unrealistic. Reality had an ugly way of reminding her she was married and had a life a thousand miles away and a daughter she had to think about. The other half of her thought it would be nice to be with Hayden, to see what it would be like to have a relationship with him. She had deep feelings for him and enjoyed all the time they spent together. Devorah even looked forward to when he'd show up randomly at Crow's place to surprise her.

And then there was Conor. The young boy without a mother, someone who was so easy to mother. Devorah already cared for him more than she thought she should and feared that if she and Maren left, he would be devasted. Could she do that to him? Although she could barely function as a human these days, and it probably wasn't smart to bring Conor and Hayden into her messy life.

Could she leave Crow and Colt behind again? There was a feeling, deep in her gut, telling her Colt and her father wouldn't allow it. They weren't going to let years go by without seeing her and Maren.

Not now.

Not now that they knew what kind of man Chad was.

The bar door opened again, and Devorah paused to see if it was Hayden letting the sunlight shine through. She shielded her eyes and said, "Bar's open," repeating the words she'd heard Colt say each time the door opened. She needed to remember a few things about being out in public. Smile and greet everyone, and if anyone said anything about that stupid-ass video, she'd remind them of who was doing the pouring.

"Devorah?"

Her head jerked, and she paused at the sound of her name as she held the dish towel. She waited for the door to close, needing the sun out of her eyes so she could see who had called out to her.

Laila Dixon, Devy's onetime best friend, stood there. Slowly, Laila set her purse on the bar top and slid onto one of the stools.

Be nice. Colt's and Hayden's voices played in her head.

"Hi, Laila." Laila hadn't really changed in the years Devy had been gone. She still had icy-blond hair, curled in all the right places to make her hair stand up, to add height to Laila's barely five-foot stature. Her eyes were as blue as the ocean, and she wore pink, which had always been her favorite color.

"Hi. Look, I want to apologize for the other night. I knew who you were, but seeing you for the first time in"—Laila waved her hand—"I don't even remember how long it's been—"

"Too long," Devy interrupted. She stepped closer to the bar, somehow needing to be closer to her former best friend.

"Yes, too long. Anyway, I'm sorry for being rude."

"You don't need to apologize, Laila. I deserve it. Honestly, I'm the one who should grovel. What I did back in high school was horrible of me. I'm sorry for hurting you and ruining our friendship."

Laila reached her hand across the bar. Devy took it. The two smiled at each other, both on the verge of tears. "Water under the bridge. Besides, you're here, and oh"—Laila waved her free hand in front of her face—"I saw you with Hayden, and all these memories came flooding back. I used to say that if I ever saw you again, I'd give you a piece of my mind, and well, there you were, and I just couldn't think of anything to say except for what I did. Anyway, how long are you here for? We have time to hang out, right?" Laila asked after they'd released hands.

Devy inhaled and lifted her shoulder. "I don't know. Life is pretty messy right now, and I can't stomach the thought of going back to Chicago. Lately, OB has started feeling like home, and I've really missed living here. I used to think this place was horrible, and some of it still is, but you coming in and sitting down to talk shows me not all is bad. And I need all the good I can get."

"I know. Again, I'm so sorry about the other night. Seeing you caught me off guard. I can't tell you how many times I drove by Crow's to see if you were outside. I thought about stopping and knocking on the door, but then I chickened out, each and every time. We have a lot of making up to do." Laila reached for Devy's hand and squeezed it. "I can't wait to meet your daughter."

"Maren." Devorah said her name with a smile. "She's the best thing to ever happen to me." An image of Maren popped into Dev's mind, taking her away from the here and now. A door slammed, shaking her reverie. "Hey, can I get you something to drink?" she asked Laila.

"A Diet Coke?"

Dev nodded and went to the soda machine. She added ice to the cup, pushed it against the lever, and waited for it to fill. She carried it back to Laila and handed her a straw.

Laila played with the straw in her drink and looked at Dev. "So . . ."

Dev knew what was coming without even asking, and somehow, she was okay to talk about it. Was it possible to fall in step so easily with someone you'd once loved like a sister?

"Devorah the viral sensation!"

Dev rolled her eyes. She hated that the video had made its way to Oyster Bay.

Laila reached across the bar again and set her hand on Devy's arm. "What she did was wrong, and she seriously needs her ass kicked. Who does this shit?"

"She does, apparently."

"What happened to girl code?"

Devorah thought for a minute of Chad and how he'd manipulated her into distancing herself from her friends and family. Something she deeply regretted.

"Chad has a way of making it seem like he's the only one who should matter."

Laila's eyes widened. "Did he pursue her?"

Devy shrugged. "I don't know. We didn't have that sit-down, what-the-hell-happened conversation."

"Are you going to?" Laila waited a beat before adding, "It might give you some closure. I can be there with you when it happens. You know, in case he gets out of line."

"Thanks. It's probably something I need to do—otherwise, I'll probably wonder what I did wrong."

"You didn't do anything wrong," Laila told her. "Men like him . . ." She paused and shook her head. "Don't let him convince you it was you."

"I know."

Another customer came in and sat at the bar. Devorah served him and busied herself for a minute before going back to Laila. The last thing she needed was one of the other staff members saying something to Colt, or her brother seeing her standing around gabbing while on the clock.

After more small talk and some back-and-forth with other customers, Devorah refilled Laila's glass and asked her if she wanted to order something to eat.

"Honestly, I heard you were working here and wanted to come in and apologize for my behavior."

"Heard? This is literally my first day." Devorah tossed her hands in the air. "Which Cathy told you?"

"No Cathy; it was Link."

"Link Blackburn?" It took Devorah a minute to remember where she'd seen Link's name earlier. "He's building Hayden's house. I saw him earlier when I took lunch over."

Laila nodded and smiled happily. "Link's my husband. We married a year after graduation."

"I'm sorry I missed it."

"Ah, don't be. We divorced five years later and didn't speak to each other for two years, and then got remarried. He's a pain in my ass, but he's my pain and I love him. No kids. We never really wanted any. So, tell me . . ." Laila leaned closer and lowered her voice. "Hayden McKenna. Are you guys together because . . ." She leaned back and fanned her face. "You go, girl! There is absolutely nothing wrong with getting yours, especially with a fine-ass man like Hayden."

She didn't know how Laila managed to do it, but she made her feel not only at ease and welcome, but like they were back in high school again and having one of their many sleepovers to discuss the boys in school.

"Hayden and I are friends. Nothing more."

Laila shook her head back and forth, all sassy-like, while saying, "Nope, nope, nope. I am not buying it. Not this time. There's a reason he's here and you're here. Get. Your. Man." Laila banged her hand on the bar to emphasize each word.

Devorah laughed and excused herself to help fill some drink orders the servers had sent in. While she and Hayden had kissed, she wasn't ready to admit there was anything going on between them. Mostly because she worried about how people would perceive her, and she was afraid her heart wasn't where it should be. Not to mention, if they were even going to go down the path of dating, they'd have to have a serious conversation about their past. The last thing she wanted to do was hurt Hayden or let herself become heartbroken again. They both deserved better.

When Devorah finally made it back to Laila, she had finished her drink. "Another?"

"If it means we can still talk, yes."

Dev took the glass, emptied it, and refilled it with ice and Diet Coke. Before taking the soda back to Laila, she placed an order for nachos. Laila might as well munch on something while they chatted.

After setting the soda down, Devorah worked on a few more orders and then went to the kitchen to get the food she'd ordered. Back at the bar, she set the nachos down in front of Laila, along with two side plates and a stack of napkins.

"They're messy but delicious," Devy said. "At least that's what Colt says."

"Haven't eaten here much?" Laila added to her plate a scoopful of the tortillas, topped with queso, chicken, bean, cheese, and lettuce.

"Honestly, I can't tell you the last time I ate finger foods. Chad isn't a fan. They're beneath him."

"He's such a—"

"Entitled prick?" Devorah blanched at her word vomit and covered her mouth while Laila cackled. "I don't know where that came from."

"I know we've just reconnected, but I feel like this is that first over-the-hump moment when you realize your ex isn't good for you."

"There's a lot I need to figure out."

"All in good time, my friend."

"Right, time." Devorah sighed. "What do you do for work?"

"Aside from still working the ticket booth at the drive-in?" Laila playfully rolled her eyes. "I own the travel agency on Main Street. What about you? What did you do in Chicago?"

"Aside from volunteering for the PTA and every other school or community function, I was—or still am—an estate curator. People hire me to sell off possessions, or the state would hire me to go in and recoup as much money as possible when a ward of the state died."

"Is that like a professional yard seller?"

Devy hated that title, but that was exactly what her job was. "Yep. I have crazy organizational skills and an eye for valuable items."

"That sounds like a fun job, Dev. Are you going to do it here?"

She shrugged. "I guess that all depends on whether or not we stay. I still haven't made up my mind. I can't believe your parents still own the drive-in." Devorah needed to steer the subject away from herself and her indecision about where she planned to live. It was something that weighed heavily on her, and the pressure made her feel like she couldn't breathe.

"They don't. Link and I do," Laila said. "My parents retired to Florida. My dad fishes all day."

Devorah looked out the window, where she could see the bay. "That water not good enough?"

"That's what I say." Laila slapped the bar and threw her hand up. "Who leaves the water to retire at the water? My parents. Makes zero sense." She shook her head. "So yeah, we own it and think about closing it every now and again, but it does a decent business."

"I had fun there. It was very nostalgic."

"Well, we appreciate you coming."

A few seats down, a man rapped his knuckles on the bar. Devy excused herself and went to him.

"What can I get for ya?"

"Are you the babe on the wall back there? The Pearl of the Ocean?" He held his hands up in a dancing motion.

Devorah rolled her eyes. "Funny. Do you want to order?"

The man placed an order for a burger with fries and a pint of Colt's house special. Devorah rang his order up, sent it back to the kitchen, poured his beer, and set it down in front of him. When she walked back toward Laila, she was smiling a bit too much for Dev's liking.

"I knew it was only a matter of time."

Devorah rolled her eyes.

"Listen, I have a proposition for you."

"Yeah, what's that?" Devy asked as she leaned on the bar.

"I'm the president of the Oyster Festival. I could really use someone like you on staff. Apart from planning, the Pearls could use guidance on their duties during the month."

Devorah laughed. "Is my reign as Pearl of the Ocean finally becoming something? Wait until I tell Crow."

Now Laila laughed. "Think about it. We meet once a week until it gets closer to the festival and then nightly for a couple of weeks."

"Where do you meet?"

"Here," she said. "Colt lets us use the room in the back."

"Right along with the CC Club?"

Laila's eyes widened. "Those gossip girls are the bane of my existence. But you know what, I'll join them in five years and be just like them."

"Do they still bring food to people in need?"

"They do. They're good people and great for the community, as long as you don't have anything personal going on in your life."

"Like me."

Laila smiled softly at Devy. "Screw Chad. He was never one of us anyway."

She was right. Knowing that should've been Devorah's first of what seemed to be a long list of red flags.

The bar started to fill with the crews from the piers. Laila told Devy she'd stop by Crow's in the next couple of days, but if she needed anything, she could find her down the street at the travel agency she owned. Dev watched her former best friend leave and marveled at how successful she'd become in their little hometown. Something Chad had said he could never be.

He was right. No one really liked him in Oyster Bay, and they probably would've made sure he knew it.

Colt relieved Devorah in time for her to get Maren from school. She could probably walk home, especially with all the other kids in the area, but Dev wasn't there yet mentally. She needed to know her daughter was safe.

Devy headed toward the school and paused when she saw a sign for THEO SHERMAN, ATTORNEY-AT-LAW. She studied the gray house where Theo had set up shop many moons ago, while a voice in the back of her mind nagged at her conscience. She wasn't going to take Chad back, and she had yet to hear from him despite him calling to talk to Maren. At least he hadn't forgotten about his daughter.

"Nope, just the vows you promised each other," Dev mumbled to herself. She pulled out her phone and called her father.

"Something wrong?" he asked gruffly when he picked up. Not a "hello" or even a "hey."

"Not necessarily. Are you able to pick Maren up from school?"

"Something happen?"

"No, I'd like to stop and talk to Theo," she told him. "See what my options are."

"I'll get her."

"Thank you . . . Dad," she said with a sigh. "I'll be home shortly." Devy hung up, saving them from the awkwardness of saying goodbye.

She climbed the steps and opened the door to Theo's office. It smelled stale, like a mixture of paper and coffee, and it reminded her of a library.

"Hello?" a male voice called out from another room.

"Theo? It's Devorah Crowley." Her maiden name slipped easily out of her mouth.

Theo came down the hallway, dressed in a white button-up, brown slacks, and suspenders. Other than his age, he hadn't changed since the last time she'd seen him. "Bea said you'd be coming by. Come on in and let's chat."

Dev followed him into his office. He sat behind a large, deep oak desk with stacks of folders piled on top of each other and a monitor in the corner with a layer of dust resting on top of it. She looked around at the shelves full of books and wondered if he had ever opened one.

"I heard about everything," he said with a wave of his hand. "We don't need to recount everything."

"I appreciate that."

Theo asked her the basics: When did she get married? Have Maren? Buy her house? How many cars did they own? The questions went on and on, each one stabbing her in the heart.

"You're staying at Crow's?"

"Yes," she told him. "How much is this going to cost me?"

"Won't cost you a thing, sweetie. Chad will pay." Theo sat back. "Now, I'm going to tell you something, and I want you to think about how you want to proceed."

"Okay."

"Illinois law forbids stepping out on your spouse. Due to what we've all seen and heard, and you unfortunately witnessed, we can call the police and have him arrested. It's a misdemeanor, but he'd be booked, fingerprinted, and have a mug shot taken."

Devorah absorbed those words. She wasn't vindictive, at least she didn't think she was. "I . . . I don't really know."

"How about this," Theo said as he straightened in his chair. "We present him with the divorce petition, which will include your list of demands. If he even tries to counter, we'll work the other angle."

"Like, threaten him with it?"

Theo nodded. "Something like that hangs out on your record for a bit. No one likes that."

"Okay," Devy said, nodding, and then she smiled. Images of Chad in an orange jumpsuit and having to be strip-searched gave her an odd sense of satisfaction. His name would be in the paper, under the police log, and then everyone would know how Devorah had taken revenge on her cheating bastard of a husband.

After another hour, Devy walked home with a preliminary petition. Theo wanted her to fill in the missing bank account numbers, note any stock and retirement plans they had, and decide on custody of Maren. Theo expected Chad to counteroffer when it came to their funds, not their daughter.

When she reached Crow's squeaky screen door, she paused when she heard laughter. She stood on the porch and listened to her dad and daughter as they told each other jokes. The sound of them laughing brought another smile to her face. She hadn't felt this at peace in a long time. Crow may not have been the best father, but it seemed like he was making up for it in the grandfather department.

Devorah opened the screen door and walked into the living room. She found Maren sitting on Crow's knee.

"Hi, Mom."

"Hey, kiddo, how was school?" Devy was concerned with retaliation.

"Great. DJ said he was sorry."

"That's good." Devorah made eye contact with her father. She hoped he understood how grateful she was. "What should we do for dinner?"

"I put a roast in," Crow said as he looked at his watch. "It should be ready in an hour."

Devorah stood there in shock. "Well, I guess I'll go set the table." She started toward the dining room and stood between the two rooms, looking at the already-set table. It was set for five.

"Who's the extra plate for?"

"Colt isn't eating with us tonight," Crow said from the other room.

Devorah already knew who was coming over before Crow could tell her.

"Conor and Hayden are coming for dinner, Mommy."

Yep, of course they were.

She looked at the papers in her hand and shook her head. "I'll be in my room." She went upstairs, shut the door, and collapsed on her bed. She'd just spent the hour-plus going through details about her life with the local attorney; the last thing she wanted to do was eat dinner with the man who confused her heart and head.

Devorah needed a break from life.

Eighteen

Hayden

By the end of the day, Hayden was exhausted. He'd done everything he could on his property, except drive or operate any of the heavy equipment. This was part of the deal he'd made with Link. Hayden would be there every day to help, and Link would give him a slight discount. To Hayden, any money off was worth the sweat. Besides, he had nothing else to do and really needed a new profession. He figured if he started working construction with Link, there might be a job for him in the future. Once he figured out what he wanted to do with his life.

For the first time, he went to his trailer. The air inside was stale and muggy. He opened all the windows, turned on the generator, and made his way to the shower. The water pressure in his camper was like a drizzle after being at his parents' place, but it was convenient. When he was done, he found some clean clothes and got dressed.

He stared at his bed and contemplated falling onto it for a long nap. Conor was with his grandparents, hopefully doing homework, and he probably wouldn't notice if his dad didn't make it home for dinner. But then again, they hadn't spent a night apart from each other in months, and while they could probably benefit from some space, this might not be the time. All Hayden's best intentions of living in his camper while construction took place seemed to have gone out the window.

At least for now.

Hayden flopped onto his bed, closed his eyes, and started to relax until Devorah's face popped into his mind. It wasn't just Devy but them together, and him kissing her. And then her standing there on his property, listening to him describe his house. When the vision of his home came into his mind, he saw Devy and Maren living with him and Conor. Those kinds of thoughts were going to get him into trouble, especially where Devy was concerned.

Hayden thought about Sofia and the last day he'd seen her. She had ridden her horse out to where he was on the property, building a new shelter for some of her father's horses. Sofia brought him lunch, and they had made love by the pond. She talked about having another child. They were both ready and felt like Conor would make a great big brother. The plan was for her to stop taking her birth control the next day.

Only the next day, he was planning her funeral. Just like that, his world had shattered. The hopes and dreams they had shared were gone, all because of her cousin. Hayden wanted her charged and in jail. It was the least the police could do for him and Conor, except Sofia's parents didn't want that and begged for the charges to be dropped. Sofia's dad had pull. Hayden didn't, despite being a respected member of the law enforcement community.

The animosity grew between them and forced Hayden to make the decision to move back to Oyster Bay with his son. He missed his wife and wiped the tears that streamed from his eyes. He hadn't realized he'd started crying. When she died, he thought he would never be ready to move on. Until he ran into Devorah. His axis had shifted that day, and for the first time since Sofia died, he saw promise. Even if nothing came of him and Devy, she would be a constant in his life. This much he knew.

His phone rang, pulling him from his thoughts. He fished it out of his pocket and looked at the screen. The text was from an unknown number, but the message was clear: Be at Crow's for dinner, 6 p.m. Bring Conor.

A nap or early bedtime could wait. He assumed the number belonged to Crow, and with that, if the sheriff wanted you at his house for dinner, you went.

Hayden spent a few more minutes on his bed, gathering his thoughts. As much as he liked Devorah, he had to respect that she was in a much different place than he was. He could easily jump in with both feet, but there was no way she was ready to even dip a toe into the dating game. The kiss they shared, while one of the best moments of his recent life, had probably scared the shit out of her. Never mind the way he was when she'd brought lunch to him earlier.

Well, lunch to the crew. She didn't know he was there. Her presence had still sent his heart into a tailspin. He wanted to be around her, more and more each day.

He sent a text to his mom, giving her an update on his and Conor's dinner plans, and then cleaned up after himself. After shutting down the generator, he left a couple of windows open to let the air circulate, hoping the fresh air would make the place smell a bit better.

On his way to pick up Conor, he detoured to the next town over and stopped at the grocery store for a bouquet and a six-pack of Crow's favorite beer. He also picked up a chocolate cake for dessert. It wasn't homemade, but he didn't want to show up empty handed.

Hayden honked when he got to his parents' place, and Conor came running out with his own bouquet in his hand. Hayden laughed and reached across the console, pulled the handle for the door, and nudged it so Conor could open it easier.

"Nice flowers, bud."

"Thanks. Grandpa took me to the store when he found out about dinner. Said the McKenna men don't show up . . ." Conor trailed off when he followed his father's gaze to the backseat. "Empty handed," he mumbled.

"Grandpa is right. I didn't think to check with you beforehand. You can give those to Devy."

Conor beamed. "I really like her," he said. "She includes me in stuff."

Hayden didn't have the heart to tell him the text was probably from the sheriff. "I like her too, bud."

"More than Mom?" Conor looked at his dad.

Hayden's heart lurched, and he shook his head. "Never. I love your mom, even though she isn't here with us. She will always be here." Hayden pressed his fist over his heart. "I can't look at you and not see her or remember her. Your mom will always be with me. With us. No one can ever take the memories we have of her away from us."

Conor's eyes welled up with tears. Hayden pulled over, released Conor's seat belt, and lugged his son into his arms. Conor cried into his father's shoulder. "I miss her lots."

"I know, bud. I wish I could take away your pain. The only thing I can do is be here for you and talk about your mom whenever you want. I don't know how you feel, because I still have my mom and dad, so you have to tell me when the pain is too much so I can try to help you cope."

"Okay," he cried.

They sat there on the side of the road, holding each other, until Conor sat up. "I'm better."

"Yeah?"

Conor nodded.

"Do you still want to go to Maren's?"

He nodded again. "She's my friend. I don't want her to think I don't like her."

"Sometimes, we can say no to things, especially if we're not feeling that great. You are more important than dinner at the Crowleys'. Just say the word, and we'll go home, or we can go to the camper and just chill for the night. The two of us."

Conor shook his head and wiped at his almost-dry cheeks. "I'm okay now."

"If you change your mind, just ask me if my headache is back, and we'll leave." Hayden signaled and then pulled onto the road. Within minutes, they were parked in front of Crow's house.

"You know he's the whole boss of Oyster Bay?" Conor said as they walked toward the wide-planked stairs leading to the porch.

"People definitely think that about Crow," Hayden told him, not bothering to explain that a mayor in town made all the decisions. Mostly because Hayden had no idea who it was or who sat on the city council these days. At one point while growing up, Lee had been on the council and laughed when he'd have to vote on whether an oyster farmer could expand his enterprise.

Conor beat Hayden up the stairs and knocked. Hayden could hear the Crowleys in the kitchen but couldn't see anyone down the hall. He was about to knock again when he saw Devy coming down the stairs in a short sundress and cowboy boots. Boots he was willing to bet she hadn't brought with her from Chicago.

"Hey," she said as she pushed the screen door open. Hayden caught the door and never took his eyes off Devy.

Conor handed her the flowers. She smiled and brought them to her nose. "These are beautiful, Conor. Thank you."

"You're welcome. Is Maren here?"

"She's in the kitchen, helping Crow. Head on in."

Conor ran down the hallway and into the kitchen. "You have a dog!"

Devorah laughed, clearly remembering what Hayden had said about Conor wanting a dog. Hayden chuckled but kept his focus on Dev.

She turned her head slowly, meeting his gaze. He swallowed hard at the sight of her with her dress showing a bit more skin than he was used to seeing from her. Tonight, she had her hair in a long braid, and her skin seemed to shimmer. He'd learned enough from Sofia over the years to know that lotions and sprays often had shimmer or glitter in them. The shimmer, he liked. The glitter sometimes got everywhere and one time had ended up in his eyes.

Whatever Devorah had on, he was a fan of it. He had a difficult time tearing his gaze away from her. Mostly because he had to stop himself from leaning down and inhaling the scent she wore. It was vanilla, coconut, and summer, and it was perfect.

Hayden adjusted himself as discreetly as possible and cleared his throat. He leaned against the door casing, kept his other hand behind his back, and crossed his foot over his ankle. "How was your first day?" he asked as he tilted his head and smirked at her. "I meant to come in, but the guys left a bit later than I planned on."

"Really good, actually. Laila came in. She apologized for the other night and asked me to join the festival committee."

Hayden's expression lit up. "Seriously? That's fantastic. Are you going to do it?"

"Yeah, I think so." Devy took another inhale of the flowers. "These are very pretty."

"What can I say, my son has taste." Hayden brought his hand up and showed her the flowers in his hand. "These are for Maren."

"From you?" Devy asked, with a slight grin.

Hayden beamed. "Of course. I can't have my son showing me up in the flower department. What would the Crowley women think of the McKenna men?"

Devorah threw her head back in laughter and thankfully didn't correct Hayden on the usage of "Crowley" versus "Campbell."

"Well, these are lovely. Conor has impeccable taste in arrangements. I'm going to go put them in water. Can I get you something to drink?"

"Shit, I forgot. I'll be right back."

Hayden jogged back to his truck and grabbed the six-pack for Crow and the dessert. He didn't bother knocking when he came in and headed right to the kitchen, where he found Conor and Maren, each standing on a chair, with Crow in between them. He was teaching them how to cut a roast.

"Crow, I brought you a six-pack." Hayden held it up and waited for Crow to acknowledge him. "I'll put it in the refrigerator, along with this chocolate cake I brought."

"Cake?" Maren turned so fast she almost fell off the chair.

"Did I hear cake?" Devorah said as she came into the kitchen.

"Well, now I know the way to yours and Maren's heart."

"Mine too," Crow said casually.

"Right, the Crowleys love chocolate cake. The McKenna men have made a note."

"All right, everyone," Crow said. "Grab a seat at the table; I'll bring everything out."

Hayden and Conor sat across from Devorah and Maren, leaving the head of the table for Crow, who brought out roast with baby potatoes, maple-glazed carrots, and a garden-fresh salad. Everyone began dishing their plates and commenting about how good everything smelled.

All except for Devorah.

"Everything okay, Devy?" Hayden asked, midspoonful.

"Yeah, I just need a minute." She excused herself from the table. Everyone was silent until they heard a door shut upstairs.

"Grandpa, should I go check on her?" Maren asked.

"No, you can eat. Your mom just needs a minute," Crow said.

Hayden set his fork down. He'd wait until Devorah came back before eating.

"I wasn't a great dad to her after her mom died," Crow began saying to Hayden. "You're in a similar situation. Don't let my mistakes ruin your relationship with your son."

"Yes, sir."

"I'm trying now, but I fear it may be too late."

"No, sir. You're not."

After a few minutes, Hayden excused himself and went upstairs. He'd spent many nights playing video games in Colt's room and knew exactly which one was Devorah's. Hayden paused at the top of the steps. He could hear Crow talking to the kids, who were laughing. Someone snorted. This brought a smile to his face. Maybe Crow wasn't so scary after all, and adolescent/teenage Hayden had feared him for nothing.

Hayden shook his head. Crow definitely scared the shit out of him back then. But Crow was much younger then and could keep up with most of the teens. There was nothing wrong with having a healthy respect for the law, and its enforcer, especially when you were trying to covet his teenage daughter.

"Devy," he said as he knocked. "May I come in?"

She didn't answer. Instead, she opened the door. He could tell she'd been crying and suspected the family dinner was the cause.

He reached for her hand, slipping his fingers in between hers. "I can't imagine how all of this feels after not having it for so long."

She nodded. "It's a bit overwhelming. I can't even remember the last time we ate at the table, as a family."

"But you'll remember tonight. Crow's trying to be a better father."

"I know. I need to let him."

"Come on. The kids are waiting."

He went downstairs while Devy used the bathroom. When she came into the dining room, she looked refreshed. Before she sat down, she kissed her father on his cheek. "Thank you."

"Eat up, Devorah. There's chocolate cake waiting," Crow said without missing a beat.

"Maybe we should skip dinner altogether and just eat cake," Conor suggested, also without missing a beat.

Crow cleared his throat, which seemed to take Conor by surprise. His eyes widened, and before Hayden could say anything, Crow set his fork down.

"Young man," Crow said as he looked at Conor. "Standing up for your friends is an honorable thing to do. I will never fault you for doing what's right, especially when it comes to my granddaughter. As her grandfather, I appreciate you. As the sheriff, take this warning with you for a long time—violence isn't the answer. Even when you didn't hurt the other kid."

"Yes, sir," Conor said. "I didn't mean to hurt DJ. But when he didn't stop hurting Maren, even after she asked him to stop, all I could think was to move him away from her. I probably pushed him a little too hard."

Hayden reached over and set his hand on his son's arm.

Conor looked at his dad and then back at Crow. "I think it's wrong not to stop when someone says no."

"You're right, son," Crow said, nodding. He then looked at Hayden. "You raised this boy right. You should be proud. I know your father is."

"Thank you, Crow," Hayden said as he swallowed the lump in his throat. "And thank you for always showing me the right path. Because of men like you and my dad, I turned out okay."

"Huh," Crow huffed. "I'd say you're much better than okay." Crow looked around and then down at his food. "Anyway . . ." He picked his fork up and began eating. Hayden waited for him to finish, but he never went back to the subject.

NINETEEN

DEVORAH

Before the sun rose, Dev sneaked out of the house as best she could. Crow would hear the door squeak and suspect either someone had left or that someone was trying to break in. She hoped for the former because she didn't want her dad scaring Maren this early in the morning.

Devorah made her way to the docks. She found a dry spot and watched the crews get ready to head out for the day. If this morning's sunrise meant anything, they should have a decent catch, which would make everyone happy. Cash in their pockets and good eats on the table were never bad things.

She couldn't remember the last time she'd been down to the docks to think. This was where they had spread her mom's ashes, and Devy would come here to talk to her mom. Her visits started out daily but slowly turned into every other day or every few days. Those turned into weekly visits, and then she'd only visit on the anniversary of her mom's passing or when it was her mom's birthday.

And then the visits stopped altogether, right around the time she'd started dating Chad. When the anniversary date flew by without a second thought, Devorah mentioned it to Chad, stating that she needed to go visit. He told her it was stupid and that her mother wasn't really there, and she was just making a fool of herself.

Devorah believed him. She stopped going and even left for college without saying goodbye to her mom.

Now, she sat there, with her knees pulled to her chest and tears trailing down her cheeks. She didn't bother to wipe them away. Devorah was angry. At herself, at her father, at life and how unfair it could be. But mostly she was mad at Chad for what he'd done. Not only now, but when they'd started dating. He should've been accepting of her need to talk to her mother, even though her ashes were long gone. If Chad had truly loved her, he would've been supportive.

Instead, he'd mocked her.

It wasn't the first time, and it definitely wouldn't be the last.

Devorah sat there with the pink-and-orange morning sky guiding the boats out of the harbor. Silently, she wished them well and recited the fisherman's prayer. Around her, the sounds of Oyster Bay soothed her. Birds squawked overhead, following the boats as they motored away. The seafood market opened its bay door, and she could hear the hum of the ice machine. Behind her, she heard footsteps and prepared for the dock to wobble from someone stepping on it.

What she didn't expect was for her father to sit down next to her. His woodsy scent, mixed with the lingering tobacco of his cigar, was a smell she'd never forget.

Crow sat as close to Devorah as he could get. She was tempted to lean into her dad, but she resisted. Since their family dinner, a few weeks back, Devorah and Crow had turned a corner. Things were good between them. Better than before.

They sat for a bit until he broke the silence. "Does she ever answer you?"

Devorah shook her head. "Nope. I haven't been a very good daughter for the past two decades. I wouldn't talk to me either."

"That's so far from the truth, Devorah. You were and still are the best daughter. Your mom and I were very proud of you, and I have continued to be since the day she passed. I . . . ." Crow took a deep inhale.

Dev glanced at him. He gazed straight ahead. "I failed you and Colt after your mom died."

"You didn—"

Crow stared at her sharply. "I did. I didn't handle your mom's passing well, and the only thing I knew to do was bury myself in work and try to make things seem as normal as possible. I thought if everything stayed the same, life would go on. By the time I realized it, you were walking out the door for college. That day, I sat in my chair and stared out the window, wondering if you forgot something and you'd be back so I could tell you how proud I was of you and how I wished things could've been different.

"I failed you as a parent. I was supposed to be there for you, to love and protect you from the likes of Chad Campbell. I'll never forgive myself for not stepping in. I wanted to forbid you from seeing him, but by the time he'd wormed his way into your life, I'd lost you."

"You didn't lose me." Devorah hugged her knees tighter to her chest.

"Short of putting you in jail, you would've continued to see him."

He wasn't wrong. Devorah nodded. "He made me believe he was all I needed."

Crow sniffled. Dev looked at her father, and her heart broke instantly. He had tears in his eyes. While they were reconnecting, she still didn't feel they were close enough for her to show him much affection, so she sat there.

"As much as this is going to hurt to hear, he's done you a favor, Devorah. You're far too good for the likes of him. The best thing is to get him away from Maren. Give her a chance to grow up without him manipulating her."

"I think I want to stay in Oyster Bay." Devorah shrugged. "It's still small-town hell, but since reconnecting with Laila, she's been showing me that living here isn't all that bad."

"And Hayden?"

She shrugged again. "He's a bonus, for sure."

"He's sweet on you."

Devorah looked out at the water before Crow could see the smile form. "You've said that before."

"I mean it. He's a good man. Comes from a great family."

"Yeah . . . ," she said, trailing off. Hayden had so many positives. There were two things holding Devy back. First, she could still see a faint line where her wedding ring used to be. She tucked her hand inside her sweatshirt to avoid looking at her finger. Second, she'd been down this road with Hayden before and wasn't willing to do it again. While the sneaking around and secret make-out sessions had been exhilarating as a teen, they were adults now, and no one had time for those shenanigans.

"I want you to promise me something, Devorah."

"What's that?"

"That no matter what, you don't give that man a second chance. He doesn't deserve one. Not after the way he humiliated you, but especially after he disrespected your vows. No man deserves a second chance after cheating on his wife."

"I promise you, I won't, Daddy." Giving Chad another chance was never going to happen.

Crow turned sharply at the sound of her voice. She saw tears in his eyes. "Hearing you call me that . . ." He pushed his fingers into his eyes and shook his head. "After all these years, it does something here." Crow put his fist over his heart. "I love you, Devorah. I know I haven't said that nearly enough in your life, but I hope you know that I do. I love you. Maren. I can't thank you enough for bringing her home to me."

Devorah somehow managed to get from her seated position and into her father's arms in a flash. She cried into his shoulder as he wrapped her tightly in his embrace. "I love you too, Daddy," she said into his neck, wet with her tears.

"I'm sorry I wasn't a better father."

Devorah nodded. "But you're here now."

"I am, and I'm not going anywhere."

After another embrace, they parted and continued to stay on the dock until the alarm on Devorah's phone sounded. It was time to get Maren up for school and then start her day at the Lazy Lamb.

Crow and Devorah walked through the parking lot and across the street, where they encountered a very angry Maren standing on the porch with her hands on her hips.

"Don't look at your grandpa like that," Crow said as he scooped her up and threw her over his shoulder. "Come on, let's make pancakes."

Maren squealed. Devorah followed slowly behind them, loving their bond. It was something she used to have with him until her mother died, and while she had missed it growing up, she was thankful Maren had this side of Crow now.

While Crow and Maren worked on the pancakes, Devorah took stock of her life. In one month, her life had changed for the better. The dark, dreary, never-going-to-survive days seemed to be behind her. Each day when Devorah woke, she vowed to make the day great. Despite her marital woes, she had a lot to look forward to each day. After walking Maren, and sometimes Conor, to school, she came home and showered and then headed to work at the Lazy Lamb. Devy wasn't killing it in tips, but her weekly paychecks made sure she could buy whatever Maren needed without having to call or depend on Chad.

Dev still hadn't called him, out of stubbornness. She didn't want to talk to him and hear about how fabulous his life was with Ester. And as far as she knew, he'd only called once to speak to Maren. Per Theo, Devy kept track. She saw it in her daughter's face each time the phone rang, and it wasn't her father on the other end.

After breakfast, Maren got ready for school while Dev prepared for work. When they opened the door to leave, Conor and Hayden were standing at the gate, waiting for them. Devorah smiled and ducked her head, trying to hide her excitement from Hayden.

She followed behind Maren. While she and Conor walked ahead, Hayden fell in step beside Devy and held her hand for a second to let her know he had indeed caught the grin she'd tried to hide from him.

They dropped the kids off and walked toward the Lazy Lamb. Every so often, Hayden would reach for her hand or put his arm around her. They passed by people, saying hi and wishing them a good day. When they came to one of the newer cafés along Main Street, they stepped inside and ordered coffee; he then walked her the rest of the way to work.

Outside the Lazy Lamb, Hayden trailed his fingers along the underside of her cheek to her chin and lifted her head gently so he could look into her brown eyes.

"Have a fabulous day, Devorah."

The moment Hayden's head tilted to the side, she knew what was coming. Yet, when his lips pressed to hers, she was surprised. He had kissed her outside, for all to see. And when he pulled away, he had a shit-eating grin on his face. Hayden knew exactly what that kiss had meant, even though it wasn't much more than a lingering peck.

He walked away, chuckling. She watched him, with her fingers touching her lips. "Evil," she said to whoever could hear her.

The rest of her day flew by. She had regular customers, could make most any drink they ordered, and had memorized the menu. Never in her life did she think she'd actually enjoy slinging drinks at her neighborhood bar, but there she was, having the time of her life.

After work, Devorah made her way from the employee break room to the room near the arcade. She'd quickly learned that Colt let most of the townspeople use the room for free, unless it was a birthday party. Even then, he kept the fee low. Each day, someone called to book the room, and on Saturdays it was only available in two-hour blocks. Devy couldn't believe how many calls she'd taken during her shift. The people of Oyster Bay liked to have meetings and parties.

She found Laila rearranging the tables and chairs to give the room more of a board-meeting-type feel. After helping her, Devy set agendas out in front of the five chairs that now faced the audience—not that many people typically showed up—and set the rest near the accordion door on a small table.

"Do you remember when we were in high school, and we had to attend at least one meeting?" Devy asked. "These meetings used to be packed."

"Yep," Laila said as she set her laptop up. "The meetings used to be at the library in the room in the basement before it flooded. Everyone came to the meetings back then. Standing room only. It's only been like this the last couple of years. There was a threat to cancel the entire thing until I took over. It's been a challenge keeping it afloat. The younger generations really don't seem to care about it, until I say this year's event is going to get canceled, then maybe one or two people will step up."

"Maren wants to be the Pearl of the Ocean. She thinks it'll be fun."

Laila giggled. "The day she becomes Pearl, we're putting you on the float with her."

Dread filled Devorah. "I probably shouldn't tell you I still have my dresses in the closet at home."

Laila's eyes widened. "You do not!"

Devy nodded. "The tiaras and sashes too. I just left it all when I went to college, and Crow . . ." She trailed off for a moment. Things between them were good. From family dinners to him calling to see if he needed to pick up Maren from school or saying he would be late. They laughed at the Crowleys' now. They hugged, and this morning Crow had told Devorah he loved her. After he said those words, she wept in his arms.

"Well, Crow never went into my room. I swear it was the same as the last time I visited when Maren was about three."

"How come you guys didn't come back more often?"

Devorah sighed. "Chad's parents moved to Chicago, and there was no need. He knew Crow didn't like him, so to him, there was no point in coming back, and you know Chad couldn't live without us." Devy made the gagging motion, which caught her off guard. Her eyes widened as she looked at Laila, who stood there shocked. "What was that?"

"Maybe your mind finally coming to the conclusion that Chad is such a . . ." Laila trailed off, looking at the ceiling as she thought. "He's such a Chad!" she said gleefully. "You know the way he is isn't normal, right?"

Devorah nodded. Each time anyone talked about Chad, she saw just how narcissistic he was. As much as she hated seeing the person she had become because of him, she needed the slap in the face to see the error of her ways.

She would come out of this mess as a better person, just to spite him.

"I wish I had seen him for what he was back when we started dating. I think even then I knew, but he was Chad Campbell, and everyone wanted to date him, and he chose me."

"I didn't." Laila lifted her shoulder and straightened a piece of paper on the table in front of her. "He was always such a pompous ass. It was a major turnoff."

"Why didn't I see him like that?"

Laila let out an exaggerated breath. "In my most humble opinion, I think it's because of Crow and how strained things were between you. Colt was gone to college. Hayden too. No one was left to protect you from Chad."

"Yeah, I guess."

"No, there's no guessing. He's a dick."

"Pretty much," Devorah said as she inhaled. "But here I am, making amends for the person he changed me into."

"Have any of your friends from Chicago called?"

She shook her head. None of the other moms from the PTA or any of the clubs she was involved with had reached out. Nor had the neighbors she'd organized block parties with. Not a single woman she had considered a friend. "I'm not surprised. Most of their husbands know Chad. They either all work or play golf together. Just a bunch of Stepford wives."

Laila came around the table and hugged Dev. "You don't need them."

"Nope. I'm a Pearl of the Ocean."

They snorted and laughed hard. A clearing of a throat had them turning around. They found the Crafty Cathys coming in, led by Hayden's mother, Darcy. Laila went about greeting everyone and told them all to take a seat.

Darcy came over to Devy, followed by Beatrice Sherman. "How are things, dear?" Bea asked.

"I'm good," she said. "I'm finding my footing."

"Theo's waiting for you to file those papers."

Devy wanted to roll her eyes. Everyone knew everything in this damn town. "I know. Soon."

"We'd love to have you and Maren over for dinner soon," Darcy said when it was her turn.

"We'd like that," Devorah said.

Up until this morning, when Hayden and Conor had surprised Devorah and Maren, Hayden hadn't been around a ton, not since construction had started on his home. Part of Devy was relieved because her feelings for him confused her. She was already mixed up enough about life; adding the little butterflies she felt when Hayden was around only complicated her thoughts.

The rest of her missed his company. She enjoyed having him around, and the brief moments, like the coy hand-holding when walking the kids to school, left her longing for more. She could always put herself in his path a bit more, but she'd never been one to put herself out there. Maybe that needed to change.

A handful of locals came to the meeting. They talked about fundraising, volunteers, and how all float entries needed to be in by July 1, along with their entry fee.

"Also, the young women in our community need to submit their applications for the Pearl of the Ocean. Remember, it's one girl from each grade. Ninth through twelfth."

"I vote to have Devorah on the float this year."

Devy looked up from her notes to the audience but didn't see who'd spoken out, and the voice wasn't from someone she recognized.

Laila looked at Dev, who shook her head and mouthed, "No." She had zero desire to be on the float and much preferred being behind the scenes.

When the meeting adjourned, Dev gathered her things and was on the way out when Maureen Stark approached her. She was one of the Crafty Cathys, who, if Devorah remembered correctly, always had something wrong with her, and she always sent out a monthly newsletter recapping Oyster Bay business, her various ailments, and what Dr. McKenna was doing for her.

"Devorah," Maureen said. "Am I to understand you organize yard sales?"

Devy blanched and masked her reaction. Her job had been more than organizing yard sales. "It was estate sales."

"What's the difference?" she asked in a made-up posh accent.

"Well, for one, usually the homeowner is dead," Devy stated more for effect than anything.

"Oh well, I'm certainly not dead, and if I am"—she paused and looked around—"if this is what death looks like, I want a refund."

Devorah said nothing.

"Anyway, when can you organize my yard sale? I have many valuable things that should fetch top dollar."

Devy smiled kindly. She could tell her again about estate sales, but she feared her words would fall on ears unwilling to listen. "I'm sorry, Maureen. With the festival planning and my job, I don't have the time right now."

"Oh well . . . I." Maureen wasn't used to being told no, and honestly, it felt good for Dev to say it to her. "I suppose I can wait until August."

"August?"

"When the festival is over."

"Sure, we can revisit the topic then. Have a good night, Maureen." Devorah left, needing to get the heck out of there before Tabitha, in her bright neon-pink spandex pants with matching fanny pack, or Anita the thrice-divorced town pauper, could come up to her. Over the last month, Devorah had learned it was Tabitha who'd kept resharing the videos Ester posted. All Dev wanted was for those videos to go away.

Devorah escaped before anyone else could come up to her. As soon as she stepped inside Crow's house, she felt oddly at peace. It was warm and inviting, something it hadn't been when she was a teen. Now there was laughter and dinner waiting for her in the oven.

She went into the living room, where her dad sat in his recliner watching the baseball game. "Who's winning?" she asked, even though it didn't matter to her, because it did to him.

"Sox by one."

"Nerve racking."

"We had pizza for dinner. Maren left it on the counter for you."

"Thank you." She leaned down and kissed his cheek without a second thought. She walked into the kitchen to grab a couple of slices of pizza. When she went to open the box, her hand froze. On it was an advertisement for a local church's annual tag sale fundraiser. She remembered having to volunteer during her reign as Pearl of the Ocean. Devorah peeled the flyer from the box and studied it as Maureen's request to organize her yard sale popped into her mind. Could she start her curating business in Oyster Bay? She loved planning. It was like second nature to her. So what if it was yard sales and not estates. She put the flyer on the table, to save for later, and then put a couple of slices onto a plate and went back into the living room. "Where's Maren?"

"Taking a shower," Crow said without taking his eyes off the television.

"How did practice go?" She sat down on the sofa, with Cordelia at her feet.

"Fine," he said with a groan. "That Noble boy is going to put me into an early grave. He's like his father. Never listens."

"He's a young kid. He'll learn."

Crow huffed. "We'll see."

The house phone rang, and Crow groaned again. He kicked his recliner into place and ambled his way toward the kitchen, where the phone hung on the wall. When Colt and Devorah were teens, the cord had been thirty feet long and coiled into a ball from the constant stretching. Crow wouldn't let them have a phone in their rooms, nor would he pay for cell phones.

"Hello?" he said gruffly into the receiver. Whoever was on the other end should've known better than to call the house phone during a baseball game.

The long pause caught Dev's attention. Crow mumbled something unintelligible and came into the other room.

"That ex of yours is on the phone."

Devorah sat there staring at her father, who had retaken his seat.

"If you don't want to talk to him, hang up. And whatever you do, don't agree to anything," Crow said as he looked at her.

Slowly, Devy stood and carried her plate into the kitchen. She wasn't in a hurry to talk to Chad and needed the extra seconds to compose herself. She set it down on the counter and looked at the cream-colored handset sitting on top of the base.

Devy cleared her throat, took a deep breath, picked the handset up, and placed it against her ear. For a long couple of seconds, she listened to the man she'd once loved—maybe even still loved—breathe. She knew he'd grow agitated the longer she took to say hello. The urge to make him wait bubbled. He needed to know he was no longer in charge of her.

Finally, she sighed and said, "Yeah?" It was childish, but she didn't care. Devy wanted him to know he no longer mattered.

"Devorah?"

Who else would it be?

"Yep." She popped the *p*, knowing it would irritate him. It gave her a bit of satisfaction in doing so.

"Hi."

"Hello, Chad. Maren's in the shower," she said. "I can have her call you when she's out."

"Yes, that's fine, but I wanted to speak with you first. She called me earlier and wants to come home for the summer."

This was news to Devy. Maren hadn't mentioned going to Chicago to visit her father. Devorah also hadn't brought the subject up. The less she spoke or thought about Chad, the less depressed she felt.

"And I was thinking it would probably be best for you to return as well. You need to live here, in Chicago. Not some time-forgotten town."

"Excuse me?"

"Things would be a lot easier for me"—Chad paused—"and Maren."

Devorah said nothing. She would never deny her child; at least she never thought she would.

"Our daughter doesn't like it there. Not that I can blame her. All her friends are here, as well as her home."

This was the first time Dev had heard this. Maren hadn't said anything about being unhappy. In fact, she was certain their daughter was thriving.

"She has friends here," Devorah squeaked out, although she suspected her statement wouldn't matter to Chad because her voice had failed her. She didn't want to sound weak but suspected that was how her ex perceived her. She wasn't weak. At least she was trying not to be.

"Don't be difficult, Devorah. What we're going through shouldn't affect our daughter."

"Yet she lost her best friend because you couldn't keep it in your pants. Do you really expect her to play second fiddle to your mistress?"

"Ester is more than a mistress."

"Right, I must've forgotten the title changes once your wife moves out."

Chad sighed. "Devorah."

She imagined him sitting there, pinching the bridge of his nose.

"I didn't want to bring this up, but the fact is, you've gone on dates when you should be focusing on our daughter. Being out, gallivanting with Hayden McKenna of all people. I thought you knew better."

Devy saw red. She didn't want Maren talking about her life to her father. What she did was none of Chad's business. "Are you kidding me?"

"I never joke when it comes to our daughter, Devorah. Her happiness is everything."

"Then you shouldn't have shit on our marriage, Chad. What I do with *my* time is *my* business. Not yours." She hung up and then picked the handle up and slammed it against the base three times before resting her head against the phone. Devy breathed in and out to calm herself.

"Mommy?"

"I need a moment, Maren." Her instant reaction was to be angry with her daughter. Her nine-year-old child who had no idea how to handle adult situations or her manipulating father. Devorah felt her father's presence in the room, and it oddly calmed her.

Devorah breathed in and out, working to slow her heart rate and curb the anger she felt. She told herself she was pissed off at Chad, not Maren. That he'd likely prodded their daughter for information. He was the one who'd fucked up. Not Devorah. Chad was the one who'd cheated, who'd destroyed their marriage.

She turned to find her daughter standing there with tears in her eyes. How much of the conversation had she overhead? Behind her, Crow stood, scowling. Was his look one of warning to her to tread carefully with Maren? Or was it a result of the one-sided conversation he'd heard?

Devorah took a deep breath. "Did you tell your father I went on a date with Hayden?"

Maren nodded as tears fell from her eyes.

She's innocent in all of this.

Another deep breath. *Inhale. Exhale.*

"Look—"

"Devorah." Crow's booming voice was full of warning. She glanced at her father and saw the slight shake of his head.

Devy crouched, putting her below her daughter's eye level. Her watery eyes matched Maren's. She clasped hands with her daughter.

"Did Daddy ask you questions about me?"

Maren nodded.

"I'm not mad at you, sweetie. I'm angry at your dad. He shouldn't put you in the middle of what's going on here. I'm sorry he did that." Devorah partially stood and kissed her daughter on her forehead, and then pulled her into a hug as she righted herself. Maren's arms wrapped around her waist as Devy looked at her father.

Mother and daughter parted. Devorah cupped Maren's cheek. "Do you want to go back to Chicago?"

Maren shrugged. "I miss my friends."

"I know you do. I'm so sorry you're having to go through all of this. We can go back if that's what you want."

Maren shrugged again.

She'd thought about whether she wanted to stay in Oyster Bay, and as of late the answer was yes, but not at the expense of her daughter's happiness.

"Devorah . . ." The deep gruffness of her father's voice was gone, replaced with sadness. She couldn't look at him. She didn't want to see the heartbreak on his face. She felt it, and that was enough. They had finally reconnected, and now she was going to leave him behind. She would leave everyone she loved behind because her daughter wanted to go back to Chicago.

"I can't, Dad. I'm sorry." She swiped her hand across her cheek, smearing makeup and tears across her face. She left her dad and Maren in the kitchen, grabbed her purse, and walked out of the house. She needed to be alone.

TWENTY

HAYDEN

Hayden had all but fallen asleep when his phone startled him. He answered groggily and rubbed his eyes clear.

"Hey, it's Colt. Can you come down to the pub?"

"Uh, what time is it?" Hayden pulled the phone away from his ear and looked. It was almost midnight. He had fallen asleep after spending all day working with Link. They were close to finishing the framing on Hayden's house. It had also been hot out earlier, and he was certain he hadn't drunk enough water. After his shower, he'd collapsed on his bed and fallen right to sleep.

"Late. Look, my sister's down here, and things aren't pretty. I'd call my dad, but he's with Maren, and I don't want to call one of his deputies."

"What's wrong with Dev?"

"I'm not exactly sure. She said something about a piece of shit and started drinking. I'm assuming this has something to do with Chad."

Hayden groaned. He liked Devorah. A lot. He was ready for more, but she wasn't, and he wasn't willing to push her. Devy didn't even have to tell him. He could sense it from her. And he was okay with that. Besides, he had enough things to keep his time occupied with building his house and making sure Conor was fitting in.

"Yeah, I'll be down in a minute," he told Colt and then hung up. Hayden sat, ran his hand through his hair, and sighed. In the time he'd spent with Devorah, she hadn't drunk a thing other than water and soda. He figured she didn't drink or didn't want to give Chad something to use against her. Hayden respected her choice. Applauded her for it.

After Sofia passed away, Hayden had spent three nights on a bender, trying to numb his thoughts. Every time he closed his eyes, he saw his wife, the tree, the damage it had done to her, and Sofia's cousin, standing on the side of the road, sobbing. If it wasn't for Conor, Hayden would still be drunk.

He pulled on a pair of jeans and a T-shirt, slipped on his cowboy boots, and hopped into his truck, only to get out and decide to walk to the Lazy Lamb. If Devorah was drunk, he'd prefer to walk her home from the pub so she could get some fresh air.

The Lazy Lamb was a hot spot, which surprised Hayden. Maybe he was just too old for any type of nightlife. He opened the door and found the place packed. There wasn't an empty seat in the entire place. People stood three to four deep around the bar or lingered where their friends sat. Music played from the back, where the arcade and meeting room were.

Hayden walked the length of the bar, peering between people until he spotted Devy sitting at the end, next to some man who looked pretty into her. A bout of jealousy bubbled in his gut. He pushed it down. He had no right to be jealous. Devy could speak to or flirt with anyone she wanted. Even though Hayden wanted it to be him.

He worked his way through the crowd, bumping shoulders and jostling other body parts until he'd made it to the end of the bar. Hayden held his finger up, and the other bartender came over.

"What can I get you?" she asked.

"Water. On the rocks," he said, trying to be funny.

The bartender didn't laugh. The bar was busy, and the water meant no tip. Hayden threw a five-dollar bill down and got a smile in return.

He stood there for a minute, sipping his water and waiting for Devorah to notice him. When it didn't happen fast enough, he slipped next to her free side and touched her hip. She turned and looked. Her glazed eyes took him in, inch by inch. A smile spread across her face when she met his penetrating stare.

"You're really hot," she said, slurring her words. "Like, really, really hot."

Hayden returned her smile.

"Hey, man," the other guy said as loud as he could.

Hayden leaned forward, pretending to give a rat's ass about what he had to say.

"We're sort of together," the guy said, which made Hayden's blood boil.

"Yeah, I don't think so, buddy. She's not going home with you."

"I beg to differ."

"The only thing you're going to beg for is mercy when I kick your ass. She's drunk, now get lost." Hayden motioned for him to scram. The man opened his mouth to say something but seemed to think better of it when Hayden set his water down. He threw some money onto the table and left. Hayden sat in the now-empty chair.

"What's going on, Devy?"

She cupped his cheek and leaned toward him. "Hi, Hayden."

"Hey. You doing good?"

She nodded, and then her lower lip quivered. "I hate him."

"I know you do," he said. "I think we all do. Why don't we head outside for some fresh air?"

She nodded as he helped her off the barstool. He motioned for the bartender to come over. "If she has a tab, tell Colt. He'll take care of it."

"Got it."

Hayden held on to Devy tightly and maneuvered their way through the crowd. At the door, she pulled him toward her.

"Wanna dance?"

"Another night," he told her as he pushed the door open. As soon as they were outside, she started crying.

"He had sex with my best friend and humiliated me," she said as she hiccupped.

"Yeah, that was a pretty shitty thing to do." Hayden held her hand as they walked toward Crow's.

"Men are pigs."

That stung, even though she knew not all men were like Chad. Despite her strained relationship with her father growing up, Crow had always set a damn fine example of how men should act.

"Not all men cheat, Dev."

"Do you?"

He shook his head. "I would never."

"He wants us to move back to Chicago, and so does Maren."

Hayden's heart twisted at hearing those words. He didn't want Devy and Maren to leave.

"Chad said things would be easier for him. For *him*." She all but spat the word out. "Better for our daughter."

"Divorce is messy," Hayden said, even though he had no idea. His parents were still married, and both sets of his grandparents had still been married when they passed away. He had friends whose parents had divorced, but he'd never experienced it firsthand.

"Maren doesn't like it here," she said, almost crying. "What's not to like?" Devorah twirled and held her arms out. "She can be Pearl of the Ocean if she wants." She stopped, swayed, and looked at Hayden. "I don't want to move back. I want to stay in OB and just be me. I don't want to be a Stepford wife or see *them* together."

"You don't have to. Maren will adjust. It's only been a month. With everything going on, these things take time." He wrapped his arm around her waist.

"He's pissed I went on a date with you. He said I should've known better. Are you bad news?"

What in the actual fuck?

They weren't dating, and even if they were, Chad had left her. He'd chosen another woman over her. What was she supposed to do, pine for him until the end of time?

"No, Dev. I'm not bad news."

She stopped walking and began crying. "He's mawipulating my daughter." Her words slurred. "Asking about me. Pretending to care so he can tell me what do to. And she tells him because she loves him. He knows this and uses her."

Hayden pulled her into his arms. "She's a child. Maren didn't do it to hurt you. She loves you, Devy, and doesn't understand what's going on. All she knows is her life got uprooted one day. If it's a lot for an adult to process, imagine being nine." Hayden expected that Chad had prodded the information out of Maren.

"I have to stop him from hurting her."

Hayden couldn't agree more.

"Come on, let's get you back to Crow's." He put his arm around her to keep her upright. After another block, she slumped against him. Hayden lifted her into his arms and carried her the rest of the way. It was a good thing he'd been slinging tools lately and had built up his strength.

When they arrived at Crow's, he was standing on the porch waiting for them. "The light's on upstairs. Take her on up."

Hayden expected to find Maren waiting, but her door was closed, as was the shared door to the bathroom. Honestly, he didn't know if he'd say anything to her. As it was, he was pretty hurt by what Devorah had told him.

He laid her down on her bed, slipped her shoes off, and pulled the blanket over her. Before he left, he brushed her hair away from her face and kissed her forehead. "Please don't leave," he whispered to her.

Downstairs, he found Crow outside, rocking in the chair.

"That husband of hers said some things on the phone, which put her in a precarious position with Maren. She wants to blame her, when it's Chad's fault. He's a piece of work and is intent on destroying what spirit she has left or has built up since she returned to OB."

"He's gaslighting her and using Maren to further his agenda."

Crow nodded. "I spoke with Maren after Devorah left. Stressed the importance of keeping her conversations with her dad about herself. She's old enough to stand up to her father. I wish there was something I could do."

"I think . . . ," Hayden started and then paused. "I think we have to be on her side. That's all she needs right now. To know she has people who support her. We can't even pretend to know how she feels. Her world is upside down. People talk about her constantly. The woman she thought was her best friend betrayed her in the worst possible way. Devy needs the people around her to stick up for her."

Crow glanced at Hayden. "I'll do better," he said gruffly. "I want to do better for her."

"That's all she wants, and from what I've seen, you already have," he said as he headed down the stairs.

"Hayden?"

"Yes, sir?"

"Since the kids have a baseball game tomorrow, what do you say me, you, Conor, and the old man go fishing after?"

"We'd love to. See you in a few hours, Crow."

The next morning, Hayden and Conor showed up at the ballpark with a giant thermos of coffee, just for Devy. Hayden figured she would need it once the noise level increased. When he came to where she sat, she looked up at him, with dark sunglasses on. He set his chair next to her and sat with a sigh. Cordelia, not to be forgotten, stood and rested her head on Hayden's leg until he'd given her enough attention.

"I'm sorry," she said right off. "Chalk it up to another embarrassing moment in Devorah Campbell's life."

"Crowley," he said.

"What?"

Hayden shrugged. "I don't know. I think you should use Crowley. It sounds better."

A small smile appeared, but not for long. "Theo asked me if I wanted to change my name back, and I said I didn't know. Mostly because of Maren. I guess it doesn't matter, if we go back to Chicago."

His heart twisted again.

He could tell her how he felt. How he wanted to date her and really get to know her. That he loved spending time with her and Maren. Conor did as well. Or he could sit back and let her make what he felt would be the worst decision of her life.

Nope.

He reached for her hand. Not giving a shit what others thought. If Devorah didn't want to hold his hand, she'd let him know.

She squeezed his hand and smiled.

"Giving in to what Chad wants isn't how you should live your life, Dev. You have a good thing going here. You and Laila are friends again. Your dad is cooking dinners. All you've ever wanted from him is an effort, and he's giving you that. Do you want to leave him?"

"Not really."

"So tell Chad no. You don't need to move to make things easier for him. It should be the other way around."

"I don't want him to move here."

Hayden laughed. "No one does. Although I'd love to see what the Crafty Cathys do to him."

"Me too."

And Crow. If he had his way, Chad would end up in the slammer for the night.

"Maren wants to move back."

Hayden nodded. "I'm sure Conor wants to move back to Wyoming, because that's what he knows. Kids like things to be easy. People move all the time. Kids adjust. She hasn't been here very long, and her father is yapping in her ear about how much he misses her. If I had to bet, I'd put money on Chad telling her she wants to move back." He shook his head and looked out to the field, where Maren and a couple of boys were tossing the ball back and forth.

"Has Maren told you she wants to leave?"

Devorah shrugged. "After I got off the phone with him, I asked her. She misses her friends, which I get."

"And she'd spoken to him beforehand?"

Devy sighed. "Yeah, I think so. Although I don't know when he's calling."

"As much as I hate the guy, at least he's calling her."

"There's that."

"Look at her, Devy. Does she look like a kid who hates it here?"

Maren stood among her teammates, laughing. Conor stood next to her, doing the same. To anyone watching them, they looked like happy, well-adjusted children.

"No, she doesn't."

"At least take that into consideration before you make a decision. And if you decide to go back to Chicago, let me or Colt help you. I don't want you making that trip alone."

Devorah nodded and leaned into his arm as it extended over her chair. She squeezed his hand again.

Hayden leaned over and pulled Devy's sunglasses down a bit. "You owe me."

"Oh God. Did I puke on you last night?"

He smiled as her eyes widened. "No, I'm only teasing."

"I'll make it up to you," she told him.

"Oh yeah? How?"

"Dinner, or I'll wash your truck."

"Dinner it is."

Crow and Colt, along with Lee and Darcy, joined them right before the game started. The six of them cheered until their throats went raw. Each time Conor or Maren came up to the plate to bat, Hayden and Devy went quiet. With every pitch and every swing, Devy would grip Hayden's arm, while his heart did somersaults.

When the last out was called, the six of them cheered wildly, along with the other parents and grandparents. Oyster Bay had won the game.

Maren and Conor ran toward them, laughing.

"Mom, did you see my hit?" Maren asked.

"I did! It went so far. You ran really fast," Devy said.

"Did you see my hit?" Conor asked.

Hayden held his hand up for a high five. "Great hit, bud. You ready to go fishing?"

"You're going fishing?" Devy asked as she looked at Hayden, then at her dad, both nodding. "Oh."

"We won't be gone long. Home by dinner," Crow said.

"Well, it looks like it's just us," Devy said to Maren. "These guys are going to go catch dinner."

Maren's face scrunched. "Fish is gross."

"Corn dogs for you then."

"Can I have corn dogs?" Conor asked.

Devy looked at Hayden and laughed. "We still need to go to Hank's Fish Fry!"

"Next weekend, for sure!"

"Maren and I will go to the store and grab a few things for dinner. Darcy, would you like to join us?"

Hayden's eyes widened in surprise as he stared from Dev to his mom.

"I'd be honored. I've wanted to spend some time getting to know your daughter." Darcy came over and put her hand on Maren's shoulder. "Come on, we'll use Grandpa Lee's credit card and buy up the entire store. Tell me, Maren," Darcy said as they started walking. "Do you like chocolate chip cookies?"

"I love them."

"Me too!"

The men stood there and watched as the women left them at the park. Lee sighed, shook his head, and looked at the others. "Happy wife, happy life. Now come on—the boat is gassed up, and I'm ready to drop a line or two."

TWENTY-ONE

DEVORAH

While the men fished, Darcy, Devorah, and Maren shopped. After buying more than they needed, they headed back to Crow's and started cooking. Devy had never cooked with another woman before, let alone someone's mother. Everything she knew how to make, she'd learned by following recipes or from the various cooking channels. Not having a mother growing up had been hard on Dev, and she was determined to make sure Maren learned everything.

Darcy took control in the kitchen. Handing out directions. Offering suggestions. And showing Maren what it would be like to have a grandmother around. Not that Darcy would ever be Maren's grandmother, but the sentiment was there. A few times during the day, Devy stood back and watched Maren and Darcy work. It was like they'd known each other forever and not just for a few hours.

A nine-year-old could only take so much cooking and eventually disappeared into her room with her new bestie, Cordelia, leaving Darcy and Devorah in the kitchen. While Dev breaded a hot dog on a skewer, Darcy peeled potatoes for a salad.

"You know we could've bought everything premade and gone to the mall," Darcy said.

She was right, but Dev needed this, and Maren needed to see what it would be like to have some type of family around. Even if nothing came of her and Hayden, Devorah knew in her heart that Darcy and Lee would always be a fixture in Maren's life. That was a benefit of small-town living.

"I've never cooked with anyone before."

"Not even your mother-in-law?"

Devy shook her head. "She likes to have things catered, and the few times we hosted holiday dinners, she sat in the other room. It's always just been me in the kitchen."

"Your mother loved to cook," Darcy said. "The CC Club should've done a better job filling in for her after she passed, but your dad . . ." Darcy sighed. "He's a stubborn old man who said you kids were just fine."

"I'm not surprised. He's very private."

"Yes, he is. But that doesn't excuse us from not stepping up and doing right by your mom. She was one of us. We owed it to her to make sure her children were taken care of."

"I think I turned out okay."

"You did, despite your father. I swear, that man." Darcy shook her head. "If it wasn't the sheriff's department, nothing else mattered."

Devy couldn't disagree.

"This is nice," Devorah said, moving the subject away from her dad. "Thank you for teaching Maren how to cook from scratch."

"It's a grandmother's job to teach. Where did you learn?" She motioned toward the batter coating Devorah's hands.

"Betty Crocker. All the cooking shows. Chad isn't big on mindless television, so I'd leave it on educational programming. Cooking is educational."

"He's a boob."

Devorah laughed. "He certainly is."

"Bea Sherman likes to gossip."

Devy snorted. "You all like to gossip."

"True," Darcy said with a sigh. "Bea's concerned for you, though. She said you haven't filed your paperwork yet?"

Devorah stabbed another skewered hot dog into the batter. She let it drip and then put it into a pot with hot oil. The sizzling sound was a bit too satisfying for her as she pictured Chad's face in the pot.

"I haven't, because I'm nervous. I'm afraid Chad will do something rash, like try to take Maren away from me. He already wants us to move back to Chicago to make things easier for him, and he says Maren doesn't like it here. I fear if I file the paperwork, he'll come get her, and then what?"

"Your father will not let him take Maren away."

"No, I'm sure he won't."

"Hayden won't either," Darcy said as she moved around the kitchen. "He likes you."

"I like him too."

"No, Devorah. My son *likes* you, and if you tell him I said as much, I'll deny it."

How could someone who liked to gossip deny the truth? Devorah laughed at her thoughts. She liked Hayden. More than she probably should for a woman going through the shitstorm she called her life. They both danced around their feelings for each other, although in the past couple of days, Hayden had been very brazen with his intent. The kiss in front of the Lazy Lamb and holding her hand during the baseball game. This was the Hayden she had longed to have back in high school. The one who wasn't afraid to show people he was interested in her. His actions spoke louder than words, and Devorah found comfort in them.

She had also bonded with Conor from the moment they met. It was like he filled a void she didn't know existed, and the thought of leaving him and returning to Chicago weighed heavily on her heart. Still, she had to do what was right for Maren.

"I enjoy spending time with Conor and Hayden," she finally said. It was the truth. Both had come into her and Maren's lives when they needed a friend, someone they could lean on. Lord knows, Devy had leaned on Hayden a lot already.

"Please don't hurt my son or grandson," Darcy said quietly.

"Wh-what?"

Darcy stood next to Devorah. "They've been through a lot. The fact that Hayden is putting himself out there with you speaks volumes. After Sofia died, I didn't think he'd recover. And Conor. He's young and has lost so much. You know what that's like."

"I do. Believe me when I tell you this, Darcy, Conor is a sweet boy, and as long as I'm in Oyster Bay, he can depend on me."

Darcy smiled. "And Hayden?"

"Anything going on between Hayden and me needs to stay there."

She sighed. "You're right. I'm meddling. I just want what's best for my boys."

"I understand. I'm sure Crow's on the boat saying the same thing to Hayden."

"Lord, help my son," Darcy said with laughter.

When the men returned, Crow fired up the grill, while Lee and Hayden gutted and fileted their catch. Conor wrinkled his nose at the smell and swore he'd never eat fish as long as he lived.

While Crow cooked, Devorah set the picnic table. Darcy took care of getting drinks for everyone. Maren brought her portable speaker outside for her and Conor to listen to. Hayden left, only to return right away with a plastic ball and bat.

"Do you want to play?" he asked Devy.

"I'm more of a spectator today," she told him, still nursing a hangover. "I'll be the media relations person and video all the bloopers."

"Yes, because there will be many."

Hayden, Maren, Conor, and Lee set up a baseball field in the backyard. Darcy joined Dev on the sidelines and rooted for only Conor and Maren. Each time Lee would come up to bat, Darcy would tease him relentlessly about being old and out of shape. He might have been older than everyone else, except Crow, but Lee McKenna was far from out of shape.

Every other play, Devorah would video the game and take photos. Other than looking at them, she had no idea what she'd do with them.

"Send those to me," Darcy told her. "I'll post them on social media."

Devy grimaced.

"Social media isn't evil, just some people who use it are."

"I know. I actually miss watching all the dog videos."

"So watch them. You know you can block her and block any hashtag she used."

"How do you know this?"

"Tabitha. She may be in her sixties, but she's a tech genius."

"Tabitha . . ." Devorah sighed. "Can you do me a favor?"

"Of course. What's up?" Darcy asked without taking her eyes off the game.

"She's resharing all of *those* videos, and as long as she does, they're never going to go away. I would like OB to be a safe place for Maren and me."

Darcy looked at Devorah sharply with wide, almost angry eyes. "No!" she said, exaggerating the *o*. "Oh, hell no. This will not do. The CC Club protects our own, and you are one of us." She took her phone out and typed rapidly on the keypad. "I told her she best knock it off, or else."

Devorah wondered what the "or else" would be in this case. Would the Crafty Cathys kick her out of the club? Banish her from Oyster Bay?

If banishment was a thing, she wanted Chad gone forever. To never be allowed to cross the bridge into town. This wasn't his home. It was hers.

Midway through the game, which didn't have a score because no one wanted to keep one, Crow yelled that dinner was done. Devorah and Darcy brought the side dishes out and set them on the table, along with the corn dogs, which Dev had kept warm in the oven for the kids.

"You ladies were busy," Lee said as he rubbed his belly. "Let's see, we have potato salad, tossed salad. Is this dressing homemade?"

"Yes, Mr. Lee. I helped make it," Maren said.

"None of that 'Mr. Lee' stuff," he told her. "You can call me Lee or Grandpa. I answer to both." He was close enough to touch the tip of her nose with his finger. She giggled.

Along with the salads, they had freshly baked rolls and green beans that had simmered on the stove all day in bacon and onions to go with the fish the guys had brought home.

"I've never been so hungry," Crow said as he heaped food onto his plate.

"We never asked—who caught all the fish?"

"Mostly Grandpa and the sheriff," Conor said as he bit into his corn dog. "I hooked one, but Dad had to help me reel it in."

Devorah looked at Hayden. "Didn't catch anything, huh?"

He shook his head slowly. "It's a good thing my family likes to share. Otherwise, I'd go hungry."

"I can't even remember the last time I went fishing," Devy said. "I must've been five or so." Crow caught her gaze and frowned. She hadn't meant to say anything to upset him, but that was the way he'd taken it. She couldn't help the past, and neither could he. What was done was done.

"This is the best corn dog I have ever had," Conor said as he reached for a second. "Where did you buy them?"

"My mom made them," Maren said.

"Duh, but from what box?" Conor asked.

"No, sweetie. What Maren's saying is, I made them. Except for the hot dog part. The rest I did by hand."

"Wow, you can do that?"

Devorah nodded. Her heart warmed with Conor's excitement. "I can show you someday."

"That'd be cool. I don't know how to cook."

"My mom can teach you," Maren told him. "We cook a lot of stuff. Don't we, Mom?"

"We do." Because there wasn't anything else to really do, unless she had a meeting to go to. Sure, in Oyster Bay she had meetings to attend, but she also had a job. One that put money in her pocket that her former husband didn't take from her.

After dinner, everyone helped clean up. Crow took over dish duty and sent the baseball team outside to finish their game. Once all the food had been divided up into containers, Darcy and Lee left. Devy put her lawn chair in the yard and watched her daughter.

Maren seemed happy. She laughed, engaged with Conor and Hayden, and even tried to play jokes on them. She didn't seem depressed, nothing like Chad had indicated on the phone. Sure, Maren missed Chicago. Part of Devy did as well. They'd had a good life there until Chad started thinking with his man parts and not his brain. It wasn't just an affair, though, at least not to Devorah. He'd ruined relationships. Maren had lost her best friend, her home, all her friends at school, and the life Chad and Devorah had worked hard for their daughter to have.

Maren hit the ball over the fence. Devorah would've thought they'd won the lottery by how loud and hard Hayden cheered. He picked her up and set her on his shoulder. With one arm in the air, he ran around the bases, declaring her the winner of the entire game.

"He's good with her," Crow said as he sat down. "Was Chad like this?"

Devy shook her head. "I'm sorry we didn't visit more often." The more she thought about it, the more she realized Chad had alienated her from her own family. She had depended solely on him and his family for everything.

"You're here now."

"I don't want to go back to Chicago, Dad. I thought I'd hate being here, but I don't. Despite everything, I had a good life. There are things I had that I want for Maren."

"You don't have to do anything you don't want to," Crow said. "Let Theo take care of things for you. It's why he gets paid the big bucks. It's his job to protect you now, where I failed."

"You didn't fail."

Crow looked at Devorah. "I most certainly did. I may have been here, but I wasn't present in your life. There are things I could've done differently. I see that now."

Devorah reached for his hand and held it. "I love you, Dad."

Crow sniffled. "I love you too, Devorah."

They sat there, watching Hayden and the kids play. The game had turned into a wrestling match, with Hayden getting pinned repeatedly. At one point, he looked at Devorah and smiled. Her heart skipped a beat and her body warmed.

She liked him. More than she would admit aloud, especially to him. It was as if hearing those words would change things between them.

Maybe it would.

Maybe it would be for the better.

TWENTY-TWO

HAYDEN

A shift had happened between Hayden and Devorah, and it all started with when he'd walked her to work and taken a chance by kissing her. He wanted to call Chad and thank him as well for being such an epic douche that Hayden had had to rescue Devy from the bar. And despite her having a hangover at the baseball game, the next day turned out to be one of the best days he'd had in a long time.

Their impromptu picnic dinner with both families had opened his eyes to what his future could be. He wanted Devy and Maren in his and Conor's lives. Hayden saw them as a family. The four of them living their best lives in Oyster Bay, surrounded by family and friends. If Devorah gave living here some time, she would thrive. The way she was meant to.

He could see everything clearly and decided it was now or never when it came to letting Devorah Crowley know exactly how he felt.

After working on his house with Link and the crew all day, he went into the Lazy Lamb and found his favorite bartender chatting with Laila. When he sat down, the two giggled like schoolgirls when Laila motioned toward him. He tipped his hat at her and Devorah and smiled when she came over to him.

"What can I get ya?" she asked as she placed a coaster in front of him.

"Three things," he said. "First, I'd like an ice water and a pint of Colt's newest brew. Second, what time do you get off? Third, will you go out with me tonight?"

Devy's expression never changed until the third question.

She took a deep, steady breath.

"That's four things, Mr. McKenna, and Colt's newest is a DIPA. Are you driving home?"

He shook his head. "Walked here."

"That's good, and I'm off in an hour."

"Good, I'll wait."

Devy took another breath. She was gorgeous, with her long, dark hair. Her body curved in ways Hayden could only imagine. And her eyes—always expressive—left him wanting to know what she was thinking at any time. Something had definitely shifted between them, and he would no longer sit back and wait to see where things would go.

"Yes," she finally said. Hayden thought about asking what the "yes" was for, but he knew and didn't want to embarrass her.

"I'll take that beer now."

He never took his eyes off Devorah as she poured his beer.

She set it in front of him. "Do you want to run a tab?"

Hayden shook his head. "Nah, not if you're off in an hour."

"And then what?"

"And then we go on our date."

"I'll need to shower," she told him. "I stink like beer and whatever else there is around here."

He nodded. "I'll wait on your porch like a proper gentleman."

"I need to see if Crow doesn't mind watching Maren."

"Already taken care of. Maren is coming over to my parents' house tonight, with your dad, for game night."

"Oh." Devorah looked flustered.

"Do you really think I'd ask you out with such little notice if I hadn't taken care of everything?"

Devy met his gaze and then shook her head. "No, you wouldn't. Okay. One hour and then home to clean up."

"I'll be here," he said, sipping his beer.

After a few minutes, Laila sat on the barstool next to Hayden. "Do you just come in to flirt with her?"

He laughed. "I've been flirting with her for over a month, and nothing works. She's got a wall up."

"Do you blame her? Between you and Chad? My girl is not taking any chances."

"Not in the slightest . . . wait, what? Me?"

Laila nodded and tapped his hand with hers while offering him a kind yet "Mess with my bestie, and I'll slay you" look. "Do you remember high school?"

"Yes, we're not that old, Laila."

"Right, but do you *remember* everything?"

Hayden shrugged and then nodded.

Laila sighed. "Dev was in love with you. Like, madly in love, but you . . ." Laila pointed at him. "You kept her hidden. You never made her your girlfriend, and that's all she ever wanted from you."

Hayden opened his mouth to speak, but she held her hand up and shook her head. "I know you were afraid of Colt and Crow, but we're all adults now. Do not sneak around with her. If you want to be with her, put her front and center. Shower her with the love and attention she deserves from you. If someone asks if she's your girl, you stand up proudly and declare your love for her because I know you love her, Hayden McKenna. It's about damn time you start showing it."

"I'm trying, Laila."

"She's trying too."

"Is she?" He chanced a look at Laila out of the corner of his eye, needing to hear it from Devy's best friend. Was she trying with him?

Did she think he wanted to keep things secret between them? Where had that gotten them before?

"She asked me yesterday if there was a right time to move on. I told her each relationship was different, and, being as she had no intentions of taking Chad back, she could probably dip her toes into the dating pool."

"I really hope I'm the only pool she's considering. I don't know how I'd feel if she dated others around here. This schoolboy crush is giving me sleepless nights."

"Ah, that's sort of romantic."

"Speaking of romance, how's the she shed Link built you last weekend? He told us all about it."

Her eyes widened with excitement. "You should see it. He built custom bookshelves, ran electricity, and bought me a new desk. It'll be perfect for a small meeting or if me and a few friends want to escape the guys while they're watching a game. He really does love me."

"He does," Hayden said. "Link said leaving you was the worst mistake of his life, and finding you again was like winning the lottery."

Laila put her hand over her heart. "I think I need to head home and show Link just how much I love him."

"TMI, Laila."

She set her hand on his shoulder. "Be good to our girl."

"I plan on it."

Hayden finished his beer, downed his water, and waited for Devorah to come out from the back room. When she emerged, he slid off the stool, tossed a twenty down onto the counter, and waited for her.

Outside, they fell into step as they walked toward Crow's.

"Where are we going?"

"It's a date," he told her. "Which means it's a surprise."

"What should I wear?"

"Clothes?"

Devorah rolled her eyes. "Fancy? Casual? Semicasual?"

"Oh, I see." He looked down at the jeans he wore. "Maybe wear one of your sundresses? It's a nice night, and we will be outside."

"Okay," she said as they arrived at Crow's. "And you're going to sit on the porch?"

He nodded and held up his hand. "Scout's honor."

She looked at him oddly. "Were you ever a Boy Scout?"

"Nope, but I promise to sit here until you're ready."

"All right, I need thirty. I'll leave the door open if you need to use the bathroom or something."

Thirty minutes later, she walked out of the house wearing a blue sundress and white strappy sandals, with her hair loose. Hayden groaned when a small breeze sent her perfume toward him. He had no choice but to put his hands in his pockets to keep them from picking her up and carrying her back into the house.

"We're walking," he told her as they took the steps down to the walkway. "It's not far."

"Okay. Probably best, since your truck isn't here, unless you planned to drive my SUV."

Hayden laughed. "I haven't seen you drive that since you got here."

"I do on Sundays, when I go grocery shopping, but other than that, what's the point? Everything is within walking distance."

"That's the nice thing about living in a small town."

"Oyster Bay isn't just small, it's like minute," she said as they crossed the street and headed toward the docks. "I think we give new meaning to the term 'small-town coastal living.'"

"I like it," Hayden said. "I'm glad I came back."

Devy paused and looked at him. "You know what, me too. On both accounts."

He ducked his head and smiled, appreciating that she was happy he was back as well. Her return to Chicago still lingered, though. "Really? Not thinking about heading back to Chicago?"

She shook her head. "I told Theo this morning to send the papers to Chad. I'm tired of him controlling my narrative."

"That's my girl," he said as he stepped toward her. Now would be the right time to kiss her and tell her how he felt, but people walking toward them had him stepping back.

They continued on toward their destination, and when the ship came into view, Devy gasped. A long vessel rested against the dock, tethered to the cleats, with white lights strung from the mast toward the land. Soft music played while people lingered on board. Some even danced.

"What is this?"

"This," Hayden said as he held his hand out for her to take, "is a floating bar. I saw a post about it last week and how it was going to be here and made a reservation."

"But you only asked me tonight."

"Because then you'd have less time to cancel on me."

Hayden gave the hostess his name, and they were led to a high-top table for two, facing the harbor. He held the chair for Devorah and offered his arm for support.

"I'm in awe," she said as she looked around. "This is such a neat idea, and the ambiance is very romantic."

"I'm glad you like it." He picked up the menu.

"Do you like sangria?" she asked him.

"I've never really had it, but I like a good red every now and again. Shall we order some? Says here we can get a pitcher."

"I'd love some. It would pair well with everything on the menu."

Hayden took her for her word. He'd only had red wine one other time, but he wasn't going to tell Devorah that, because he wanted her to be happy. If that meant he had to drink something he'd never had before and had no idea what it was, so be it.

They put their napkins on their laps, and both smiled when the waiter came to their table. Hayden ordered the pitcher of red sangria, along with their dinner order. Hayden went with a capicola and spicy honey pizza with mozzarella and pomodoro sauce, while Devorah chose roasted vegetable tacos with guajillo salsa, pickled jalapeños, and cotija cheese.

"Can we also order the chips and salsa, as well as two orders of the street corn?" she asked as she handed the menu to the waiter.

Hayden leaned closer to Devorah. "We just ordered a ton of food."

"I know. We can always take some home," she said. "Leftovers for breakfast."

He scrunched his nose. He loved pizza the next morning but wasn't sure about the one he'd ordered. Not to mention, he'd looked online for photos of the food but could not find any. He hoped the portions weren't tiny, and they'd end up starving later.

Their pitcher of sangria came. Hayden poured a glass for Devy and then one for himself. He held his glass up and said, "To a beautiful evening with an even more beautiful person. Cheers."

Devorah's cheeks flushed. "Cheers."

Hayden took a sip and then another one. He had to admit: the sangria was tasty. "I'm a fan," he said.

"I'm going to have to look up how to make it," she told him. "Colt needs better drinks at the bar."

"What does he have?"

"Beer and liquor. None of those low-calorie drinks, or hard seltzers. I told him I need to start ordering for the bar."

"How'd he take the suggestion?"

Devy shrugged slightly. "Doesn't seem to bother him. He joked that I'm slowly turning into the manager anyway, which was never my intention."

"I'm sure he appreciates having you there, knowing he has someone he can trust to help run things."

"I like it there. I never thought I would, but it's fun, and I've been able to reconnect with a lot of people."

Hayden took another sip, enjoying the fruitiness. "How's parade planning coming?"

"Really well, actually. I'm very thankful to Laila for asking me to join. It gives me a purpose, and I really do love planning. One of the big things is finding people to help every year. No one volunteers, and when the festival is on the verge of being canceled, a few people step up."

"People are the first to complain when their favorite event is canceled and the last to volunteer."

"You know, now that I'm here, I want Maren to experience Pearl of the Ocean and how it feels being on that float, with her friends and family waving to her from the sidewalk," she said. "I remember being up there, with the other Pearls on the float. We'd wave and people would yell out our names. We were front-page news. For the entire month, we'd do community service around town. That doesn't happen now. I find it sad that the Oyster Festival has lost some of the prestige it used to have.

"People from all over used to flock to our town for the week, booking every mom-and-pop motel and B and B within miles. I want to help change the mindset and bring back the way things used to be. Crowded streets, vendors selling their goods by the docks. The fire department giving demonstrations to groups of kids all throughout the day. We have a lot to offer people outside of OB."

"You can count on me, Mayor Crowley."

Devorah smirked and rolled her eyes. "It starts with volunteers. Without people helping, you can only do so much."

"Well, with you and Laila leading things, I'm sure this will be the best year yet. Until next year."

Devorah smiled. "I like the sound of that."

"Good, because I'm not sure Conor and I would like it in Chicago," he said as he picked up her hand and held it.

Hayden looked at her when she didn't respond.

"Wh-what? Why would you move there?"

"Devorah, in case you haven't figured it out yet, I like you. A lot."

"I like you too, Hayden." He swore her eyes twinkled when she spoke.

"Do you need more time?"

She shook her head. "No, I don't."

"Perfect."

◆ ◆ ◆

After dinner, Hayden took Devorah by the hand and led her onto the dance floor. He was determined to make this first date unforgettable. So far, the evening had been a triumph. The boat's ambiance oozed romance, the food was delectable, and he'd even savored the taste of the sangria. He held her as they swayed to the soft jazz coming from the sound system. The music wasn't overbearing. The cool breeze, mixing with the floral aroma and the salt air, made this the perfect night for them.

They shared a few glasses of sangria at the bar before deciding to call it a night. As they walked off the boat and onto the dock, Devorah slipped her hand into the crook of Hayden's elbow. She stopped walking, forcing Hayden to turn and face her.

"Thank you for tonight," she said. "I don't remember the last time I've had so much fun."

"Me too, Dev." Hayden stepped forward and trailed the back of his hand down the curve of her jaw. "You're so beautiful."

"You're biased."

He shook his head. "I'm not. Every guy in town thinks this. Everyone wants a chance with you."

"I—"

His heart did a double tap, and he dropped his hand from her cheek.

"All of this is wonderful." Her hand trailed down his arm until their hands linked together. She brought their hands up. "But there's something I need to know."

"What's that?"

"Are you over your fear of my father and brother?"

Hayden choked. Laila had been right. His actions in high school still plagued Devorah to this day. He nodded and came clean.

"Not asking you to be my girlfriend back then was a big mistake. I was in love with you and afraid to admit it to anyone because of Colt. Your dad I could've dealt with, but losing my best friend seemed unimaginable back in the day.

"What you don't know is after I left for college, I was so homesick and missing you that I came back and was ready to tell you how I felt, but I saw you with Chad." Hayden shrugged. "You looked happy."

"So, you just left?"

He nodded. "I went back to Idaho and met Sofia shortly after."

"Wow." Devorah shook her head. "Life could've been so different."

Hayden shrugged. "It could, but I don't have any regrets, Devy. I loved Sofia, the life we had, our son. I can't imagine my life without either of them."

"I feel the same way. Although Chad . . ." She trailed off.

"Here's the thing." Hayden stepped closer and once again trailed his fingers along her jaw. "You're the one I want to be with, and while sneaking around, making out in the park at night, or playing seven minutes in heaven is a lot of fun, kissing you in public—for everyone to see, for everyone to know you're mine—is much more thrilling."

"Yeah, I like that," she said breathlessly. "But back to what you said, how everyone wants a chance with me."

He nodded reluctantly.

"I only want a chance with you."

Hayden's smile spread from ear to ear. "You don't have to say it twice." With the music from the boat still echoing in the night air, Hayden pressed his lips to her soft, luscious, still-tasting-like-sangria lips. He pulled away and smiled again, and before he could even muster another move, she leaped into his arms and smashed her lips against his.

Devorah moaned, and Hayden pulled away from her. This wasn't the time nor the place for a serious make-out session. Unfortunately for both of them, they lived with their parents and had kids at home.

There wasn't anywhere they could go, and something about the camper he'd parked on his property didn't scream romance.

He also wasn't ready to drop her off at home.

"What's wrong?"

"Absolutely nothing," he told her as they started walking toward the parking lot.

"How's the house coming?"

"We finished the framing on the first floor already," he told her.

"Can I see it?"

"Uh, sure."

They walked in relative silence until they reached his property. He used the flashlight on his phone to give them a bit of light until he could reach the switch for the construction lights. He pressed the button for the lights and lit up his property.

"Wow."

"Yeah," he said, sighing. "It's a work in progress, but I'm happy with how it's coming along."

They walked up the temporary stairs and looked inside. He reacquainted her with the layout, pointing to the living room, dining room, and kitchen. "And back there, I think I'm definitely adding the three-season room off the kitchen."

"This is going to be such an amazing home."

Hayden agreed as he looked around and imagined what the space would look like once the construction was complete. He was proud of the house and the work he'd put into it, and he was learning a lot from Link.

"Hayden?"

"Mm-hmm," he hummed as he looked at Devorah.

"I think you should show me your camper."

He looked at the camper and frowned, and then he glanced at Dev. It took him a second for what she meant to set in, and when it did, he wondered if he had left a mess in there. Hayden wasn't going to tell her no.

Hayden held her hand as they went down the rickety steps and made their way across the yard. He unlocked the door, turned the light on, and then motioned for her to go ahead of him.

"It's not much," he said as he stepped in behind her. "Someplace for me to escape to."

"It's perfect," she said as she pulled him toward the bed.

Hayden inhaled her scent; it had been wafting off her all night and did something to him. Now he could smell the slightest bit of the coast combined with her perfume, and he stepped closer before nuzzling into her neck. Dev inhaled sharply and gripped his biceps as she leaned into him.

Hayden wrapped his fingers around her hips, squeezing as he trailed kisses down her neck to her shoulder. He felt her shudder but was sure she enjoyed his touch. "Do you want to stay awhile?" he asked, not sure what else to say. The moment could go a lot of different ways, and Hayden didn't want to scare her off just when things were moving in the right direction.

"Well, you arranged the sitter," she said jokingly. "Do I have time to stay for a while?" Her fingertips were trailing up and down along his triceps, making it hard to think.

Hayden chuckled and replied, "You definitely have time to . . . get comfortable." He glanced at the queen-size bed they were still standing next to and inhaled deeply, waiting for Dev to make the next move.

Dev pulled him closer and backed up until the back of her legs hit the bed. "Then let's get comfortable," she whispered, pulling him down with her gently.

Hayden could barely contain his desire as he moved over her, kissing her passionately and caging her underneath him. Dev scooted back and pulled Hayden between her legs, causing the hem of her dress to rise to her thighs.

As they continued to kiss, the heat between them rose to the level of full teenage make-out session, reminiscent of their teenage days. Back then, they'd spent many clandestine moments together, making out and grinding on each other. But they never went further than touching each other over their clothes.

Is that first or second base?

Dev began pulling at the buttons on Hayden's shirt, slowly opening it to reveal the soft patch of chest hair.

"I want you," she whispered between kisses.

Hayden wanted to be perfectly sure he'd heard her. "And what do you want? Tell me." His voice was husky and laden with lust. He wanted her in more ways than he could count.

Dev gave him a bashful smile. "I want you—all of you. This," she said as she cupped him.

His eyes rolled as he fought to gain composure. He couldn't lose it now, not with the girl of his dreams under him. Somehow, he found the strength to turn on the charm.

"That's my girl." Hayden grabbed Dev's hips and rolled them both over so Dev was straddling him. His cock strained against his jeans, but the friction of having her on top of him was worth every agonizing moment.

She leaned over him and finished unbuttoning his shirt, then began trailing kisses down his chest and back up under his earlobe. He was hanging on by a thread, running his hands up her thighs under the dress she was wearing.

Then, a moment of panic struck him. Protection. He didn't have any. Hell, he wasn't totally convinced she'd even go out with him tonight, and even when she'd said yes, he definitely didn't assume they'd be half-naked in his camper. "Dev?"

She panted, still rocking her body gently over his erection, which was driving him mad. "Hayden."

"I don't have any protection," he confessed. "I didn't think—"

Dev bit her bottom lip, then grinned before she let out a small laugh. "I do."

Confused, Hayden asked, "You do? Were you expecting . . . did you think . . . you didn't know I was going to ask you out . . ." He didn't know how to feel until Dev hopped off him and grabbed her purse and began to dig inside.

She held up a condom like she was raising a paddle at an auction she knew she'd win and laughed. "Laila gave it to me before I left the bar with you."

"Remind me to thank Laila later. Now, come here. I want to finally make love to you."

Hayden toyed with the ends of her dress and looked at her for permission. With her help, he pulled it over her head, revealing a matching bra and panties that were also the same shade of blue as her dress.

He swallowed hard as he took her in, gripping the sundress in his hand until the silver packet caught his attention. "Jesus, Devorah. You're so fucking sexy." He worked to remove his shirt while Devy undid his belt, stopping to kiss him. To tease him.

With his jeans undone, she gripped his cock in her small hand, causing Hayden to hiss. He reached around her and undid her bra, letting her round breasts free. He settled her back on the bed, took his jeans off, and then returned to her, immediately sucking one of her puckered nipples into his mouth.

Dev moaned and arched her back slightly while gripping the sheets beneath her. The sounds coming from her only drove Hayden more, and he knew he wasn't going to be able to drag this out much longer. He gently ran his finger over her now-soaked panties, gently stroking her and moving to give his attention to her other nipple. Gently pushing her panties to the side, he slid one finger inside and pumped lightly while rubbing her clit with his thumb.

As Dev began to spasm around him, she cried out. "Oh my God, Hayden." She panted harshly and sat up a bit. "Put that condom on. Right now."

Hayden stopped, grabbed the condom, ripped the foil open, and did as he was told while Devorah rid herself of the last garment she had on. He wanted her with every bit of himself but had to check with her one last time before there was no going back.

"Are you sure?"

One word was all she said. "Yes." She leaned back, welcoming him.

He hovered above her again, his cock at her entrance. The anticipation in her glistening eyes was unmistakable, and he thrust forward, letting her warmth surround him. She moaned loudly and began to rock her hips to meet his rhythm.

"That's my girl," he said as she began to tighten around him, her climax near.

"Don't stop!" she called out, willing him to pump into her with the rolling of her hips into his. Unable to contain himself any longer, he rubbed circles on her clit while chasing his release, and they yelled out together, rocking the camper as they finished as one.

Twenty-Three

Devorah

They lay there with the blanket draped between their legs. Devy rested her head on Hayden's chest while her fingers rubbed back and forth over his smattering of chest hair. He was only the second man she had ever been with, and she was surprised by how good she felt, by how Hayden had made her feel. Alive and sexy. Wanted and satisfied.

It was her idea to come into the camper, but not something she had planned. It could've been the sangria talking or her heart. Either way, she was happy. She wanted to be with him, to explore what a relationship with him could be like.

The only thing holding her back was fear. She was afraid to give him her heart. Not that she expected him to hurt her. It was more her than anything. Chad had really done a number on her, causing her to have trust issues.

Hayden moved onto his side to face her. He twirled the end of her hair around his finger and then kissed her forehead. They hadn't said much since they'd made love. Mostly nuzzling and touching each other. Words seemed to fail her, and she didn't want to say something stupid. She didn't know what to do in this situation. Her first time had been in the back of Chad's car, and then they'd sneaked around until college. Now that she was an adult, she couldn't help but feel like she was sneaking around again.

In a sense, they were. Neither of them could go to each other's houses. What would their parents think? Their children? Deep down, Devy knew Chad would somehow get Maren to spill. Devorah didn't understand the hold he had on her. She wanted it to break. For him to go away and live his life with Ester.

One day.

"As much as I want to stay in this space with you," Hayden said, combing his fingers through her hair, "and make love to you again, we should get home."

"But here, we're free, and it's quiet."

He chuckled a bit. "I actually think if my neighbors were outside, they might have heard us."

Devy's cheeks burned. "Good thing it's dark then, and no one will see us doing the walk of shame."

"There's zero shame in what we've done. I don't have any regrets."

"Me neither." She sat up on her elbows and kissed him. "This was the most exceptional evening. Thank you."

"Thank you," he said. "We'll make plans with the kids for tomorrow. I read in my single-parent handbook that it's important to include the children in dates."

"It's a good thing Maren and Conor are friends."

"Definitely."

They got up, dressed, and began walking toward Crow's, holding hands the entire way. She loved the way her hand fit in his, and also loved how Hayden was taller than her. Chad was her height, and he didn't like it when she wore heels. Now, if she wanted, she could put a pair on, and she'd still have to look up at Hayden.

When they reached Crow's porch, Hayden kissed her lightly on the lips and said he'd see her in the morning. Devorah waved to him when she got inside and then watched him walk away. She closed the door, kept her hand on it for a moment, wishing the night didn't have to end, and then went to find her father.

Crow sat in his recliner, with the news playing on the television.

"How was your night?"

"Maren and I are a formidable team," he told her. "We beat Lee and Conor at checkers, Monopoly, and some other card game she taught us. We're taking our show on the road."

Listening to him describe their night brought tears to her eyes.

"Why are you crying?" he asked as he kicked the recliner closed and stood. "Did he hurt you?"

She shook her head and let the tears fall. "I'm happy you and Maren have bonded. It means the world to me."

Crow brought Devorah into his arms and hugged her tightly. He continued to hold her until she'd stopped crying.

"I'm trying, Devorah. I know I messed up with you, but Maren's my second chance. Right now, I'd like to thank that horrible husband of yours for screwing up because I'm the victor in the situation. I have my daughter back and now my granddaughter."

"I love you, Daddy."

"I love you too." He pulled back a little. "Did you have a good night?"

"I did," she said as she wiped her tears away. "Hayden took me out to this restaurant on a ship. It goes from port to port, so it's pretty unique. After dinner, we danced and then we walked around town, remembering how awesome it was to grow up here."

"Really?" His eyebrow popped up. "I recall many times while you were growing up, yelling and screaming about how you hated it here and couldn't wait to move."

Devorah shrugged. "That was before I became a mother. Now I love it. Good night, Crow."

"Good grief, I can't keep up with you kids and your ever-changing minds," he mumbled. "Good night, Devorah."

She went upstairs, sneaked into her daughter's room, and crawled into bed with her. The slight dip in the bed caused Maren to roll into her mom.

"Mom?"

"Go back to sleep, my sweet girl."

Maren opened her eyes and looked at her mom. "Did you have a nice dinner?"

"I did. If the boat we ate on is still there in the morning, I'll take you to see it. Did you have fun with Crow?"

Maren nodded. "Grandpa is a lot of fun."

Devorah wished she could've had this version of her father when she was younger, especially when she was struggling with her mother's death.

"We went out for ice cream, but I'm not supposed to tell you."

"That's okay. Let's not keep secrets, okay?"

"Okay, Mommy."

"Go back to sleep. I'll see you in the morning."

"Good night, love you."

"Love you more."

Devorah kissed Maren and then went into the bathroom to take a shower. While the water ran, she undressed and looked at herself in the mirror. She wasn't sure if she expected her body to be different or if there would be some remnant of what she and Hayden had done, but she found none except for a bit of beard burn.

She stood under the hot water for what felt like five minutes before she washed her hair and body. Every time she closed her eyes, Hayden was there, moving his body over the top of hers, bringing her to ecstasy. The way he kissed and held her, the way he made her feel when he was inside her, the way he brought her to new heights that she didn't know existed, all made her feel like she wasn't broken. That Chad hadn't destroyed the very essence that made her, her.

Devorah rinsed, shut the water off, and got out. She wrapped herself in a towel and went into her bedroom, dressing in a tank top and shorts. Before she got into bed, she towel-dried her hair and doused herself with lotion.

She turned on the bedside lamp and crawled under her covers. It had been over a month since she'd looked at any videos, and tonight, she felt brave enough to do so. Devorah lowered the volume and opened the app.

Devorah watched five videos before her anxiety spiked. She closed the app, not wanting to come across anything having to do with her humiliation, Chad's affair, or even a glimpse of what Ester was up to. Devy wanted to move on and get past everything, but that didn't mean she had to watch it play out on her phone.

She set her phone down on the charger and reached for the light switch. Her hand stilled when she heard a loud thump and then something crash into the floor downstairs. Quietly, she got out of bed, tip-toed across the floor, and opened her door a smidge. She listened for footsteps.

Nothing.

Opening the door farther, she walked as deftly as possible, avoiding the squeaky floorboards. She and Colt had long learned which boards would alert Crow downstairs. At the top of the stairs, she peered down and saw the hall light was on.

Had she left it on?

The house was silent except for the ticking grandfather clock in the living room. Devy descended the stairs, against her better judgment.

"Dad?" she called out when she came to the second-to-last stair, figuring if she needed to retreat, she could. She heard nothing.

"Crow?" she yelled louder. If he had left, wouldn't he have said something or at least texted her?

Devy finally took the last two steps and turned toward the kitchen. Cordelia ran past her and started barking wildly. She saw his foot and part of his leg sticking out from behind the counter, a place it shouldn't be. Rushing into the kitchen, she dropped to her knees and shook her father.

"Crow?" She then said his name louder and continued jostling his shoulders. "Oh God. Daddy, wake up. Please don't do this to me."

Devorah held her ear to his heart and heard nothing. She felt for a pulse, and again, nothing. Tears streamed down her cheeks and onto her father, who lay still.

She ran to the phone and fumbled with the handle. Her fingers shook as she pressed 911. She went back to her dad and knelt beside him.

"Emergency services, what's your emergency?"

"I need help. It's my dad. I think he had a heart attack."

"Have you started chest compressions?"

"No, but I am now." She cradled the phone between her ear and shoulder and pushed on his chest, the way she'd learned from a cardiopulmonary resuscitation class she had taken years ago. She, like many, thought she'd never use CPR again and had never gone back to recertify.

The operator asked other questions and assured Devorah that an ambulance was on the way. When she saw the lights pull into the driveway, she dropped the phone and ran to the door.

"He's in the kitchen, straight ahead."

From there, she stood and watched men rip open her father's shirt, then push and press things to his chest. Tears continued to stream as the men pressed paddles to his chest, let them recharge, and then did it again. And again.

And again.

Maren came down the stairs, and before she could see what the medics were doing to her grandfather, Devorah wrapped her daughter in her arms and held her head against her shoulder.

"You don't want to see this," she whispered. "Just let me hold you."

Maren cried. She may have been nine, but she knew.

Behind them, Cordelia whimpered. She'd started off as Colt's dog, but she'd quickly turned into Crow's.

"Ma'am," a medic said as he came to her. "We're sorry . . ." Devorah heard nothing after those words. She'd lost her father, a man she'd had a troubled relationship with until recently. Things were better between them, more loving, nurturing. Crow had been happy she and Maren were there, and he'd wanted them to stay.

Devorah continued to hold Maren in her arms as they wheeled Crow out of the house, a white sheet covering his body. The medic left the front door open, and so did Devy. She didn't move or get up to close it until the lights had disappeared.

Now what was she going to do?

"Mommy?" Maren's voice was soft, scared.

"Yeah?"

"Is Grandpa going to be okay?"

More tears streamed down her cheeks, and she choked on a sob. She shook her head and somehow found her voice enough to tell her daughter, "No."

Footsteps thundered on the porch steps, and Colt shot through the open door. "What happened?"

Devorah looked at her brother, and she could tell by the way his face dropped that he knew. She wouldn't have to say the words. She wasn't sure she even could.

Colt leaned against the wall and slid down, his own tears coming in hot streams.

It wasn't only Colt, Devorah, and Maren who'd lost someone at that moment; their entire community had.

Devorah finally asked Maren to go upstairs. She didn't have to go back to sleep, but Devy and Colt had to talk and take care of adult things. Things a nine-year-old didn't need to hear about or be a part of.

When she heard the bedroom door shut upstairs, Devorah recounted the noise she'd heard and how she'd crept downstairs. "If I wasn't afraid, maybe I would've gotten to him sooner."

"Don't you even blame yourself, Dev. He didn't exactly take care of himself."

She nodded, but the guilt was there, building with no end in sight. Just when she thought she'd found her footing, her father had to die on her.

Now what?

Devorah brought her knees to her chest and sobbed. Despite their strained relationship, he'd been a rock for her the past few weeks, reminding her to put herself first and to grasp all the happiness coming her way.

Colt moved next to his sister and wrapped her in his arms. "It's going to be okay," he said to her, but she didn't believe him. She didn't know how.

Crow hadn't been gone an hour before the news spread, and people began showing up. One by one, the Crafty Cathys entered the house on Main Street and took over while Colt, Dev, and Maren mourned.

When Hayden walked in, he found Devorah on the couch, with her knees tucked under her. She was exhausted, and her eyes burned from crying. He sat down next to her and said nothing. He didn't have to, because everyone else in the house had said it already.

"I'm sorry for your loss."

Twenty-Four

Hayden

In the week since Tremaine "Crow" Crowley—the long-standing and beloved sheriff of Oyster Bay—passed away, life in town had come to a standstill. Everyone mourned the loss of Crow. Residents and businesses on Main Street draped black coverings over their windows, and the governor had given the town special permission to fly their flags at half staff. Crow's passing had made statewide news, and thousands were expected to attend his funeral.

Hayden finished tying his tie and then helped Conor with his. Hayden could count on one hand how many funerals he'd attended in his lifetime: five. Both sets of grandparents and his wife's. He felt odd knowing the number off the top of his head, and the feeling was compounded when he looked at Conor. He was nine, and this was his second within a year.

The McKenna family walked to the high school, where Crow's services would be held. It was the only place in town big enough to accommodate the masses of mourners coming. Every law enforcement agency in the state sent at least one delegate, if not more. Crow had friends on every force and in every emergency service industry, as evidenced by the coast guard ship docked at the pier, blocking everyone's view of the harbor.

Local people walked to the service, leaving parking for out-of-towners. Hayden had offered his land up for overflow parking, which the Crafty Cathys appreciated. The CC Club handled everything, with Colt's and Devorah's permission. The club, for all the gossip they spread, knew how to get things done.

Since Crow's passing, his home had been a revolving door of people coming and going throughout the day; the phone rang off the hook, and food deliveries arrived almost every hour. People came to pay their respects and leave cards, and, with the sheer number of bouquets on every free surface of the house, they made the inside look and smell like a florist's shop.

Standing on the outside—Hayden.

He hadn't seen Devorah since the night her father passed away, and they'd barely spoken. He'd chalked it up to her not having a moment of peace. It was easier to think that than the alternative. When he saw Colt, he'd told Hayden that Devy had locked herself in her room, that she barely came out to eat, and that Maren wasn't going to school.

Hayden worried about Maren and hoped her lack of attendance over the past week wouldn't be something Chad could use against Devorah. The last thing she needed was to give her ex any ammunition to use in their divorce.

Of course, with Crow gone, who knew if she would even stay in Oyster Bay?

That thought plagued him. Hayden was serious when he'd told Dev that he and Conor would move to Chicago if she and Maren went back. Devy probably thought he was joking, and maybe at the time he was. No one knew Crow would have a massive heart attack and die, though, and Hayden didn't want to lose Devy. Not when his high school crush had finally turned into reality.

Staff at the high school had converted the gymnasium into an auditorium of sorts with a podium at one end, numerous white chairs facing it, and the bleachers pulled out. The first ten rows of chairs had been reserved for friends and family. Those people had received a special notice, hand delivered by someone from the CC Club, letting them know they'd sit with family.

Hayden showed the attendant at the door his invite, stuffed it back into the inside pocket of his suit jacket, and then led Conor to their designated row. His parents hadn't made it past the school entrance before people wanted to talk to Dr. McKenna about their heart health. It didn't matter that Lee had retired; he would always be the one people trusted.

Devorah and Maren sat in the front row. Both wore black dresses. Hayden was about to go up to her when he saw Chad walk by. He bent and kissed Devy on her cheek and then picked Maren up and held her in his lap.

Clearly, this wasn't the first time they'd seen Chad. Not by the way Maren reacted. If he'd just shown up, she would've been excited and surprised to see her father.

She wasn't.

And neither was Devorah.

As much as Hayden wanted to tell himself that what he'd seen was nothing, that it meant nothing, a nagging voice in the back of his head told him otherwise. How come he hadn't heard Chad was in town? Certainly, this type of news would've spread like wildfire. The man who'd cheated on Oyster Bay's Pearl of the Ocean had returned to town, a man whose mistress had publicly humiliated her, and no one had anything to say?

Hayden dug his fingers into his legs as anger threatened to erupt. A funeral honoring Devorah's father wasn't the time nor the place. Neither was after the service. How long would he have to wait to confront her? To demand answers?

Wasn't he at least owed the basic "Hey, thanks for the fuck, but I'm going back to my ex" talk?

His father crossed in front of him, blocking his view for a brief second.

"What's eating you?" Lee asked.

"What? Nothing."

"Bullshit. You look like you're about to put someone in the coffin next to Crow. What's going on?"

Hayden kept his eyes focused on the back of Chad's head. Lee was right. Hayden would like to put Chad in a coffin. Just not next to Crow's. He wouldn't damn the man through eternity with the person responsible for breaking his daughter's heart.

"Ah," Lee said. "You feel you should be up front with her?"

"No, it's not that," Hayden said through gritted teeth. "It's the man next to her."

"Colt?"

Hayden shook his head and looked around the room for Colt, spotting him in the corner speaking to a police officer. "That's Chad Campbell."

"No shit? Pretty ballsy showing up at Crow's funeral. He's liable to come back to life and beat his son-in-law."

"I wish he would," Hayden said. Then he wouldn't have to spend the night in jail for doing it himself.

A police officer stepped to the podium, and everyone rushed to take their seats and quieted down. The man spoke about why they'd gathered there today and asked that if people needed to excuse themselves, to please use the gym doors off to the right or left. His last request was that everyone silence their cell phones.

One of the local preachers took the podium and began Crow's service. By the end, there wasn't a dry eye in the house, including Hayden's. For as gruff as Crow was, he was going to be missed, and not just by the community, but by his family.

Crow's family stood, and, led by Colt, they walked to Crow's coffin and said their last goodbyes.

Chad did not. He stood there and waited for Maren and Devorah to return, and then he held his daughter's hand and placed his other hand on the small of Devorah's back and guided them out of the gymnasium.

One by one, rows were excused. Some went to Crow's coffin, while others made their way to the cafeteria, where the wake was being held.

Hayden thought about leaving, heading back to his parents' place, where he could shut everyone out of his mind.

Only, doing so would serve no purpose. He wasn't going to stop thinking about Devorah and Chad. Or be able to forget how she hadn't spoken to him all week. Or how Chad was in town, and his presence wasn't a surprise to anyone. Except Hayden.

The receiving line to get into the gymnasium had already backed up down the hall because of all the people waiting to pay their respects. Hayden grew irritated, but he knew that if he didn't go to the wake, Devorah would ask him why he hadn't been there. Or would she?

Would she even notice he wasn't there?

Probably not, with Chad there.

"Behave," his father's voice said in his ear. He turned and glared at his father.

"I'm at a funeral," he told him. "It's not like I'm going to punch the guy."

"Or her," Lee said. "She's going through a lot right now and needs support. She doesn't need you pissing on her to mark your territory."

As if the thought crossed my mind.

When it was Hayden's turn, he shook Colt's hand and then pulled him in for a hug. "I'm so sorry, man."

"Me too. Nothing feels the same without him."

Hayden understood.

Devorah was next.

Their gazes me, hers with unshed tears. Hayden pulled her into his arms and nuzzled her neck. "I'm here if you need me."

She nodded against him.

Before she could pull away, he kissed her just below her ear.

"Hey, Conor," Devy said.

"I'm sorry about your dad," he told her. "We're the same now." Hayden turned and watched Conor interact with Dev. She crouched to his level.

"What do you mean?"

Conor shrugged. "My mom went to heaven too."

Devy smiled softly and tugged on the end of Conor's jacket. "We are the same, aren't we?"

Conor nodded, and Devy stood, meeting Hayden's eyes. She didn't smile or offer any other words.

When Maren saw Conor, she hugged him. "I'm sorry about your grandpa," Conor said.

"I'm so sad. But I'm also happy. Weird, right?"

Hayden paid attention to Maren and Conor's interaction.

"Why are you happy?" Conor asked.

"Because my daddy's here, and we're going back to Chicago. Maybe you can visit someday."

"Sure," Conor said, without understanding the magnitude of her words. Hayden took Conor's hand and led him out of the cafeteria. They didn't need to stick around and wait for their hearts to break anymore. They'd had enough in their lifetime.

Hayden and Conor walked to the park. With everyone at the funeral, the space was empty. Hayden sat down on a swing with Conor next to him.

"Dying is weird."

"What makes you say that?" Hayden asked.

"I dunno." Conor shrugged. "When you die, people throw you a big party."

"It's not exactly a party, bud. People want to pay their respects. It's what we do. Sometimes the gatherings are small, like your mom's. But other times, like with Crow, they're big."

"How come Crow's is so big?"

"Because he grew up here. He was the sheriff for a very long time. Everyone knew him, and a lot of people loved him. Or they love Colt, Devorah, and Maren."

"Is that why Maren's dad is here?"

He had no idea.

"I think so." Hayden wanted to know, though, and he wanted an explanation. It was one thing for Chad to be there, but to act like they were a family or together was a whole other ballpark. He was in love with Devorah and had known it for a while but hadn't found the right moment to tell her. And now Chad had sat next to her and Maren, in a spot Hayden thought he would be in.

"Do you think Maren will say goodbye before she moves away?" Conor asked, sadly.

Not if Chad had anything to do with it.

Hayden sighed. He had a hard time fathoming how Dev would want to go back to Chicago. She had started to build a life in Oyster Bay. She had friends, a purpose, and . . . him. They had each other, and Hayden wasn't going to let her go so easily. He'd already told her that if she went back, he and Conor would follow. Hayden intended to keep his word to her. There was no way he'd let her go.

"Yeah, I'll make sure you get a chance to say goodbye to her. You were a good friend to her. She doesn't want to forget you."

Conor was sad, and Hayden's heart broke for his son. He watched him push the swing back and forth. Conor had known far too much hurt in his young life. Hayden would be damned if he was going to lose his best friend. When the time was right, he'd talk to Devy and get to the bottom of what Maren had said.

Before it was too late again.

After the parking lot had started to clear and cars headed out of town, Hayden and Conor walked back home. Lee and Darcy were there with dinner in the oven. As soon as Hayden walked in, Darcy hugged him.

"Where have you boys been?"

"The park," Conor told her. "We had to do some deep thinking."

Hayden tried not to laugh. His son was wise beyond his years.

"Is that so?" Darcy asked.

Hayden nodded.

"And?"

"And what?" He looked at his mom in confusion.

"And are you going to go get her, or are you going to let that sorry excuse for a man take her away from us again?"

Hayden's eyes widened at his mother's outburst. He opened his mouth to say something and then shut it.

"Don't act like a fish looking for water, Hayden McKenna. Go get Devorah, tell her you love her, and, by all means, don't let her go. I can't bear you or her suffering any more heartbreak. You've both had enough to last a lifetime."

Hayden looked at his dad for some help.

"Don't look at me, son," Lee said as he checked the oven. "The longer you stand there, the longer it's going to take you to get over to Crow's and save the girl." Lee closed the oven and looked at his son. "If I were you, I'd run."

Hayden ran.

Twenty-Five

Devorah

Devorah ran out of steam before the wake was over. She was past the point of exhaustion. Her emotions were all over the place, and she was tired of Chad hovering over her. The fact that he was even there grated on what nerves she had left. But she couldn't very well toss him out on his cheating ass. Not with Maren there. Even though that was exactly what Devorah wanted to do.

Growing up, she'd always loved her name, even though she couldn't buy already-monogrammed items at the store, like notebooks, pencils, and a slew of other things. None of the material things mattered because everyone knew her name. And when they mispronounced it, which was easy to do, she calmly corrected them by saying, "It's Debra but with a *v*."

Now, when Chad said her name, her blood boiled and her skin itched. Violence flashed through her mind, images of her hands around his neck and her violently shaking him until he stopped talking. That was all she wanted, for him to shut his mouth so she could think, and for him to stop the incessant "Things will be better" line he said every ten seconds.

Nothing would be better with her father gone. Not a single thing. He was the glue that held them all together, whether Crow knew it or not. He was the one Devy had turned to after her husband betrayed her, even though they had a rocky relationship. Crow was there when she needed him the most.

Devorah stood in the middle of the living room. Crow's recliner sat there, worn out by age and use. From there, she could see the dining room table. Every square inch of the mahogany wood had a vase of flowers on it. The strong and sometimes pungent odor of flowers permeated throughout the house and made the place smell like a funeral home. She wanted them gone and didn't care where they went.

Without even going into the kitchen, she knew what she'd find—food. More food than they could eat. This death was different from her mother's. Crow was different. He had touched so many lives. Both good and bad. People would miss him. The community would mourn and honor him the best they could.

Devorah longed for one more day with him. Just one more hug. Just one more time hearing him tell her he loved her. Just as she had when her mother died. That was all she'd wanted when she was younger, one more moment with her mom, to ask her every important question she could think of about becoming and being a woman.

Was that too much to ask?

It seemed it was.

The front door opened. Devorah wiped at an errant tear and turned to face her soon-to-be ex-husband and her daughter. Maren rushed to her mom and wrapped her arms around her. Dev patted her hair down and then bent to kiss the top of Maren's head.

"Hey, why don't you take Cordelia upstairs or go outside and play?"

"I want to stay with you and Daddy."

"I know, but right now, your dad and I need to talk."

"Adult stuff?"

Dev nodded, and Maren rolled her eyes. She let go of her mom and crossed her arms, letting out a huff. "I can't wait until I'm an adult, and then I can have adult conversations."

"Oh, how I wish I could've recorded you saying as such so I can remind you of it later," Devorah said. She touched the tip of her index finger to Maren's nose. "Go let your imagination run wild in the back. I'll be out in a minute."

Devy watched her daughter go to Chad and then head into the kitchen, with the dog following behind. She waited for the door to close before she opened her mouth.

"You need to go. I don't know why you're here, anyway. It's not like you were close to my father."

"Devorah," he said as he moved toward her. "Tremaine was my father-in-law. Of course I'd be here for you and Maren."

"Crow," Dev said quietly.

"What about him?"

"That was his name. No one ever called him Tremaine. Especially his friends."

"Crow's a silly old nickname."

"Not to him, Chad. It was his name, and as his son-in-law, you should've known that. But the truth is, you didn't, because he didn't like you, and he wouldn't want you in his home."

"Devorah . . ."

"Stop saying my name. You give me the ick when you say it."

"All right. What do you want me to call you?"

"I don't. I want you to go."

"Not until we talk."

"We have nothing to talk about." She wanted a glass of water but didn't want Maren to hear them talking. Knowing her daughter, she would be sitting under the window, trying to listen. Devy held her hand to her forehead and sighed. "Please just go."

"Listen," Chad said as he walked closer to her. "I know I did some things—"

The way he said "things" had Dev laughing.

"And I'm paying the price by my family packing their things and coming out here to stay."

"Are you kidding me right now?"

Chad shook his head. "Have you ever known me to joke about my family?"

Devorah stared at him for a long time.

"Yes, actually, when you cheated on me with Ester. No, I take that back. My father said you shit on your family."

"I made a mistake," Chad said, pleadingly. He clasped his hands together, as if he was about to pray, when in reality he was begging. "I regret everything that's happened, and I'm sorry. Can we please sit down and talk?"

She shook her head but sat in Crow's recliner anyway. Chad sat across from her, perched on the edge of the couch as if he was going to make a run for it.

"Talk," she said.

"When I got the papers . . ." He paused. "It was like an anvil had been set on my chest. We had the perfect life, and then—"

"You slept with my best friend, and then you told me you were moving in together."

Chad hung his head. "Regardless, when I saw those papers, I realized this wasn't what I wanted, and I knew I had to make a change."

"And Crow's death just happened to be your light bulb moment?"

"Is there a more perfect time to bring your family home?"

"Excuse me?"

"Come on, Devorah. You can't honestly tell me you plan to stay here."

She nodded, and he stood.

"And do what? Bartend at the Lazy Lamb?"

"It's better than being the laughingstock of the PTA, Chad. How can you expect me to show my face there, huh? After what you did."

"Because it's better than living in this time-forgotten town."

"No, it's really not."

"I didn't want to do this, but you're leaving me no choice. You and Maren are coming back to Chicago with me. We'll be a family again, go to counseling. We'll work on our marriage."

"The hell we will," she said. "To all of it. I'm not leaving Oyster Bay, and neither is Maren. We're happy here. She's thriving—"

"Is she?" he asked with a tilt of his head. "She tells me otherwise."

Dev scoffed. "No, Chad. It's because you tell her otherwise. You twist and turn words to suit your narrative. Not mine. Not hers. Maren is happy." She stressed the word "happy," hoping he would finally understand. "She loves it here and talks about the future. She's an integral part of a baseball team, and her grades are stellar. Maren matters here.

"The only time she talks about going back to Chicago is when you call. That's it. She never mentions it because it's not what she wants. Sure, she'll tell you this now because she's nine and wants her parents to be together. It's what every kid her age wants.

"But do you honestly think I'd take her back there so people can point fingers at her? Everyone knows what you did, Chad. It's not a secret. It's not something we can sweep under the rug. Do you really want her going to school with Rita? And having their classmates point fingers at them?"

Devorah got up and paced. She finally went into the kitchen, looked out the window, and saw her daughter on the tire swing Crow had put up for Maren just days ago.

Her father. His voice rang out in her head: *Stand up for yourself, Devorah.* She fought back a wave of tears. Crow hadn't been gone long, and she missed him fiercely. There was no way she was going to let him down now. She took a centering breath and pushed away the tears. Chad would think they were for him. He hadn't earned any more of her tears, and she'd be damned if she was going to let him see her cry.

After drinking a glass of water, she went back into the other room with her head held high.

"Sign the papers, Chad."

"Devorah."

She shook her head. "I'm not leaving here, and neither is Maren. I don't care if I've been here three minutes, three months, or three years. This is our home, and this is where we're staying."

"So that's it, huh? I just leave my family behind?"

Dev pinched the bridge of her nose momentarily and then looked at her ex. "You left us behind the minute you thought about sleeping with Ester. The second the thought entered your mind, you should've reminded yourself of your vows. But you didn't. We didn't matter then, and we don't matter now."

"That's not true."

Devorah had had enough. She went to her purse and pulled out her phone, ignoring the slew of text messages and missed calls. She opened the video app, went to Ester's username, and pressed the first video there, posted two days ago. Dev pressed play, then turned the phone around to show Chad. Someone had sent it to her the other day. That someone, she was sure of, was Ester.

The video showed Chad walking to his car with his overnight bag, and Ester talking:

"Babe, where are you going?"

"To a funeral."

"Whose?"

Chad shook his head as he stared at Devorah. "Turn it off."

"No, I want you to watch and tell me why in the hell you think I should go back there and subject myself to this. Subject our daughter to this?"

"My former pain-in-the-ass father-in-law." Chad's voice rang out.

"Sounds like a waste of time."

"Thank God I can't see you kissing her. The sound effects are enough," Dev said as she continued to hold her phone out and glare at Chad.

"Hurry back. My kitty will miss you."

The video went blank and restarted.

"Two days ago, Chad. And here you sit, telling me how you made a mistake and want to be a family."

"Devorah . . ."

"Are you still sleeping with her? Living with her?"

Chad's silence was deafening.

"You disgust me, Chad. My life with you has been nothing but a lie." She shook her head. "I want you to sign the papers and leave. Maren stays here. I will fight you with everything I have, and believe me, it's a lot more than you've given me credit for."

"You're making a mistake."

"Oh well. At least it'll be my mistake. One I can live with and won't be judged for."

Chad went to his bag and pulled out the papers. He handed them to Dev.

"You already signed them?"

He nodded. "I had to try."

"And you failed," she told him.

He went upstairs to Maren's room to get his things. While he was up there, Devorah went to the back door. She opened it and found Maren still on the swing and Cordelia lying on the ground, watching her every move.

"Are you done having adult conversations?"

Dev nodded. "I am. I don't plan to have another one for a very long time."

"Phew," Maren said as she came toward the house. "Maybe I don't want to have them when I'm older. They take forever."

Dev held out her hand for her daughter and pulled her in for a hug. "Never grow up," she told Maren. "It's a trap."

Inside, Maren saw Chad's bag by the door. "Are we leaving?"

"No, just your dad."

"What? No. He said we were going back to Chicago." Maren ran up the stairs, yelling for her father. She returned, moments later, with her backpack. "Where is he?"

"I'm right here, Maren. What are you doing?"

"I'm going with you. Last night you said you were taking us home, that we belonged in Chicago."

Chad looked up at Dev, who turned away. Would he tell her he was still with Ester?

"Look, sunshine. You'll come back to Chicago soon. Once I get settled."

"What does that mean?"

"It means Daddy's going through some stuff right now."

"With Ester? Are you living with her? I don't want to live with her, Daddy." Maren tugged on Chad's shirt. "Please. You promised. You said we were going to be a family. You, me, and Mommy. You said."

"I never said your mommy, princess. Me, you, Ester, and Rita."

Devorah saw the realization in Maren's face as she stepped back from her father. Her head shook slowly. "I hate you. I hate you," she said as she hit him with her fist. "I hate Ester and Rita and you. I hate you so much." She screamed the last one at him with tears streaming down her face. "You're a liar and I hate you."

Chad looked at Devorah. "A little help?"

She shook her head. "No. I'm not your savior, Chad. You did this. You broke her, but I'll sure as hell fix her and give her the unconditional love she deserves without lying to her."

Chad said nothing. He picked up his bag and headed out the door.

Maren stood in the hallway with her backpack on, sobbing. Divorce was hard on kids, only made worse when one of the parents had chosen a new family.

TWENTY-SIX

HAYDEN

Going to Crow's meant Hayden had something to lose.

When Sofia passed away, Hayden had gone through the "I'm never going to love again" stage. Mostly, he meant it. He didn't want Conor to get hurt. Hayden didn't care about his own well-being, only his son's. He could easily live the next ten years without dating or being in a relationship.

That was, until he ran into Devorah.

She was the shift for him. The light at the end of a never-ending tunnel of blackness. Even when she had her darkest days, his were bright because of her. Without even knowing it, she had given him hope. Devy gave him something to look forward to each day.

She was also a challenge.

Hayden knew she wasn't ready for any type of relationship, at least not the type he'd want. He'd already had his time to mourn the loss of his wife and had come to terms with his future as a single dad. Her wounds were fresh and still bleeding. Coupled with the anxiety of knowing that everyone knew about everyone else's business, Devy needed time to heal.

He'd hoped to give her that time, but with Chad in town and showing everyone at Crow's funeral that they were a family, Hayden's time was running out. Taking most of Lee's advice, Hayden hopped into his truck and sped over to Crow's. He parked in what he considered his normal spot along the curb and stared at Chad's car, nestled behind Devorah's. They matched with their Illinois license plates, which squeezed Hayden's heart a bit. He also wondered why the busy hotshot finance guy had driven all this way from Chicago rather than flying.

After getting out, he walked around the fence, avoided the gate, and climbed the steps, only to pause when he heard raised voices. The right thing to do would be to turn around and head back to his truck, call Devy, and plead his case, but he couldn't bring himself to leave.

Hayden sat in one of the white rockers and eavesdropped, waiting to hear the words that would send him back to his truck. If Devorah chose to go back to her husband, then Hayden would respect her decision, whether or not he agreed with it. They had years of history and a daughter together. Devy and Hayden had a couple of moments and one fabulous night, which had ended up being the night her father passed away.

He sighed and felt what little energy he had left dissipate. Even if Dev stayed, their night of passion would be marred by the passing of Crow. Devy would never forget the aftermath, no matter how hard she tried. Hayden either.

Maybe their short-lived relationship was all that was in the cards for them.

Maybe there was a reason their middle and high school make-out sessions had gone no further.

Maybe you need to stop looking for excuses and give her a chance.

Hayden could come up with an entire list of maybes when he was desperate, but the one that kept nagging him was that if Devorah didn't want to be with him, she wouldn't have been.

Voices rose, and he didn't even attempt to ignore them. If Devorah got mad at him for sitting there, he'd take the punishment. Besides, he had a few things to say to Chad, and he'd use that as an excuse to sit there and wait.

What he heard made his stomach turn and revolt. It threatened to heave its contents all over the porch. Chad wanted—no, he demanded—that Devorah and Maren return to Chicago with him to be a family while he continued his relationship with Ester.

Hayden's blood boiled. He gripped the side of the rocker, the whites of his knuckles painfully exposed. It took everything in him to not go into the house and confront Chad. This wasn't the time nor the place, nor was this his battle. It was Devorah's, and from what he could hear, she was holding her own.

Each time Devorah told Chad to sign the divorce papers, Hayden smiled. This was a victory for *her*. Not for him. As her friend, Hayden wanted Devy as far away from the man who'd cheated on her as possible. Crow would want that as well. He realized then that Chad had ignored the papers Theo Sherman had sent until now.

Why not tell Devorah all this over the phone? Why show up to Crow's funeral and make these demands? Was it because Chad felt Dev would be vulnerable and cave?

Hayden would call Colt home before he allowed that to happen. Her brother at least could reason with her, show her how Oyster Bay was a great place to raise Maren.

When Devorah asked Chad if he was still sleeping with Ester, Hayden stood. He was ready to barge in and . . . do what? Protect Devorah from the truth? She was doing a stand-up job on her own.

"You disgust me," Devorah said. Hayden sat down, having his answer. Chad the Cad hadn't changed a bit. He was the same guy he was in high school, only with even more money in his pocket.

Hayden had heard enough and started regretting being there. He shouldn't be listening in, not to something like this. If Devorah wanted to, she'd tell him later.

He stood and was walking toward the stairs when he heard Maren. Where had she been this entire time?

"Are you leaving now?" Her sweet voice cracked, and another jolt shot straight to Hayden's heart. What came after would live with

Hayden for a very long time. He witnessed the agonizing cry of a child needing and wanting a parent she couldn't have. He'd lived it when he'd had to tell Conor his mother had passed away, that she wouldn't be there in the morning for breakfast. Hayden had been there through the sleepless nights filled with gut-wrenching sobs because all his son wanted was for his mom to tuck him in.

Tears formed, and Hayden batted them away. The urge to run in and wrap Maren in his arms pushed him to his limit. He gripped the railing to hold himself in place, to keep from embarrassing Devorah. He refused to be like Chad. Hayden would put her feelings first.

"I hate you. I hate you. I hate Ester and Rita and you. I hate you so much."

No child should ever feel this way about their parent, and no parent should ever give their child an excuse to feel this way. This wasn't normal. This wasn't the run-of-the-mill "Why can't I go out with my friends tonight?" hatred often spewed by angry teens.

No, this hatred was deep seated, and it had festered for months. All those phone calls between Chad and Maren, filled with broken promises, had finally done their job. Maren now saw her father for what he was: a selfish prick.

The door opened, and the screen door squeaked. "You'd think—" Chad froze when he came face to face with Hayden.

For a minute, neither man said anything. They appraised each other, as if sizing up one another for battle. Hayden would win. He already had when Devorah told Chad to get out.

"You must be Hayden," Chad said as he looked Hayden up and down.

"Don't act like you don't know me."

Chad lifted his shoulder just barely. "She'll always think of me. I'll never be far from her thoughts."

"Nah, that's where you're wrong," Hayden told him. "The only time she'll think of you, in any capacity other than you being Maren's father, is when she's cleaning dog shit off her shoe. You, on the other hand, will always wonder what she's up to and how much better off she is without you, and how you did her a favor."

Chad scoffed but said nothing.

"You should probably go," Hayden told him. "It's a long drive back to Chicago, and while you may think that with Crow gone, no one will do anything, think again. The people of Oyster Bay will protect their own. Give them an excuse to run you out of town."

Chad heaved his bag over his shoulder and shook his head. "She'll be back," he said as he walked past Hayden.

"I wouldn't hold your breath." Hayden walked toward the door. He waited for Chad to leave before knocking on a door he hadn't knocked on in a long time.

It swung open, with a frazzled-looking Devorah on the other side. "Why are you knocking?"

Hayden looked from her to the driveway, at Chad's receding taillights.

"How much did you hear?"

"Enough," Hayden said as he stood on the other side of the screen. "Look, I know I shouldn't have eavesdropped—"

"But you did."

He nodded.

"I should be mad."

Hayden nodded again.

"But I'm not." Devorah pushed the door open and welcomed him inside.

"Where's Maren?"

"Out back," Dev told him. "She wanted to be alone."

"I'm sorry," Hayden said. He touched her hip and left his hand there. "This has been an epically shitty week for you."

She ran her hands through her hair and walked toward the kitchen. "Do you want something to eat? I didn't eat at the wake and left the second I could. I think Colt's still there, being the dutiful son and all."

"I'm not sure there are rules when it comes to wakes and how long you need to stay."

"Chad—" Devorah groaned. "His presence at a time like this . . ." She shook her head. "He made my father's funeral all about him and how he had to take time off from work to come and how he couldn't get a flight out, so he drove the fifteen hours to be here. Let's not forget there are no hotels in the area and no room at any of the inns, so he had no choice but to stay here." Devorah sat in one of the chairs and rested her head in her hands.

Hayden went to the refrigerator and pulled out a casserole dish of lasagna. He plated three squares, heated them up, and set them on the table, one in front of Devorah, and then he went out back to see Maren.

She was in the middle of the tire, resting on her belly, still wearing the dress she'd worn to her grandfather's funeral. She held a stick in her hand and was drawing lines in the dirt while her pretty dress shoes moved her and the tire swing back and forth. Cordelia couldn't take her eyes off the stick, waiting for her friend to throw it.

Hayden leaned against the tree. He had a million things to say, but none of them sounded right. So he started with what he knew. "I was about your age when my grandma died. She was like my best friend. I'd go to her house after school, and she'd always make me cookies. Sometimes, when she had a Crafty Cathy meeting and my parents weren't home yet, she'd take me, and all those ladies would fuss over me. We'd always go to the park or do the grocery shopping together. I spent a lot of time with her, and then one day when I get to her house, she's not there. My dad is, and he tells me my grandma died. I didn't get to say goodbye or tell her I loved her. She was just gone."

"And then what?"

He turned his back against the tree and pressed into it. "And then I still walked to my grandma's, only I didn't go in because she wasn't there, and my grandpa was working. I think I stood there every day for two weeks, just waiting for her to come back, even though I knew she wouldn't. Finally, I started going to my parents' office, but it was never the same. It took me a long time to understand how much life changes from day to day."

"My daddy left."

"I know," Hayden said. "I saw."

"He's not very nice."

"Being an adult can be confusing, especially for kids. We make decisions, and not everyone will understand them. Heck, sometimes we don't even understand them."

"He has a new family."

That hurt Hayden to hear. He took a deep breath.

"You've got your mom," Hayden said. "She'd move heaven and earth to be with you. And you've got your uncle Colt."

"Yeah."

"Know who else you have?"

Maren finally looked at Hayden and shrugged.

"You have me and Conor. My parents. My dad told me he had so much fun with you when you were at the house. He can't wait for you to come over again."

"Really?"

Hayden nodded. "Yep. He really likes you, Maren."

"He's pretty funny."

"You'll have to tell him that when you see him at your next game." She shrugged.

Hayden pushed away from the tree. "If you're hungry, there's lasagna on the table. Your mom's in the kitchen, and I think she misses you."

"Daddy made her angry."

"Well then, I bet a hug from you would make her happy."

Hayden went into the house and sat down. Devorah had added a garden salad and garlic bread to the table.

"This looks like the best impromptu lunch I've had in a while."

"For all their faults, the CC Club knows how to take care of their own."

"That's for sure," Hayden said as he raised his fork, pausing when the back door opened. Cordelia came in first and went to her water dish. Maren followed, shutting the door behind her.

Devorah turned in her chair and welcomed her daughter into her fold. They hugged for a long time, both sniffling. When they parted, Hayden put some bread on Maren's plate and got up to get her some juice.

"Thanks for lunch, Hayden," Maren said as she sat down.

"Thanks for joining us," he said as he retook his seat.

While the three of them ate, Hayden's thoughts drifted. He was in love with Devorah and already looked at Maren as part of his family. Now, he just had to find the right time to tell Devy about his feelings. Unless he was too late.

TWENTY-SEVEN

DEVORAH

In the month since Crow had passed away, life moved faster than Devorah thought possible. The dreary spring days turned into beautiful, almost summer days, with the nights getting longer with each passing day.

Maren counted down the days to summer break and had a list of activities she wanted to do with her mom—everything from taking a cruise on the big giant ship (according to Maren) to camping on the beach. Devorah would make sure they checked everything off the list, even the trip to the zoo that Maren had learned about in school one day, and they would head back to the Pizza Palace so she and Conor could play all the games while their parents munched on cardboard pizza.

They were surviving. Devorah and Maren.

Devy finally put her estate sale knowledge to good use when she cleaned out Crow's house. It was hers and Colt's to do with as they pleased, and since neither of them wanted to move, they decided to keep it. At least for now.

A week after he passed, Dev opened his closet door and groaned. Her father hadn't gotten rid of anything in all his years, including his first sheriff's uniform, which was, by all accounts, five sizes too small for him. Room by room, box by box, she went through her parents' things.

On some days and nights, Colt would help her. He'd often come across something he thought would be perfect for the Lazy Lamb and take it to the bar. Other times, Maren sat on the bed and helped her mom sort old clothing, books, and jewelry.

The day Devorah came across her mother's wedding dress, she sat on the floor and cried. She had very few memories of her mom, and any photos had long since faded with time. Still, when she opened the box and softly touched the silk, she knew she'd never part with the gown. It was her hope that Maren would want to wear it someday, and if not, then Devorah would keep it in the box, tucked in the corner.

After everything had been gone through, she invited people into their home. This was the first time she'd done an estate sale while someone still lived in the home, and she hoped people would respect the **Do Not Enter** signs she had posted. Unlike her previous sales, she offered cookies from the local bakery.

Most everyone in Crow's generation had been through the house, but this time it was different. His booming presence, while Dev still felt it, was absent. As was his ratty recliner, which Colt had put out front with a **Free** sign on it. He hadn't even made it back to the house before it was gone.

Still, having people go through their things and second-guessing whether she should sell them unnerved Devorah. With this sale, she had attachments to the items, whereas before, she'd had a job to do. One she did very well.

What surprised her was the number of people who came to the sale. When she helped someone she didn't recognize, she asked where they were from. She couldn't believe when they told her they'd come from New Hampshire or Vermont.

What really threw her for a loop was when someone asked if she could hire her to do an estate sale on a home once it cleared probate. The only issue Devorah saw was the location. Setting up took time, sometimes days on end. Then there was the sale and the cleanup afterward. Traveling out of town would be a big ask, and a costly one for some people. Colt and Hayden had a solution. Colt would make sure he was home to take care of Maren, and Hayden told Devorah he would help when he could, but that she could use his truck.

Without even trying, she was back in business, and now she was the head of the local church's annual tag sale fundraiser.

As well as cochair of the Oyster Festival, a title handed to her by Laila, who had retaken her rightful place as Devorah's best friend.

When all was said and done, Devorah and Colt stood in the living room of their childhood home and grimaced. The walls, the floors, and everything in between needed a deep clean and a good paint job.

During what spare time she had, Dev got to work.

Devorah filled Maren's water bottle, tightened the cap, and then set it in her bag. "Maren, are you ready?"

"Yes," she yelled from upstairs. Within seconds, the thumping sound of her cleats hitting the wooden staircase echoed. Devorah rolled her eyes. It was pointless for her to say anything about Maren wearing them in the house; after today, the season would be over.

"Okay, I'm here," Maren said as she came into the kitchen. "Did you make my water?"

Devy nodded.

"Thank you." Maren came over to her mom and hugged her. They'd hugged every day since Chad walked out. He paid support monthly, not only to Maren, but to Devorah as well, and that was because Theo had asked the court to set up an automatic withdrawal from his paychecks. If Chad were to quit his job, his retirement would pay. Chad was on the hook for support until Maren turned twenty-two. Theo was adamant and the judge agreed that support wouldn't end until Maren graduated from college. All the support in the world wouldn't make up for the fact that he never called.

After he left, Maren had watched the phone like a hawk before gradually stopping. Now, she didn't even show excitement when it rang. To her, her father had moved on to his new family. She had a strong support system around her and two men who would do anything for her in Colt and Hayden.

Devorah had made out well financially in the divorce. She received the profits from the sale of their home, half of Chad's investment portfolio, and 40 percent of his retirement funds.

All she wanted was her name back.

After a long talk with Maren, it was her daughter's suggestion for Devorah to return to the name Crowley. She, too, planned to change hers to Crowley, once she was old enough, and she asked when she could start using her family's last name. Chad had ruined what was left of his relationship with his daughter.

Devorah had never been so happy to sign the name Crowley on everything.

"Are we walking?"

Devorah nodded. "It's too nice to drive over to the school." She shouldered the bag, leashed Cordelia, and picked up her chair from the porch as they left.

They made their way to school and went right to the McKennas' house. Lee stood and stopped them both in their tracks. Devorah read his shirt and then waited for her daughter to comprehend the words: PROUD GRANDPA TO CONOR & MAREN. Lee had told Maren after Crow passed that he could fill in for the grandpa role whenever she needed him. Every Saturday since, Maren had gone over for game night with Lee and Darcy.

"Wait," Maren said as she reread the shirt. "Why does your shirt have my name?"

"Because," Lee said as he came a bit closer. "As a grandpa, I gotta cheer for both my grandkids."

"But that says you're my grandpa," Maren pointed out.

Devorah bit her lower lip to keep from crying.

Lee shrugged. "Yeah, I guess it does. What do you think—are you okay with me calling you my granddaughter?"

Maren looked at Devy, who smiled at her daughter.

"Can I call you Grandpa?"

Lee smiled brightly. "I wouldn't want it any other way."

Maren closed the gap between them and wrapped her arms around Lee's waist. When they parted, Darcy cleared her throat to get Maren's attention.

"And what about me?" Darcy showed Maren her shirt, which was identical except for the switch from Grandpa to Grandma.

Maren beamed. "I've never had a grandma before."

"Well," Darcy said, as if out of breath. "I'll have to make sure I'm the best grandma you ever had, then, won't I?"

Maren nodded and fell into Darcy's arms. Lee sat down and pulled all three into one giant hug while Devy looked on.

After their lovefest, Maren took off toward the field, where she ran right up to Conor. Dev set her chair up, set a blanket out for Cordelia to lie on, and collapsed with a sigh.

"You guys have no idea what this means to me," she said to Lee and Darcy. "She's really missing Crow."

"Don't think you're getting off so easily," Darcy said as she patted Devy's hand.

"What do you mean?" she asked as she looked from her to Lee.

"A long time ago, I told Crow I'd always look out for his kids, and I intend to follow through. Sunday dinners start this week," Lee said.

"And we'll discuss the holidays later," Darcy added.

Devorah opened her mouth to say something but closed it. She needed people around her who would help her thrive. Those people were the McKennas.

"Now tell me, what's this 'I never had a grandma' crap?"

Devorah rolled her eyes. "Chad's mother wouldn't allow Maren to call her Grandma. It was the most asinine thing in the world. You and Lee have done more for her since we moved here than the Campbells have done her entire life."

"Grandchildren are a gift," Lee said. "They have no idea what they're missing."

Hayden walked toward them. Devy cupped her hand over her eyes and took him in. He was a tall drink of water, according to most of the women in town, and he only had eyes for Devorah and the patience of a saint.

She had all but put the brakes on where their relationship had been headed. Sure, they still went out on occasion, but it was nothing serious, and they each went home to their own places at the end of the night. There were times when she thought she was ready, but then something would spark a memory and she'd want nothing to do with romance.

Still, she hadn't given up on falling in love with Hayden.

Hayden never pressured her and let her dictate their path. She wondered when he'd give up on her and was thankful each day that he hadn't. Devorah liked him and wanted to be with him, but she worried about Maren.

He set his chair up next to hers, squatted to pet Cordelia, and sat down, stretching his long legs out in front of him. Dev watched him and then laughed.

"What's so funny?"

"Nothing," Devorah said as she tried to hide her grin. Her eyes told a whole other story, though, as they went from him to the group of the opposing team's mothers.

"I'm afraid to look." Hayden grimaced.

"But then you'd miss the blatant gawking."

"They'd stop looking if you kissed me," he said quietly. She wouldn't, not with Maren in the vicinity. Knowing this, Hayden leaned toward her and acted like he was about to whisper in her ear, only to place his lips there instead.

The best she could do in public was hold his hand. She reached for it and set their conjoined hands on the armrests of their chairs.

True to his word, Lee stood up when Maren came up to bat. "Let's go, Maren. Keep your eye on the ball," he yelled as she stepped up to the plate.

"You know," Hayden said so only Dev could hear him. "Christmas is going to be nuts."

Devorah looked at him sharply and then directed her attention to Maren. "What do you know? Your mom mentioned something about the holidays earlier after she all but told me I had to be at dinner on Sunday."

"Just that Lee's been going on and on about a promise he made to your dad years ago."

"Which I get, but I'm an adult now." She gritted her teeth.

"I don't think it matters to Lee," Hayden said.

"Well, I . . . let's go, Maren!" Everyone stood as Maren smacked the ball toward center field. Devorah jumped and clapped as her daughter rounded first base and headed toward second, where she stopped.

Devy turned to Hayden, and they high-fived each other.

"That's my granddaughter," Lee said to anyone who would listen as he clapped loudly.

"Your dad is one of a kind," Dev said as she sat back down. "I'll never be able to thank him for filling the void Crow left."

"He'd never accept it."

After the game, in which the Oyster Bay squad won the championship thanks to a home run by Conor, everyone met at the Lazy Lamb, where Colt made every video game free. Parents clogged booths and tables, while some of the dads took turns showing they still had what it took to be the pinball wizard.

Devorah helped put food out, while Hayden assisted with drinks, and then everyone sat down to eat.

Dalton Noble stood and tapped his fork against his glass to get everyone's attention. "I want to thank all the parents for a successful year. They say it takes a village to raise a child, but what they really mean is it takes a village to raise an athlete. Every one of you stepped in when one of our players needed help. We all appreciate you."

Everyone applauded.

"Like last year, I handed out three awards. These are not indicative of how I feel but how the team feels. The players voted. The best defensive player of the year goes to our catcher, Charlie Street."

More applause.

"Our best offensive player goes to our first baseman, Conor McKenna."

Hayden, Devorah, Lee, Darcy, and Colt cheered loudly for Conor, who looked embarrassed as he walked up to accept his award.

"And finally," Dalton said and then inhaled. "When I asked the team to write down the player who exuded the best qualities when it came to sportsmanship, leadership, and all-around team play, each member wrote the same name. I'm happy to give the most valuable player award to Maren Campbell."

Devorah was out of her seat instantly, cheering for her daughter. The others followed, but Dev and Maren needed this moment. They hugged tightly. "I'm so proud of you."

"Thanks, Mom."

When Maren reached Dalton, he stood there for a minute. "You are the first female baseball player I have ever coached. I'm thankful you joined our team this year and am looking forward to next year."

"Thanks, Coach."

Maren took her trophy back to where her family sat and then posed for an ungodly number of photos.

Later, when they got home, Maren put the trophy on her shelf.

"It's funny, that's where I put my first Pearl of the Ocean tiara," Dev said from the doorway.

"Yeah, I figure I can move this one when I get my first tiara."

Devorah pushed off from the door casing and went into Maren's room. "You want to be a Pearl, huh?"

Maren nodded. "It's tradition, isn't it?"

Dev shrugged. "Maybe." She put her arm around Maren's shoulders. "We're gonna be okay, kiddo."

"Yep, we are."

Epilogue

On the night before the Oyster Festival officially kicked off, Hayden called and asked Maren and Devorah to meet him at his new house. There was something he wanted to show them.

Due to parking restrictions in place because of the festival, Dev and Maren walked to Hayden's property. It wasn't far, but far enough that driving would've been easier. But like he had with Crow's funeral, Hayden had offered his land for parking.

As soon as Devorah and Maren stepped onto the property, Hayden turned on all the lights and sat down next to Conor. Dev had picked out a bench for the front porch on one of their many trips to the "city."

"Hey, we're glad you ladies could come over," Hayden said as he stood and reached for Devy's hand. She climbed the couple of stairs and linked her fingers with his. Over the past week, they had decided to give their relationship the green light but had yet to tell the kids. The progression seemed natural, and both were happy with their lives.

"What's going on?"

"Conor and I want to show you something."

Hayden had spent every free moment he had working on his house, on top of the normal crew during the day. He'd also been offered a job with Link Blackburn, doing construction, which Hayden absolutely loved.

He had yet to accept.

After Crow passed, the obvious choice to replace him as sheriff was Miller Farnsworth. When the town council approached him, he'd passed, saying he was afraid he wouldn't be able to fill Crow's shoes.

The council planned to open a state- and nationwide search for a sheriff. That was until someone from the CC Club casually mentioned that Hayden had been a deputy in Wyoming, and Oyster Bay wouldn't want an outsider.

Without even asking if he was interested, the council had offered him the job.

Now, he was faced with a conundrum. While he loved working with his hands, being the new guy meant he'd be laid off first once the season slowed down. But taking over as sheriff had its pros and cons.

The pros were easy. Hayden had loved being a deputy and serving the community he lived in.

The con was simple: Crow. The man had been a well-respected member of society. Everyone revered him. If Miller couldn't do it, could Hayden?

The council had given him until the end of the Oyster Festival to decide.

He escorted Devorah into the house, with Maren and Conor behind them. The kids chatted among themselves.

"Whoa," Devy said when she entered. "When did you paint?"

"The past two days," he told her. "Link has these amazing paint machines that take very little time. I did most of it last night."

Devorah walked around the living room, nodding. She had suggested Hayden keep things light in color, and while he'd agreed, he'd wanted an accent wall and had opted for navy blue.

"Did you do anything in the kitchen?"

Hayden's somewhat stoic expression turned into a grin. Devorah didn't wait for him to take her there. She'd given her two cents when Hayden had taken her shopping for countertops, appliances, and cabinets. She walked in and gasped.

"Oh, Hayden, it's gorgeous."

The back wall of the kitchen faced the backyard, where apple trees still grew. The hole for the pool had been dug, but not until next year would Hayden have it installed. The farmer's sink was on the back wall, surrounded by marble countertops and a glass backsplash. All the appliances were stainless steel, and the flooring was wide-plank bamboo. The kitchen was designed for someone who liked to cook.

Like Devorah.

Next, they toured the upstairs. Only one of the four bedrooms still needed to be painted, and the primary suite—bathroom and closet—hadn't been finished yet.

"Everything is so perfect, Hayden. How does it feel knowing you built this with your own hands?"

"Honestly? Pretty damn good. I look around and think, 'Wow. This is mine and Conor's.' It doesn't belong to the bank. Sofia was able to do this for us with her life insurance and the trust her parents set up for his college education. I'd like to think she'd love this place."

"Mom wouldn't like it here," Conor said.

"No? Why do you say that?" Hayden asked his son.

"Not enough wood," Conor said. "She wanted wood all over the house. Remember?"

Hayden nodded. "Ah yes. I do remember."

"She would've loved it because you built it," Devorah said.

"Thanks."

They went back downstairs and into the dining room. In the middle of the floor sat three pizza boxes. Devorah looked at Hayden suspiciously.

"Those weren't there when we went into the kitchen."

"Nope," he said as he sat down. The kids did the same, leaving Devorah no choice but to sit.

"Is there a mysterious pizza person living in town?"

"Yes, your brother," Hayden said as he put two slices of cheese pizza on a plate and handed it to Maren, and then did the same for Conor. "I asked him to bring the pizzas over so we could have our first meal here, together." Hayden looked at Devorah and smiled.

She opened one of the boxes and took a slice of mushroom and sausage out, forgoing a plate. Devorah took a bite and watched Hayden the entire time, wondering what he was up to.

"So, tomorrow is the big day," he said, and everyone nodded. "Aside from our beautiful Devorah marking her first Oyster Festival as cochair, my time has expired on whether I want to be the next sheriff or not."

"Have you decided?" Dev asked as she took another bite. They had discussed, in detail, what it would mean to become sheriff. Not only to her and Colt but also to Conor and the McKennas. The Crowleys were in full support of whatever Hayden decided to do.

"I think it'll be cool," Conor added.

Hayden caught Devy's expression and kept his thoughts to himself. To her, it was, in fact, not cool when you were a teen and your father was the sheriff.

"I think Grandpa would be proud if you took the job," Maren said, seeming to catch Hayden off guard.

"Thank you for saying that, Maren."

Hayden inhaled and looked at Dev. He gave her a slight nod. "Well, you're looking at the new sheriff of Oyster Bay."

"Woo-hoo!" Conor cheered.

"You say that now," Devorah said to him. "Someday, I'll tell you all the stories."

Hayden laughed as Conor's face drained of excitement.

"Well, now that decision is made. As far as tomorrow goes, I'm going to get up early, way before the sun is up, and go get us our spot for the parade."

"Do I have to go with you tomorrow, Mommy?" Maren asked.

Devorah shook her head. "I was thinking Hayden and Conor could spend the night tonight. I'll sleep in your bed, and they'll sleep in mine. This way, when Hayden and I have to leave in the morning, Uncle Colt will be there with you."

"Why not just say we're having a sleepover?" Maren asked, eyeing her mother suspiciously.

"Yes, okay."

Maren narrowed her eyes and then went back to eating her pizza. Hayden stared at Devorah until she looked at him, and he, too, narrowed his eyes at her. In return, she rolled hers. Hayden wanted her to come clean to Maren about the dating, which was the whole point of them eating dinner together at the new house.

"Maren, I thought I should tell you, before you hear from anyone else, Hayden and I are dating."

She continued to eat her pizza. "That's like old news, Mom."

"What do you mean?"

Maren rolled her eyes this time. "Remember when we moved here, and you said everyone knows everything in a small town?"

"Yes."

"Well, duh! Everyone except for you knows you're dating Hayden. I think the town is tired of waiting for you to catch up."

Devorah opened her mouth to say something back to her daughter, but she couldn't think of anything. Instead, she looked at Hayden. "This has your mother written all over it."

Hayden choked on a bite but agreed. Darcy McKenna was a blabbermouth.

"Hayden?"

He looked over at Maren and smiled. "What's up?"

"Do you think I can paint my room pink?"

"Mine is going to be green," Conor said. "I'm thinking I want a baseball diamond on the wall."

"Oh, that sounds fun," Maren said.

"What's going on?" Devorah asked them.

Hayden shrugged as he dug in his pocket. He pulled out a key and handed it to her.

"Will you move in with us?" Conor asked before Hayden could say the words himself.

Dev opened her mouth to say something but closed it quickly when she met Maren's gaze. "Do you want to live with Hayden and Conor?"

Maren nodded excitedly. "I really like them. Hayden treats me like his daughter."

Hayden coughed to clear the lump forming in his throat at what Maren had said. He hadn't told Devorah about the conversation he'd had with a former classmate of theirs when the person had asked how many kids he had. Hayden had answered two without even thinking. He couldn't pinpoint when he'd begun to think of Maren as his daughter, but he was grateful for it happening.

"And you treat me like I'm your son," Conor said to Dev. "Ever since the day we went shopping and you did the thumb test."

Devorah wiped at her cheeks. "Wow, this is so . . ."

"Perfect," Maren said, shrugging.

"I like that," Hayden said. "So, what do you think? Would you and Maren like to live with the McKenna men?"

Devy nodded. "Yeah, I think we would."

"One condition," Conor blurted out.

"What's that?" Dev asked.

"Cordelia moves in too."

"Duh," Maren said, as if this was a no-brainer.

Conor fist pumped. "Finally, I get a dog!"

Devorah and Hayden ambled toward the Oyster Festival headquarters under the cloak of darkness. It wasn't even right to be up this early and have to work before the sun had even thought about peeking over the horizon. Dev sighed as she sipped the hot coffee Hayden had brewed and kindly put in a thermos for her. This caffeine jolt wouldn't last long, and she was thankful a local coffee house was sponsoring the festival. In a couple of hours, she'd need an IV of the black tar to survive.

Soft white lights illuminated the tent where the festival committee would be for most of the weekend. Laila was there with her headset on, holding her own cup of coffee.

"Morning," Devorah mumbled. "Remind me to send you my letter of resignation on Monday." Although joking, Devorah wanted to quit. It had been years since she'd been up this early and functioning.

Laila set her cup down and gripped both of Devy's hands. "I won't accept it," she told her pointedly. "Without you, I'd be stressed, and I'm not stressed. You saved me this year, Dev. You'll never know how grateful I am to have you here. To have you back in my life."

If Devorah wasn't so tired, she'd weep a bit.

Hayden kissed her temple. "I'm with Laila. Our lives are so much better with you in it, here in Oyster Bay."

Dev closed her eyes and leaned into Hayden. "I appreciate you both. So much."

Laila clapped her hands and looked at Hayden. "Hey, I hear congratulations are in order!"

Hayden's eyes widened in shock as Devorah shook her head. "The CC Club must have speakers buried everywhere. He literally decided last night while we were eating dinner."

"I didn't even tell my mom," Hayden said, laughing.

"Huh, well, Link knew. He told me." Laila shrugged. "Are you the new sheriff?"

Hayden nodded. "I start on Monday, once this festival is over. The only part I want in this is to support you ladies."

"He's a keeper, Devorah," Laila said.

"Wait, I thought I was the funny guy?"

The three of them laughed.

"Let's get to work," she said as she handed Devorah a headset. "Parade participants will start arriving shortly, and we have an issue with the Pearl of the Ocean float."

"Anything I can help with?" Hayden asked.

"I'll let Link know you're available, but for right now, I think he has it covered."

"All right then. I'm going back to head over to my property and open the gate for parking, and then I'll be back at Crow's to set our chairs out and make breakfast for the kids." He leaned down and kissed Devorah. She was extremely happy their relationship was out in the open now.

"Call me if you need anything," he told her.

"I will."

She watched him jog toward his property and didn't take her eyes off him until he'd rounded the corner.

"When's the wedding?"

Devorah turned sharply to face her friend. "Uh . . ."

Laila laughed and took a sip of her coffee. "He's got it bad. You've got it bad. By the way, in case you've forgotten, my favorite color is lavender, which is the perfect color for a late-spring, early-summer wedding."

Devy stepped toward Laila and put her hand to her forehead. "Do you have a fever? Did you fall and bump your head last night? Should I call Link?"

Laila batted her hand away. "We *all* see it. You're just blinded by the crap Chad did to you. Hayden doesn't care that your divorce was final weeks ago. He wants to be with you."

"You forget, he's a widower."

"No one's forgotten," Laila said. "When you find your soulmate, nothing else matters."

"And you think he's my soulmate?"

Laila nodded. "I know he is. It's time for you to see it."

Devorah turned back to where Hayden had been. Did she believe in soulmates? She wasn't sure, but she knew Chad wasn't the one she was meant to be with. He'd been convenient, a means to an end to get out of town and piss her father off. She never wanted to say she regretted Chad because of Maren, but part of her wondered what her life would be like if she hadn't left Oyster Bay. Chad had convinced her that nothing good came of the people who stayed.

He was wrong.

She looked at her best friend and smiled. Later, after the festival was over, she'd tell Laila about how Hayden and Conor had asked her and Maren to move in with them. Right now, she wanted to hold on to the news a bit longer because she wanted it to be their news and not Oyster Bay's.

By the time the parade was over, Devorah was exhausted. She wanted to go home, crawl into bed, and sleep until the next morning, but she couldn't. She had promised two kids and a grown man they could go to the carnival. It was the last place she wanted to be.

Hayden, Conor, and Maren came toward the Oyster Festival headquarters, looking as cheery as the day was bright. The kids said hi, while Hayden kissed her good and proper for all to see. Everyone in their booth hooted and hollered, while Conor and Maren made gagging noises.

Perfect.

"Did you kids enjoy the parade?" Laila asked them.

Maren nodded. "I'm going to be Pearl of the Ocean when I'm old enough to enter."

"I don't doubt it," Laila said. "Your mom will teach you everything she knows. What about you, Conor?"

"All the fire trucks were cool, and the candy. I don't want to be Pearl of anything, though."

Laila looked at Devorah and smiled. "I think it's about time we have something for the guys. Clam of the Ocean."

Everyone laughed, while Conor grimaced.

"The name needs work, but I think we should do it," Devorah said.

"I'm not wearing a crown, ever," Conor added with a shake of his head. "No, sir."

"Come on," Hayden said, giving his hand a tug. "The rides are screaming our names." Hayden walked away with both kids, leaving Devorah to finish with business. When she was done, she told everyone she'd see them tomorrow, bright and early.

When she caught up with the kids and Hayden, she stayed back for a second and watched them. Conor walked next to Hayden, while Maren and Hayden held hands. Every few seconds, Hayden would stop and point to something, or he'd look at what the kids were gesturing to.

The sight of him with her daughter, treating her as his own, made her fall hard for him. She'd been on the cusp for a long time but was now fully over the edge. He was there too. She just didn't know what they were waiting for. If he asked, she'd marry him tomorrow.

In the time since they'd returned to Oyster Bay, Hayden McKenna had been a constant in her life. Someone out there knew they needed each other.

"Hayden!" Devorah yelled loudly to get his attention. He turned and smiled.

She ran to him and, when the timing was right, jumped into his waiting arms. "I thought you should know before we move in together," she said as her hand caressed his face, "I'm in love with you."

His smile was brighter than the lights from the carnival rides. "It's about time," he said. "I've been waiting for you to catch up ever since we played seven minutes in heaven back in middle school."

Devorah laughed. "Yeah, well . . . I'm ready for the sequel."

Hayden tightened his hold on her and pressed his lips to hers. The timing of their kiss was perfect and magical as fireworks shot into the night sky.

About the Author

In 2012, Heidi McLaughlin turned her passion for reading into a full-fledged literary career. She is now the *New York Times*, *Wall Street Journal*, and *USA Today* bestselling author of The Beaumont Series, The Boys of Summer, and The Archer Brothers. McLaughlin has written more than twenty novels, including her acclaimed first novel, *Forever My Girl*, which was adapted into a film that opened in theaters in 2018, starring Alex Roe and Jessica Rothe.

Visit the author at www.heidimclaughlin.com, and keep up with new releases by subscribing to her newsletter.